T0108027

SHOCKING PINK

STUART CANTERBURY

RUNNING
Wild
PRESS

CONTENTS

For Ian and Sandra

The problem with pornography is not that it shows too much of the person,
but that it shows far too little. — Pope John Paul II

CREDITS

THE PRODUCERS

Travis Lazar
The Duchess
Miles Flannigan
Blimp Pullman
Alec Zig
Menachem Amsalem

THE STUDIO EXECUTIVES

Duncan Hathaway, American X-Rated Entertainment
Evelyn Hathaway, American X-Rated Entertainment
Nicholas Pasquale, American X-Rated Entertainment
Beppo "The Bear" Bari, Majestic Movies
Selwyn Felwyn, Paradise Media, Inc
Sylvia Bern, New York Pictures
Motti "The Destroyer" Sunbeam, Sunbeam Video

Maya "The Dragon" Sunbeam, Sunbeam Video

THE STARS

Tiffany West
Traci Gold
Ginger Vitus
Mariana Trench
Summer Rainfall
Storm
Colt
Sebastian Barge

THE CREW

Howard Finkel, Production Manager
Jack Limo, Director of Photography
Tommy Hargis, Chief Lighting Technician
Maria Blush, Make-up Artist and Hair Stylist
Willard Fingerbrand, Special Pyrotechnic Effects

THE TALENT AGENT

Billy Dallas, Global Models Management

THE FOREIGN SALES BROKER

Oscar Lowport, Lowport International Licensing

THE AUTHORITIES

Officer James Fleet, Los Angeles Fire Department, Film Unit, Supervising Officer
Detective Sergeant Luis Perez, Los Angeles Police Department, Vice Squad
Special Agent Frank Hassenger, Federal Bureau of Investigation, Racketeering and Organized Crime Division
Judge Bernice Grundle, Presiding Judge, Van Nuys Small Claims Court

THE EUROPEANS

Klaus Ulrich, Hamburg Film and Book Company, GmbH
Luigi Pinocchio, Pinocchio Films Italy

A TRAVIS LAZAR VIDEOGRAPHY (PARTIAL)

Hard Time
Starlight
Dreamboat
High Risqué
High Risqué Part 2
High Risqué Part 3 (all-girl)
Fireworks
The Love Life of a Loser (Executive Producer)
Cheats

CHAPTER ONE

WHAT HAPPENS IN VEGAS

If anyone were watching Travis Lazar, one crisp January morning in Las Vegas, where the illustrious producer was attending the largest adult entertainment convention in the world, that observer would have been mystified.

Dressed impeccably in a dark designer suit, with a burgundy tie swelled at the throat in a Windsor knot, Travis weaved his way down the crowded aisles lined with a phantasmagoria of stands, displays, banners, and enormous advertisements to promote the brands, studios, stars, and movies which comprised the billion-dollar, global X-rated industry. There were scantily-dressed young women everywhere the eye could see. Flimsy garments could hardly contain the bulges of flesh, overflowing from tight bra-cups, sheer stockings, short skirts, and plunging cleavages. There were costumes of lace, leather, and latex. There was a rainbow of glitter, platinum blonde coiffeur, shocking pink nail-polish, flamboyant body art, and vivid streaks of color. The scent of powder and perfume and hair-spray mingled with perspiration and liquor. Although there were some well-worn troupers, for most of the starlets, this was their first convention; everyone wanted to see the latest newcomers. They were all very busy, signing autographs, posing for photographs, engaging in interviews, and running back and forth on heels as high as stilts from the makeup chair to the hotel room to the bathroom to the booth; all while trying to talk on cell phones. Music blared in competing fanfares. Touts yelled into microphones like carnival barkers. Models in bikinis or lingerie demonstrated the latest in whirring vibrators and humming accessories. Packed with fans, crawling with photographers, filled with wannabes and hopefuls and hangers-on, the passage from one end of a noisy thoroughfare to another was not easy to negotiate. With such a feast for the senses, no-one knew where to look or which way to go. Most shuffled along mesmerized, each following another. The hordes halted as one to collect free giveaways flung to the crowd, including buttons, t-shirts, posters, souvenirs, sample packs of lubrication, and the odd item of frilly underwear. There was always a crush of admirers gathered around a porn star who might have stopped to pout for a camera. To protect the attendees from the dangers of nudity, local sheriffs on patrol through the convention hall at taxpayer expense issued warnings to likely perpetrators. Occasionally, an illicit nipple appeared, provoking a stampede of excitement. There were roars and cheers and whoops of encouragement. Fans whistled and applauded. Lights flashed. Bottlenecks jammed the aisles.

But Travis Lazar, threading through the throng, was closing a deal.

At the far end of the aisle, two German men, in mustard colored jackets and green slacks, sat in a roped off area at a small round table upon which there was a stack of catalogs of recent pornographic movies available for distribution under exclusive license in territories outside the United States. Without missing a beat, Travis unbuckled the clamp holding

SHOCKING PINK

the velvet rope to the catch on a stanchion, and slipped into the VIP section, an entitlement granted by the complimentary all-access credentials on the industry badge hanging on a lanyard around his neck. He was not the type to have to wait to present his pass to a functionary, and no official presented himself. Travis looked like he belonged. He broke into a white-toothed grin as he approached the men, who reciprocated with the same dazzling show of teeth. They rose to shake hands, a gesture, which was wrestled into a clumsy hug by the lean producer, whose cold-blooded instincts always warmed at the prospect of business.

The first thing that the producer produced, when they all sat down again, was a notepad followed by the swift appearance of a pen, both of which he placed on the table before him, and adopted a serious but earnest expression. One of the two Germans kept gravely quiet, but the other man, Klaus, became as serious and earnest as Travis, who wrote down notes on the pad, and underlined some of the words in hard strokes. If any neutral witness had seen what he had written, the random list on the paper would have been baffling: *Pegging. Uniforms. Secretary. Brazilian. Grandma.*

Wearing the same earnest expression, he rose to his feet, an example followed by the two Europeans who shook hands with him again before they sat down again, exchanging a hopeful look between them, probably in the expectation that Travis could source the movies with the necessary requirements, or, perhaps, because they had avoided the culture shock of another awkward embrace.

Travis then slipped out the way he had come in, and set off down the obstructed aisle again, trying to get back to the other side of the room.

Halfway down the aisle, Ginger Vitus, a tall, pale redhead with five-thousand-dollar breasts, was getting ready to take a

3

break after three hours of standing in sparkly heels that matched her sparkly dress and signing glossy photographs of herself on a bed of roses for a line of devotees. She was obliged to have a few words of conversation with each of them. Every fan - and they were mostly men - in a reach to elevate his importance above the fray, tried to explain why he was not just a fan, why he was much more than a fan, why he was not only a fan, until it was revealed that he was exactly a fan and nothing more.

Travis Lazar, who was never at a disadvantage in the company of beautiful stars, stopped when he noticed Ginger, cutting discreetly to the head of the line of overweight men in loose, loud t-shirts, who had been waiting for what seemed like a few hours for a few moments with the statuesque beauty, and whispered a word in her ear; she breathed something in response, and planted a kiss on his cheek, leaving an outline of red lipstick.

His next stop on the far end of the aisle was at one of the more modest booths with a grand sign, which read simply: MAJESTIC MOVIES. The acting president of Majestic Movies, a lumbering, slovenly man in his fifties who lived up to his ursine nickname, was Beppo the Bear. He wore baggy pants, into which a faded dress shirt was meant to be tucked, and a colorless windbreaker. Travis showed Beppo the list of key words inscribed on his notepad, which impelled Beppo to deliberate action, sifting through a large assortment of colorful, glossy flyers which were each used to promote a different movie. Between the two of them, Travis and Beppo selected a stack of flyers thematically suitable based on the requested list and that were subsequently deposited into a pale yellow folder that Travis secured with a rubber band.

He then set off down the busy hallway again, trying to make his way back to the Europeans, as challenging an expedition as if he were on a voyage across stormy seas to visit them at home on the continent itself.

On the way, there was another unscheduled stop as he passed the point where Ginger Vitus was moored, this delay initiated by the star herself, who wiped the red smear of her tell-tale lipstick from his cheek with a lick of spittle and the heel of her hand. To her apparent disappointment, Travis indicated that he was just passing through her port of call but gave her his solemn pledge that he would return.

The Germans were waiting apprehensively, but had assured each other that Travis Lazar would be able to offer them aid in their predicament. The producer sat down again at the round table in the VIP section, slipping off the rubber band securing the folder, and, one by one, presented his potential buyers with the slicks for the movies which Beppo had entrusted to him. The Germans examined each one with deliberation and discussion, creating three piles representing yes, no, and maybe. Travis agreed with all of the selections in the yes pile, but, from time to time, he challenged the wisdom of the choices in the other piles, and, from time to time, the buyers saw the error in their original decisions.

As soon as the entire presentation had been reviewed, Travis counted up the titles, which were to be acquired, thumbing through the slicks like a bank teller counting hundred-dollar bills. He frowned at the end of his calculations, clearly not satisfied with the final tally, which was short of a round number, so, after some further debate, a few more selections found their way from the no and maybe piles into the yes. Now, as if by a trick of prestidigitation from the producer, a contract suddenly appeared, which Travis signed with a flourish, and the senior of the two buyers countersigned where Travis laid the pen for him on the dotted line.

The producer presented his stoniest poker face to conceal

his emotions, in this moment of completion, but the best was yet to come.

Without much in the way of prompting, Klaus brought forth a large wad of American dollars, with much the same magical effect as if he and Travis had attended the same conjuring school. The cash hardly hit the table before it was in Travis' pocket. That was it. A producer of Travis' caliber knew better than to hang around after the close, in case the buyers exhibited the remorse for which buyers were well known. He stood up at once, and they all shook hands again with polite formality.

Travis slipped out of the VIP section again, but did not yet make his way down the aisle. He turned his back on the room, with his face to the wall of a booth, so that his body could mask his actions. Extracting the money from his pocket, he divided it into two stacks, one slightly larger than the other. From the smaller pile, he peeled off a couple of bills, which he put into his breast pocket; he separated the rest of the cash into the side pockets of his jacket.

He began his trek down the hall back to Beppo the Bear, interrupted again by Ginger whom he once again placated by a promise that he would be back within minutes, and two mysterious taps of his own breast pocket which contained a small percentage of his recent profit.

An unlit cigar in his mouth, Beppo was pacing up and down in the Majestic Movies booth like a grizzly in the zoo. Travis, understanding his concern, offered him a thumbs-up signal of assurance as he approached. Beppo gave a visible sigh of relief. In the back corner of the Majestic Movies booth, Travis handed Beppo the richer of the two piles of money, since he was the legitimate copyright holder of the movies the producer had just sold to the German-speaking territories. The next step in the process would be the production of the masters, documentation, and artwork to create German packaging to be shipped to Hamburg, as per the contract, but the deal was done, and Beppo would owe him a favor, which was just the way that Travis liked it.

With money literally in their pockets now, they could each turn their attention to satisfying other urges. Beppo headed off for the lunch buffet, which was serving prime rib. Travis made one final trip halfway down the aisle, where Ginger Vitus, who had lost all patience, got hold of his crimson tie, by which she led him in the direction of the exit into a mass of people in which they both disappeared from view.

Essentially, what the producer had done was to buy something on one side of a room, and sell it on the other side.

Any observer would have been mystified. As it turned out, not only was Travis Lazar being watched. He was being scrutinized.

* * *

Howard Finkel, the long-suffering production manager for Travis Lazar Productions, was on a mission of his own. And it was not going well.

It had begun with some asshole security guard with a potbelly like a balloon in a white shirt and a huge badge. He did not want to let Howard into the hall, apparently because Howard was not wearing a red wristband.

"I work for Travis Lazar Productions," he explained, trying to convey a sense of his own importance, which was belied by the grungy, informal attire on his scrawny frame, "We got our badges months ago. They never sent any wristbands."

"We only got the wristbands yesterday," the security guard revealed, with gruff authority, "So nobody knows what color they are in advance."

A stream of people was nodded through by the security guard. There was a news crew with blinding lights, following a stable of starlets, led by the talent agent Billy Dallas, who, given the propensity for performers to wander off, kept them moving like steers on a cattle drive. In Las Vegas, to augment this effect, Billy added a Stetson to the trademark cowboy boots and belt buckle of his attire, a fashion statement which he could not get away with in the chic metropolis of Los Angeles. He touched his fingers to the brim whenever he offered a greeting. The courtly touch was not only a polite throwback, but also helpful since the wide circumference of the hat limited the tall Texan's peripheral vision. This was fortunate for Howard, who turned his head, because he did not want to be recognized by anyone he knew, with the humiliation of being refused entry.

"Can I just go in, please," Howard argued, "I've got a badge."

"I'm sorry. You also have to have a wristband."

"Travis Lazar is nominated for an award for best picture," he submitted.

The security guard did not recognize the prestige of the nomination. "You still have to have a wristband."

At that moment, making a grand entrance, the stars, Summer Rainfall, and her chiseled-jawed husband, Storm, swept past him towards the double doors on the way into the hall.

"Hey, Howard," said the busty actress, with wispy dark hair, who was wearing a sequined gown, slit in strategic places.

"Aren't you coming in?" asked Storm, his muscles glistening in a cut-off tank top.

Howard turned pink all the way to his pate. "Just working it out with my friend here."

The security guard said, "You have to go back to the front entrance, and ask for a wristband. Or I can't let you in."

"We'll see you inside," said Summer, waved through by the vigilant guards, by virtue of nothing other than her aura as a personality.

Howard had to go all the way back to the front entrance and stand in line with a bunch of retard fans, dealing with a bunch of idiots behind computers, which compounded the stupidity to an exponential level, and the longer he waited the more he had to urinate. He was not sure whether to try to hold it in or lose his place in the line so he could relieve himself. He hated having to line up among the plebeians given what he considered his pivotal place in the industry. After a brief argument with the white-haired lady at the counter, who seemed to disapprove of sex in general and Howard in particular, and a brief bathroom stop on the way back, he made another attempt at entry into the hall.

"Wristband!" the security guard shouted, as Howard walked towards the double doors.

Without breaking his stride, Howard held his arm upright, so that his sleeve slipped down, revealing the requisite red wristband, an appropriate underscore for Howard's middle finger which, to convey his opinion of the security guard, he also held upright.

Inside the hall at last, his first objective was to find Traci Gold, the lean, tanned brunette, who was his favorite porn star, both on the set and in his personal collection of complimentary movies.

She was scheduled to sign glossy photographs of herself at the booth for New York Pictures, but, just as overwhelmed as anybody else by the motley confusion of competing attractions in the hall, he set off in the wrong direction, and collided with the abundant bosom of Tiffany West.

"Howard! You four-eyed, dick-headed geek!" snapped the blonde diva, towering over him in her perilous heels.

"Sorry, Tiffany," he mumbled, still face to face with her chest. "Do you know where Traci is?"

"Get out of my way, you nightcrawler." She squinted her clear blue eyes. "My cleavage is not a tracking device."

"Good luck for the awards tonight." Howard tried to end the encounter on a positive note, by referring to a matter which was sure to put her at ease, namely her nomination for Best Actress.

"Puh-lease," said Tiffany, with a flick of her fingers, indicating that the whole affair was beneath a star of her magnitude, unless, of course, she happened to win.

* * *

For Travis Lazar, closing the German deal for Beppo was not the main item on his agenda in Las Vegas. He was not even concerned about the awards, even though his blockbuster movie, *Dreamboat*, was held in high esteem. The other contenders in the paramount Best Picture category were his friend, The Duchess, for *Forbidden Desire* from New York Pictures; Miles Flannigan, who was also a likable ally, for *Wake*, from Paradise Media; Blimp Pullman, who was a buffoon, for his big shipwreck parody, *Titanus*, also from Paradise Media; and, the creative wizard, Alec Zig, whom he despised, for the science fiction epic, *Future Foxes*, from American X-rated Entertainment. American X-rated Entertainment, or more typically, AXE, was also the studio behind Travis' movie, *Dreamboat*. In his estimation, the contest was between Miles and Alec, largely because of which distributor had spent the most money on advertising. It also meant that the contending directors were really proxies for Duncan Hathaway, the studio boss at AXE, and Selwyn Felwyn, his rival at Paradise Media.

For Travis, the chief purpose of his agenda at the convention was to make peace with Duncan.

His plan was to use the award as leverage, but he had to make his move before the winner was announced, in case the honor went to somebody else.

Because *Dreamboat* had garnered so many plum nominations, and was a critical favorite, Travis Lazar, as the director of the movie, had been invited to sit at the mogul's front-row table. There had clearly been an internal discussion at AXE, the studio which had financed and distributed the picture, as to whether or not Travis should be invited, as a result of a conflict between the president of the studio and the director, which could most diplomatically be described as artistic differences. Magnanimity had prevailed. In addition, following the maxim of all or nothing, an invitation had been extended to the director to join Duncan and a few guests for a few cocktails before the event. No matter how many guests had been invited, in light of the legendary reputation of Duncan's hospitality notwithstanding his endless thirst, Travis was sure that there would be fewer guests than there would be cocktails. After all the build-up, he was not looking forward to the gala, a tedious affair in which awards would be given out for an endless list of ridiculous categories, so that as many nominees as possible went home with a door prize to avoid crushed sentiments. The private cocktail party beforehand would be a political minefield, with the potential for many unpleasant squibs and petards, although the drinks at Duncan's open bar would surely provide some effective liquid girding for the long night ahead. To prepare himself, he planned to track down Nicholas Pasquale, the Head of Production and Creative Affairs at AXE, who would best be able to educate him as to the prevailing mood within the giant corporation.

On his way back to the convention hall, after spending his

lunch hour in Ginger's delightful company, he spotted Nicholas in a glass cage for smokers and foliage squeezed between the slot machines and a country-and-western bar offering barbecue ribs and cotton candy. There were four other primates, in business suits with name tags, milling in the greenery of the enclosure, all sucking on cigarettes, although it was only necessary to inhale the trapped air to receive an infusion of nicotine.

Nicholas, in stovepipe black pants and a shirt with a bolo, was gesticulating with a cheroot in the terrarium, when Travis stepped into the haze of smoke and ferns.

"Mister Pasquale, I presume," said the charming director, falling into conversation, with a nod at some of the other primates with whom he was acquainted.

Nicholas flicked the ash off the slim brown cheroot. "Hello, Travis, come into my jungle."

"It's better than the jungle out there, I can tell you."

"Oh, it will be all right. You have a good chance of winning. You have the best picture."

Travis understood that, with the exception of Nicholas and his small faction of allies, everyone at AXE would be rooting for Alec Zig, who was the in-house director under exclusive contract, to win the award. "Look, at least, we got the nomination," he tried to make the best of it, "Duncan must have been pleased with that."

"You got a seat at our table, didn't you?" Nicholas noted, without going into the details of the meeting that had taken place where Travis Lazar had been described in the most expressive of adjectives.

Travis realized that it must have taken some finessing for Nicholas to engineer his invitation. "Are you going to be at the cocktail party tonight?"

"No, Evelyn wants me to do something for her," Nicholas

was referring to Evelyn Hathaway, the mogul's wife, "There was a show trailer with all our upcoming releases that missed its deadline. The buyers only watch the first thirty seconds, so it was really a minor thing. But Evelyn wants to screen it anyway, so I have to oversee a post-production session that may run late. You know how these things take longer than they should." He clapped Travis on the shoulder, with the cheroot clinched in his teeth. "But I'll be at the awards. Duncan wants me to go up on stage with you, if you win." He drew a puff, and stroked his goatee. "Of course, you understand that you will accept the trophy, and you can hang onto it for a few days, if you like, but it has to end up in the display case in Duncan's office."

"Whatever it takes to satisfy him," surrendered Travis, wondering how his wife would appreciate the statuette of a naked Venus in the house.

"Just take it one slow step at a time," advised Nicholas, with a wave of the cheroot, "We need good pictures."

Then Blimp Pullman, whose obese bulk was a stark contrast to the slim frame of his rival nominee, waded into the terrarium to light up a cigarette, taking up so much space that even with everyone squeezing up against the glass walls, there was hardly room for the ferns. His signature floral muumuu blended well with the vegetation, as if they were all congregating on a tropical island utopia instead of the smoking section of a Las Vegas casino floor.

"Hello, Travis," said the large director.

"Good luck for the awards," responded Travis, who had last seen Blimp on a movie set in Budapest, where, in his consideration for the ease of his performers, he was prodding the rectum of a nubile Hungarian in preparation for her anal scene.

"I already know I'm going to win," Blimp bragged, brushing the same fleshy finger against the side of his nose to signal confidentiality, "Inside information. It's all rigged. Selwyn bribed the committee with advertising dollars. So, luck has nothing to do with it."

Travis did not know if Blimp believed what he was saying, but Nicholas concentrated on the end of his cheroot and Travis studied some of the botanical specimens because they were both convinced that what he was saying was total poppycock. In addition, it seemed that Blimp had no idea who Nicholas was, but Travis saw no need to introduce his competitor to the Head of Production at AXE, and through his body language, intimated that he was heading for the exit of the glass cage, which Blimp was blocking. In the normal course of events, he would not have left the two of them alone together, with poor Nicholas defenseless against Blimp's professional ambitions, but, in truth, he was finding it hard to breathe. It took some maneuvering to circumvent the rotundity of his fellow director in the enclosed space, but, avoiding collisions and asphyxiation, Travis made it out, into the sweet honeysuckle air of the casino.

All dressed in black, with the exception of a vibrant paisley scarf, a petite brunette with a tapered haircut and jangling earrings was waiting for him. It was his close friend, and friendly competitor, whom everyone called The Duchess. The Duchess was the contract director for New York Pictures, where Travis also had a deal.

"I saw you in there, but I wasn't venturing into that gas chamber," she said, pointing to the glass-walled terrarium, "Blimp Pullman is a crowd of one." She wrinkled her nose. "Not only that, but I can't tell if his body odor is perspiration or flatulence."

"Which way are you headed?"

"To the main hall. I have a meeting. You?"

"Let's walk together," Travis suggested, falling into step with her, "I have Sylvia Bern in an hour."

"New York? That's just a formality. I saw her yesterday.

We're both locked in on a checkerboard. You shoot one month, I shoot the next."

"I wasn't worried," he assured his stable-mate, "Are you ready for tonight?"

"I don't have a prayer. It's always an award for who spends the most money, so it has to be between Selwyn and Duncan, just based on studio advertising expenditure. They're never going to give anything to New York Pictures. But you might have a shot."

Travis shook his head. "The front-runners are Miles and Alec."

"Alec? I hope not." She made a sour face. "Yuck!"

"What's your meeting about?"

"You can't breathe a word of this to anyone." She glanced around to see if she recognized anyone in the cluster of fans around them. "I mean it."

Travis flashed a white smile, also meaning it. "Absolutely."

They presented their all-access badges to the security guard at the entrance to the hall, who responded with a respectful nod.

The Duchess made sure that nobody else was listening. "There's a new Internet company looking to buy out one of the big studios. And they have plenty of money to make it happen. It's going to have a female slant, and they want a woman to run it. Guess which woman they're talking to?"

"They're talking to the right woman," Travis said, processing the news, "But which studio?"

"Well, that's the question, isn't it?"

* * *

Something besides the irritating morsel of prime rib lodged between his upper molars at the back of his mouth, was bothering Beppo the Bear. He had finished his meal at a leisurely pace, but he was never in any race to get back to work. With an inscrutable expression, like the immobile statue of some Oriental sage, he sat resting and digesting. From a distance, he seemed to be the picture of patience and discernment, but he was waiting for his stomach to settle. Beppo never moved too quickly. He was a slothful man, a trait which could often be confused with caution, but wariness was in his bones, and, out of old habits, ingrained over the years, his instincts never slumbered.

He knew when he was being watched.

He had a sixth sense about it.

Alone, he occupied a half-moon table in a horseshoe-shaped booth, facing the buffet. The old mobster scanned the faces in the eatery, one by one, and picked his teeth. Most of the patrons rolling through the restaurant were on the portly side. There were entire families with the same chubby features and wide girths waddling merrily to gather more fodder, and contented couples who had found compatibility by tolerance for their partners' weight. It was unusual to observe such heavy individuals in the competitive society of Los Angeles, but they were at home in the forgiving comfort of Las Vegas, which catered shamelessly to all human appetites, encompassing greed, lust, and gluttony. There were numerous stations, including a carvery presenting the aforementioned prime rib, as well as roast turkey and pork, cut to order by a vigilant attendant in a tall hat, with ready cutlery which was kept sharp on a grinding instrument between servings; chicken, fried, baked or swimming in a cream pond; pasta in sundry shapes and strings, with a choice of lumpy red or white sauce; cooked fish or raw sushi served at the same lukewarm temperature; an international alliance of Italian pizza, Mexican favorites, and Chinese cuisine; bowls of salads safely shielded behind a sneeze guard; metal containers of steaming vegetables, with an emphasis on potatoes; baskets of soggy fruit, platters of tepid cheese, frozen tubs of brick-hard ice-cream, trays of thick cake, and syrupy selections of dessert. Food swilled together on the dishes and down the gullets, leaving only the olfactory collage of aromas steaming thickly through the room. Quantity won out over quality. Accepting the all-you-can-eat inducement as an existential challenge, and in the prudence of maximizing their money's worth, everyone sought to sample as much of the offerings as possible.

Beppo ran his eyes over the eager individuals with large empty plates waiting in line along the troughs, and those returning even more eagerly to their tables, their plates heaped with food, which they devoured rapidly so as to be prompt for seconds. He was not sure what he was looking for, but, other than the extravagant grazing, he would know anything out of the ordinary when he saw it. There were holiday makers, bach-elorettes, honeymooners, cheating spouses, divorcees, senior citizens, cowboys, southerners, easterners, mid-westerners, foreigners, and kids who had gulped down too much sugar.

He spotted two heads that he recognized. One was plumped on top of the shoulders of a large man with no neck, in a muumuu like a circus tent, whom Beppo recollected as someone from the industry. The other face was more ominous. It was an official from Los Angeles, oddly located out of his habitat in Las Vegas, which was already a clue. The man was formally dressed in an off-the-rack suit, so it seemed that he was not a tourist, and he wore no convention credentials. He sat at a table on his own, hardly touching his serving, and, although he was trying to keep his onion-shaped head behind a newspaper, it bobbed up and down behind it like the bosom of an old-time burlesque dancer behind a fan of feathers.

But Beppo knew who he was. He never forgot a cop.

His name was Luis Perez, and he was a detective on the L.A. Vice Squad. Beppo had encountered him at a raid on a stage in Chatsworth while he was dangerously involved in motion picture production. There was no doubt that it was the same round saffron face and shellacked hair. All that was missing was the badge swinging on a chain around his neck. He was from the LAPD, but Perez was assigned to the FBI Organized Crime task force. That meant that wherever Perez was, the Feds were not far behind. That also led Beppo to the uneasy conclusion that they might be there for him.

* * *

"You want me to do what?" demanded Traci Gold when Howard had finished explaining to her the broad strokes of his new business venture. The hard-bodied brunette, who was wearing nothing more than a bikini, put down the black marker with which she was signing posters of herself for New York Pictures. "Are you serious, Howard?"

Holding up the line of fans, Howard leaned up against the counter of the booth, as if he were a proprietor. "Yes, I've been working on this project for a long time."

"I bet you have," she said, with a knowing twist at the side of her mouth. "Does Travis Lazar know about this?"

"No." Howard looked sheepish. "It's my own thing. He doesn't know."

"Well, duh, Howard," Traci advised, doing a character, "Dontcha think ya better ought to tell him?"

"Travis would interfere." He moved out of the way so that the line could proceed, not so much because the fans at the back were giving him stink-eye, but because a bony, bespectacled woman from New York Pictures was glaring at him. He had a feeling it was Sylvia Bern, to whom he had never been introduced, her abode being on the East Coast, but who ruled the studio with a rigor that made other mortals quake. Traci was going to have to leave soon to begin the process of getting ready for the gala, and Howard was taking up the porn star's valuable time. "He's as greedy as a miser! Travis would try to stop me, or, knowing him, try to take a cut."

"Try to take a cut," Traci agreed, "But he's going to find out in the end, Howard." She smiled for a photograph, and picked up her felt-tip pen again to autograph a poster for a patient admirer. "Then what?"

"Forget Travis." Howard got to the point, because he had an itchy feeling that the producer himself might show up at any moment. "What about you? Will you do it or not?"

* * *

Travis had trouble with the bow-tie, even though it was one of the easy, clip-on types, and, after being frustrated for a few attempts of trying to hook the catch around his neck, he wondered if he might have to go back to L.A. to get his wife to help him dress. He managed to snag it by fluke, and, in the mirror of his hotel suite, tense as he was, he flashed a gleaming smile at himself, dressed in his tuxedo.

Duncan's suite was on a penthouse floor of the same hotel, a sumptuous two-story spread, with floor-to-ceiling windows overlooking the lights of the Strip, a private bar, and soft sofas with checkered cushions. The door was ajar, and there was the mutter of subdued conversation from inside the room. Travis entered and suddenly got the sense of attending a funeral with well-clad mourners sharing private sentiments. Everyone was attired for the event in evening gowns and tuxedos, but the atmosphere was so dismal that all they needed was a dressed-up cadaver in a wooden box to make it a wake. The attendees comprised a leggy blonde with an overbite, who was the AXE art director, responsible for designing the box covers and posters; a greasy sales agent named Oscar Lowport with a five-o-clock shadow and long, dark curls shiny from hair oil, who handled the international sales of the studio's movies and had dragged a few of his foreign buyers in tow; the head of domestic distribution and some lower level domestic sales executives who were taking advantage of the open bar and complimentary cocktail wieners; Duncan's wife, Evelyn, who was playing hostess like a dowager at a charity function instead of a reception for pornographers; and the mogul himself, whose booming voice soared over the low undertone of discussion from the rest of the guests.

Nicholas Pasquale, the producer's only potential ally, was nowhere to be seen, but, to his relief, Alec Zig was not there either. Everyone looked uncomfortable, not sure of how to handle the web of office politics in what passed for a social setting. Nobody wanted to say the wrong thing, so little was exchanged, but the chance of that increased, as did the volume of chatter, with the level of alcohol which was steadily being consumed in an effort to settle the general nerves. Because of his rocky recent history with the studio, Travis' popularity was uncertain, and so, to be on the safe side, he was largely kept at bay by most of the guests.

Duncan, wearing a purple cummerbund around his waist, and a scowl on his face when he saw the producer, greeted Travis with a wave of his arms from across the room. "Lazar, you're here. Have a drink. There's *hors d'oeuvres* too, if you're hungry. Fill up a plate."

This was as hospitable as Duncan could be, under the circumstances, so Travis agreeably complied with his invitation, and promptly had a glass of vodka and tonic in his hand, and balanced a plate of appetizers on his lap on one of the soft sofas. He had been too edgy to eat all day and took advantage of the free food to staunch his constitution. This also gave him something to do while nobody spoke to him.

When he had finished eating, he clambered out of the pillows into which he had sunk, just as Evelyn Hathaway approached him, smiling from across the room.

She was always gracious. "I just want to wish you good luck for the awards tonight."

"Thank you. You too. You have two horses in the race with me and Alec, so I am sure one of us will bring home a prize for you."

"I really liked your picture," she encouraged, "You should talk to Duncan about doing something else."

At these words, as if he were making an entrance from behind a stage curtain in response to the evocation of his name, the president of the studio himself lumbered over, with a swing to his stride that suggested his tuxedo trousers had just a little too much room in the crotch so as to prevent his presidential testicles from pinching. The purple cummerbund clasped like a girdle. He was always more comfortable in baggy shorts and golf shirts, and tugged at his tight collar with his forefinger. "You get something to eat?"

Travis gestured at the empty plate he was holding. "Thank you, yes."

"I was just saying that Travis should do something else for us," nudged Mrs. Hathaway, backing away to attend to other duties of hospitality.

The mogul dismissed the suggestion. "Let's see if he wins the trophy first."

"Well, it's really about the nomination," the producer defended himself.

"You have something you want to make?" Duncan asked, glowering through his gold rims.

21

Travis responded, "I've got an idea."

It was hard for Duncan to refuse him on the night of the awards, while they were all having such a jolly time. Duncan needed to make a statement through the industry that he had kept Travis Lazar in check, and did not want the producer allied with his competitors, or sniping at him from the outside, and he also understood that Travis had the support of his brilliant right-hand man, Nicholas Pasquale. Travis wanted the prestige of the AXE brand on his movies, and Duncan spent more on production budgets than anyone else in the industry. *Better the devil you know* was the theme. The mogul and the producer both realized that, no matter what they felt for one another on a personal level, peace had to be declared, and the only way to do that was through another project.

"Fine," Duncan growled, reluctant to mar the ambiance, "Let's talk about a deal when we all get back to L.A."

Then Alec Zig walked into the room in a camel beret augmenting his tuxedo, and there was a murmur of excitement, and most of the guests, including Duncan and Evelyn, went over to pat the creative wizard on the back, leaving Travis holding a conversation with his empty plate. As he twirled the wisps of his red beard, Alec began to tell a long anecdote in such a low rasp that the group that hunched around him to heed his remarkable account gasped and tittered at his wittiness, while those just outside of his circle could not hear the narration, offering the impression that he was unfolding arcane insights to a select few disciples. Despite this handicap, some of the audience who lurked on the perimeter, taking their cues from the listeners close by and not wishing to be excluded, responded with appropriate awe and mirth in reaction, just as if they could actually catch the discourse of the spellbinding wag.

The hubbub following Alec's entrance was soon replaced

when Tiffany West, who was running late, charged into the room in a glittering gown that barely restrained the contract player's exclusive breasts, between which dangled the AXE studio logo in polished gold. She was squired by a block-jawed, crew-cut Irishman in a velvet jacket. It was Miles Flannigan, the in-house director for the arch-rival studio, Paradise Media, and the star's recent bridegroom. Now everyone who had flocked to Alec abandoned him and crowded around Tiffany to compliment her on her appearance, which had been much assisted by the wonders of makeup, and to congratulate her on the coveted nomination. This distraction struck Travis as a superb opportunity to refill his plate of appetizers, keeping himself occupied in picking at cold shrimp and warm pigs-in-a-blanket, which also served as his companions, while he was otherwise ignored.

He finished up the last mouthful, as Miles strolled over, also seeking a friendly face in the tundra of the soiree. "So, by your presence, can I assume that all is calm and cozy between you and the big guy?"

"Sure." Travis broke the news of his recent deal without delay. "We're doing another picture."

"He doesn't like you, but he loves your movies," concluded Miles.

"How come you're not warming up with Paradise?"

"Selwyn is waiting until after the gala to give his party," said Miles, "So he can crow over his spoils." He gave a sigh in the direction of his new wife. "Besides, somebody has to keep an eye on Tiffany."

"How's married life treating you?"

"Oh, it's like a fairy tale," Miles answered, with a roll of his eyes.

"I understand." Travis was sympathetic. "This industry is not easy on relationships." He was relieved that he did not bring his wife to these events. "There are jealousies, tempta- tions, and all kinds of stress, but mostly, you just get jaded."

Suddenly, Miles confided, "Sometimes, life seems so hollow I feel like sucking on the end of a gun barrel." Then he put a cocktail wiener into his mouth, followed by a piece of cheese, which he chewed vacantly.

Travis was not sure how to respond to such a bulletin so he attempted a joke. "That sounds like one of my movies."

"I'm sorry, Travis," Miles said in a forlorn voice, "I don't mean to sound so operatic. But you understand."

"Absolutely." He flashed a white smile.

The star herself walked over to them now, searching for her husband, and Miles slid his arm around her waist, claiming possession.

"Travis Lazar," Tiffany proclaimed, by way of greeting her least favorite producer.

"I haven't seen you since your wedding," Travis said, "Congratulations."

"We're just two love-birds in a nest now," she declared.

This was not the impression that Travis had gleaned from Miles' remarks, although he thought it would be indiscreet to disagree with her.

"What?" she demanded, studying his face.

With the noblest of intentions, Travis said, "I mean it. The best of luck. I was saying to Miles that this business is not always easy on relationships."

"Oh, eff you, Travis," snapped Tiffany, "Why do you always have to be such a prick about everything?"

The greatest commotion of the night now buzzed from the group, in response to an announcement, not of the arrival of another luminary at the level of Alec Zig or Tiffany West, but of the limousine. There was a scurry towards the door of the authorized chosen, who were to be taken to the awards by livery.

"Okay, limo's here," Duncan declared, in his booming voice, "All of those of you who are going in the limo, head downstairs. The rest of you, party's over. We'll see you at the awards."

The guests all dutifully downed the last of their cocktails, ate the last of their shrimp, and lined up towards the exit.

On the way out, Travis made sure to express his gratitude to his hostess. "Evelyn, I just want to thank you for your hospitality."

"How did it go with Duncan?" asked the mogul's wife.

"We're supposed to talk in L.A." said the producer.

"Don't talk to Duncan. Follow up with Nicholas."

"I understand." The boss always had to win. He realized now why Evelyn had made sure that Nicholas was not even at the party.

Like a nightclub doorman at closing time, Duncan stood at the hotel suite door to watch everybody depart, and the group traipsed down the hallway to the bank of elevators. Everyone crowded in together, and as the elevator began its descent, the tone was just as somber as it had been at the party, but, on the way down, Oscar Lowport, in the back corner with an intoxicated Swede, cracked a few jokes, which were not funny, but lightened the mood, so that by the time they all poured out at the bottom, it seemed that everyone had shared a rollicking occasion.

They all stepped out into the bracing winter air, whereupon the women in evening gowns scurried straight back inside, as quickly as they could manage in heels, while the men braved the elements to arrange transportation. This was not easy, as there was a line of shivering guests waiting for taxis, and it was clear that anyone at the back of the line would never make it to the front of the line to arrive at the ceremony on time, but possibly frozen.

Tiffany and Miles roared off in a two-seater convertible with the top down, and both the heater and the sound system turned up to the maximum.

Duncan's limousine was double-parked, and, without waiting for the chauffeur to open the door, the mogul helped his wife into the back of the car, followed by Alec Zig, rubbing his hands, the toothy art director, with the long legs, and the head of domestic distribution. They shut the door, forgetting Oscar Lowport, who was also authorized to ride in the presidential vehicle and who came jogging up – narrowly avoiding a collision with a luggage cart – to get in just before they drove away.

Stranded, Travis watched the red taillights of the limousine disappear, and weighed his prospects for conveyance.

There was a fleet of limousines for hire at one hundred dollars an hour, but the parsimonious producer was not going to be extorted. In addition to which, there was nothing less glamorous than one lonely traveler being chauffeured to an awards show without accompaniment. His producing skills came in handy. With hardly any hesitation, Travis strode right up to the front of the taxi line, where a group of three drunken businessmen, in town for a colleague's bachelor party, were about to get into a cab. On a roll, the producer, who had already negotiated a successful agreement with the mogul, made his second deal of the night – with a taxi passenger.

"Wherever you're going, I'll pay your fare," offered Travis, his formal wear adding a much needed touch of class to his proposition, "I just need a ride across the street."

"Sure, come on in," one of the trio said cheerfully, spilling some of the margarita from his plastic cup in his *joie de vivre*.

Travis slipped into the front seat, almost unnoticed, and,

with a twenty-dollar bill in his hand, said to the driver, "I just need to get dropped off at the awards."

The taxi driver nodded, as he had been ferrying this shuttle all night, and swung the car out into the stream of traffic on the Las Vegas Strip.

"Hey, who's this guy?" someone demanded from the back, perceiving their additional companion for the first time like an apparition.

"Dude, he's paying for the trip," announced the man with whom Travis had concluded the arrangement.

"Awesome," was the overall consensus.

As they drove beneath the neon marquees welcoming the adult industry to Las Vegas and approached the hotel where the awards ceremony was to take place, the passengers in the back began talking about the big porno convention that was in town, imagining what it would be like to be involved in such a business, provoking each other with colloquialisms in the vernacular like porking and bazoombas, and fantasizing about how it would be to do one of those chicks. Discretion being the better part of valor, Travis maintained his anonymity, refrained from offering his expert opinions on the industry, and allowed the fans to run wild with their imaginations.

As they pulled up to the entrance to the hotel, in the hubbub of press and spectators, they could not miss Ginger Vitus waiting out front, in a coral gown with silver beading which hardly distracted from her expensive mammary glands, and an anxious expression on her face.

"Oh lordy, there's one of them right now," a fellow from the back seat of the cab could hardly contain his enthusiasm.

"What's her name?" inquired another.

"That's Ginger Vitus, you dummy," said the third, "I wonder what she's really like."

Travis got out of the taxi, with a wave of thanks to his fellow travelers, as Ginger came up to him in a panic.

"Where have you been?" she threw her arms around him, "We have to go in right away, or we will miss the red carpet."

Travis glanced over her shoulder as the taxi pulled away, and, oblivious to his identity, all three passengers were staring at him through the rear window, their wide-eyed faces rooted in astonishment.

Always thinking one step ahead, the producer put on a pair of dark sunglasses, and linked arms with his shiny partner.

Bulky security men in tight suits, with earpieces and haircuts like bristles, guided the stars through a maze of metal barriers and then along a red carpet between velvet ropes, on the other side of which a horde of onlookers cheered, whistled, and called out the names of their preferred performers. There was a non-stop burst of a camera-flash lightning storm erupting as Ginger stopped every three feet to adopt a pose for anyone holding a camera. She batted her eyelids and lowered her chin and pursed her lips, and turned this way and that. She loved having her picture taken. Travis was not so unabashed, and angled his face away anytime a lens was pointed in his direction, as if it were a firearm.

"Lazar!" someone shouted from the crowd, "Travis Lazar!"

He looked to see where the voice was coming from, and, through his dark sunglasses, Travis recognized Howard, squeezed in among the fans watching the cavalcade with a goofy grin.

Leaving Ginger posturing for the porn paparazzi, the producer went up to the velvet rope, which demarcated the border between the famous and the unknowns. "What are you doing?"

"I've been here for two hours, watching everyone go in," said the production manager.

"You couldn't get a ticket?"

"Not at these prices, and nobody would comp me," he complained, with a slight dig at his patron, who had not paid for his own ticket, and would certainly not shell out for anyone else.

"I wish I could give you mine," he said, turning back to Ginger.

That momentary distraction from Howard proved to have an embarrassing consequence.

Left to her own devices without her chaperone and over-whelmed by the encouragement of her many admirers, Ginger took it upon herself to offer a treat to everyone in sight. Before Travis could get back close enough to restrain her, to his horror, the busty actress – in a spontaneous act of daring – tore open the folds of her shimmering coral gown, and, with a shimmer of her own, she proudly exposed her naked five-thousand-dollar breasts to a frenzy of public jubilation and extensive photo-graphic documentation.

The security guards descended en masse, like football players diving upon a loose ball, Travis seized her by the arm and, giggling, Ginger covered herself up while the crowd was jeering and hooting as she was rapidly shepherded down the red carpet and into the hall before the inspiration of the moment could incite her to any further anatomical revelations, or possible repercussions from law enforcement.

Through the double doors manned by more security guards, they marched into the cavernous ballroom. Struck blind for a moment, Travis removed his dark glasses and peered at the spectacle. There was a stage with a podium, front and center, adorned with a logo that looked like one of those silhou-ettes on truckers' mud flaps. Behind it, against a backdrop of glitter, was a ten-foot statue, replicating the award trophy, with a band set up to one side. Even though no food was to be served, banquet tables with white cloths and floral centerpieces filled the space closest to the stage, with standing room on the dance-floor behind them stretching all the way to the bustle at the bar along the back wall. Theatrical spotlights swept through the hall.

The event was to be televised and there were cameras on platforms at strategic angles, and cameramen prowling among the guests with handheld units. The spacious venue contained most members of the adult industry, many of whom had dallied together on or off screen, but, even with all the stars, executives, producers, distributors, retailers, agents, technicians, journalists, and international players, it did not feel crowded, notwithstanding the activity at the bar. There were many people buying each other drinks, and many people drinking them, and there was a festive tone, with handshakes, hugs, and kisses, in close quarters, and, for acquaintances at a distance, everyone was beaming, pointing, and waving across the room. On their best behavior, the women were so elegantly dressed and so perfectly made up and coiffed – like high school virgins at a homecoming – that nobody would have ever imagined they all made their living from fornication.

Travis led Ginger to Billy Dallas' table, midway down the hall, where she took her seat among the bevy of starlets who surrounded the talent agent. He wore an *aw-shucks* expression because he was the only man at the table, licking his lips like the cat that stole the cream, as they all fawned over him. With his hair sculpted into a pompadour, he had forgone his ten-gallon hat for the affair, although he had cowboy boots sticking out at the bottom of his tuxedo trousers.

"Howdy, Travis," he greeted the producer, "Thanks for walking Ginger down the aisle."

"No problem." The producer decided not to mention the

slight clothing malfunction, which had electrified the media. "How's business?"

"It's always dead this time of the year," said the granite-faced Texan, "With the holidays. Nothing happens before Vegas." The agent kept his sharp eyes on the cliques forming among his feminine companions, now that the pecking order had to be readjusted to accommodate the inclusion of Ginger. "But it's going to be busy as hell on a Saturday night when we get back. Everybody's shooting. So, let me know who y'all want to book as soon as possible."

"I have something coming up with Duncan."

"Not if you don't collect an award tonight." Billy laughed, and cocked his head to one side, a newly developed tic as a result of struggling with the visibility issues presented by the low brim of his recent Stetson. "Don't count your chickens, as we say where I come from. You'd better hope you win the enchilada. If the Best Picture goes to Alec Zig, Duncan will pour all his whiskey into his exclusive guy and put you on ice."

"I'm used to the cold," the producer shrugged, as if his veins coursed with reptilian blood.

They shook hands again, and Billy wished him luck, turning his attention back to the challenges of talent management as Travis continued towards the AXE table in front of the stage.

Passing the table for New York Pictures, he almost did not recognize The Duchess who was not attired in her usual garb, and blended into the background in formal wear like she was successfully camouflaged.

"Travis," she hissed.

"Good luck," he said, "If I don't win, I hope you do."

"I hope I don't," she responded, "This dress is so tight that if I have to go up on stage, I swear it'll split and I'll reveal more than any of the performers." She slithered about within her garment, trying to get comfortable. "How was the cocktail party?"

"Nicholas wasn't there," Travis informed her, leaving the Duchess to draw her own conclusions, "How was your meeting?"

"Later," she said, indicating that there was more to discuss with him in private, "Where are you sitting?"

"Duncan's table in the front."

The Duchess was aware of what the opinion of Travis was at AXE. "Make sure your drink's not poisoned."

"We're doing another picture," he said, ignoring the admonitions of Billy Dallas with respect to the numeration of poultry.

The more one talked about a movie, the producer believed, the more momentum was created, which was how producers got projects off the ground. Rumors bred results. Everybody wanted to jump on the bandwagon of something that was moving. Of course, if one talked about anything for long enough, one never had to do it, so Travis made sure that he maintained a solid track record of doing the things he talked about doing and had learned the important lessons of when to speak–and when to keep silent.

He made his way to Duncan's long table, which was so close to the front that it was practically on the stage. There were nameplates at each seat, but it was not necessary to consult them because all the other guests, who had had a head-start in reaching the destination, were already in their places; only one chair remained empty, like it had recently been occupied by the first victim in a horror movie. In the center sat the mogul; on one side of him, leaning in close enough to breathe in his presidential ear, was Alec Zig; on the other side of Duncan was his wife, flanked by Nicholas, who was the only one to acknowledge Travis when he arrived. All down the rest of the table, each seat was taken by someone in descending rank and favor with the boss, until finally at the end of the table beside Oscar Lowport, was a nameplate marked *Travis Bazaar*.

Notwithstanding his designation as some sort of Arabian souk, the producer took his place beside the foreign sales agent, who, as if he were trading rugs or spices in just such a market, immediately began his pitch.

"You know what your problem is...?" Oscar postulated, by way of greeting his neighbor, "You don't own the rights to your movies."

"I sell the worldwide rights before I make the movies," explained Travis, who felt like an overbearing uncle had sat down beside him at the children's folding table at a family Thanksgiving dinner.

"Right. But if you parceled it out, you'd be making lots more money." He turned over a cocktail napkin, whipped out an expensive pen and drew a large dollar sign with four vertical stripes. He started writing down numbers, pressing hard on the napkin. "I could get you Scandinavia, United Kingdom, Italy, Japan, let me see now, France, Sweden – did I say – and Australia, although they don't pay much because the place is so full of pirates that the Australian flag should be the Jolly Roger. When you add up all of the international sales, you could be making, let's say, double what you're making now, and it all just keeps rolling in. Not counting my royalty, of course. I usually get thirty per cent, but for you I will do twenty-five, and not a penny less." He wrote the number on the napkin, and under-lined it firmly. "If I say twenty-four, I'm not doing it."

Oscar had neglected to mention Germany in his list of imperial territories, which Travis knew very well was the tent-pole of international distribution, and that his close ally, Klaus, with whom Travis had signed the Majestic Movies deal that very morning, was the pivot in that fertile soil.

"You didn't say Germany," he threw out at the sales agent.

"Right. I'm working on something there. You have any good contacts?"

Travis shrugged. "I don't do much overseas." The producer, keeping his mouth shut, was not going to give up his ace in the hole in Hamburg. "You have your network."

"Well, you don't really need Germany. Besides, when you sell Germany, you have to give away Austria, Sweden, Liechtenstein." Oscar caught himself and referred to the napkin for inspiration. "I mean Switzerland. I always mix up those two. Which one has the cuckoo clocks?" He consulted the napkin again, where the answer was not to be found, but he charged on, undeterred. "Believe me, Travis, I'm going to make you so much money from the rest of the world that you won't need the Germans, and isn't that a good position to be in?" He gave a chummy chuckle and concluded in a rising tone. "They can keep it, the wurst and the beer and the leather shorts and marching songs. Who needs it?"

Travis was not obliged to answer Oscar's rhetorical question, because at that moment everyone was startled by a premature crash of cymbals, indicating that the band had taken up their position on the stage, and the lights in the ballroom dimmed, although it took a few more minutes for the high-spirited audience to settle.

Then there was a roll of drums, and an enthusiastic rock and roll fanfare from the musicians, and the spotlights raked the hall, as the lights came up to reveal Summer Rainfall and Storm heading to the podium from opposite sides of the stage. They joined hands when they met in the center, and approached the microphone as the music and applause fell silent.

They welcomed everyone to the awards, exchanged pleasantries, and, by way of getting things started, introduced a female comedian with a raunchy mouth, who bounced up and down the stage, describing in comical terms all the genitals which she had ever seen in porn, and rounding up with a shocking description of her own pink petals which left people groaning and gasping and wiping their eyes with napkins.

She relinquished the microphone, and the band struck up for the host and hostess again, who announced an endless roster of presenters and prizes to nominees in diverse categories, such as Best Orgy Scene, Best Interracial Three-way, and Best Anal Newcomer. One ingénue, receiving recognition for sodomy, thanked her own sphincter. Another laureate thanked her parents, who were not in attendance but basking proudly in Kentucky, and sobbed that this was the happiest moment of her life, and had to be cradled off the stage in tears by one of the presenters. Blimp won for Best Movie Title for *Titanus*, but was too out of breath to deliver his acceptance speech after ascending the short flight of steps to the stage, and the proceedings were momentarily halted while he was restored with a glass of brandy. Majestic Movies was passed over for the award for Best Box Cover for Travis' prison movie, *Hard Times*, starring a pre-contract Tiffany West, but Beppo suffered no disappointment; he had gone to sleep early with a muscle relaxant and did not even bother to attend the event.

A long printed program listed all the categories and nominees, with plenty of advertising pages and boxes to check off the results, but nobody could keep track of the copious amount of winners, themes, and intercourse. There were two large screens on either side of the stage which displayed clips from all the nominated scenes, although since the glamorous event was being broadcast live, the explicit content had been edited down to create very short snippets that played as swiftly as subliminal messages. The band belted out an interlude between each of the categories, the intermittent repetition of which should have been outlawed like water torture.

The interminable program was only made bearable for the audience by the numbing of the collective consciousness through constant visits to the bar which ran out of vodka about two-thirds of the way through the ceremony but still had plenty of ice.

The only salvation for Travis was that the music was so loud it completely obliterated any chance of additional yammering from Oscar Lowport or anyone else in the room. People had to shout to make themselves heard by their neighbors. After about two hours of prize giving, everyone was completely bored with the proceedings, but bombarded into shell-shocked submission by a combination of sensory overload and alcoholic sedation. There was only so much pomp that anyone could absorb over the course of an evening. The audience as a whole bonded over a shared longing for the function to come to an end.

Travis had a stake in a few nominations beside his own. Firstly, the nomination for Best Lesbian scene, featuring Tiffany West and Traci Gold, was from his movie, *Starlight*, distributed by New York Pictures. He remembered that, during the production, the two quarreling performers had been more at each other's throats than at each other's pudenda, but fortunately, that animosity had either not translated to the screen, or had been perceived as passion by the reviewers, because they won the prize.

Tiffany and Traci mounted the stage together, kissed without any contact whatsoever so as not to soil their lipstick, and pressed their curvaceous bodies together in a hug, which was recorded for future generations by the media.

Tiffany spoke first, "One of the great perks of this job is getting to munch on Traci." She squeezed the statuette to her chest with even more fervor than she had embraced her co-star. "Not counting my dog, Coochie, and my husband, Miles, I love her more than anyone, and I am so happy to share this award with her. Girlfriend, you are the best."

"Same for me," Traci added, holding up her statuette in triumph, "I really enjoyed working together. Thanks to New York Pictures and a shout-out to our director, Travis Lazar."

At the mention of the director's name, Oscar took the avuncular opportunity to elbow Travis in the ribs, and Nicholas looked down the table and raised his glass of champagne to toast him. There were no other reactions at the AXE table, and Alec waved around to summon a waiter, but when the portentous nomination for Best Actress was announced, everyone stiffened up and paid attention because Tiffany West, the AXE contract player, won the award for starring in Travis' movie, *Dreamboat*.

The role, in which she portrayed an emotionally unstable protagonist, troubled by lurid nightmares, had been written especially for her, and everyone agreed that she was perfectly cast.

Her victory seemed to bode well for *Dreamboat* to receive the Best Picture accolade, alarming Alec who knocked over an empty bottle by mistake.

"Well, here I am again," Tiffany said, as she accepted her second award, displaying a blasé sense of entitlement now that she was already in the record books for posterity. "Best Actress. Wow!"

She thanked Duncan, Evelyn, Nicholas, the art director and everyone at the company, and, for a second time, referenced her lap dog (Coochie, not Miles), but in her elation, she once again overlooked the director. The emission was running a little long, so the omission was probably helpful for broadcast purposes. Tiffany left the stage to a standing ovation, partly in recognition of her thespian talents, but also because, after more than three hours of sitting, some members of the audience wanted to stretch their legs.

The coveted Best Picture prize was the pinnacle of the night, so they were all obliged to wait stoically until the end. As everyone else in the room became anesthetized into lethargy, the five nominated directors tensed up and became more alert, as the suspense tightened and the culmination of the evening grew closer. At long last, the critical moment arrived.

CHAPTER TWO

INSIDE THE WINNER'S CIRCLE

I t was Tiffany herself, making her third appearance on stage, twice as a winner, and, at the culmination of the gala, as a presenter, who was to bestow the coveted award for Best Picture. She was quite at home at the podium now, with all eyes riveted upon her, and effortlessly took over the show and the microphone when it was her turn to be the center of attention.

"The five nominees in the category of Best Picture are..." Tiffany announced, taking her sweet time about it, especially for the benefit of the television audience who were waiting with bated breath just like the attendees in the ballroom. "... Alec Zig for – oh, one for my home studio – I'm in this movie – *Future Foxes* from AXE..." A rattle of applause sputtered from a table in the front, "Blimp Pullman for Paradise Media for *Titans*....I mean, *Titanus*...oh, you know what, I just got it...." There were some titters from the audience. "*Forbidden Desire* by The Duchess for New York Pictures, and *Dreamboat* from my home studio again – AXE - oh, and, yeah, I'm in this one too....directed by Travis Lazar." She winced, and squinted towards where the filmmaker was seated at the end of Duncan's table, with a silent prayer that someone else would receive the favor of the gods. "Miles Flannigan. *Wake* for Paradise. I'm in that too..." Her voice reverberated in the hushed auditorium. "I hope it's you, honey."

To add to the suspense, Tiffany took a pregnant pause before she opened the embossed envelope, containing the name of the winner, then her full red lips swelled into a smile. "It's you. Miles. *Wake* for Paradise Media."

Cheers erupted from Selwyn's table at the corner of the stage, and somebody popped the cork on a bottle of champagne, which, buoyant, landed to bubbly delight in the décolletage of one of the table guests. At the same time, in symmetrical contrast, a black cloud of doom descended over the crestfallen guests at the AXE table in the front. Duncan's jaw fell open and his jowls shook. Nicholas sank his head into his hands. Evelyn remained stoically composed, as if the venerated lady were restraining tacit flatulence against a rumble. Alec Zig went white as the tablecloth.

The band of long-haired, gangly-legged rockers reached the musical crescendo of the evening, and everyone clapped – even the polite losers with their heads down and grimaces masquerading as smiles clenched on their faces. From the stage, Tiffany could see Travis in the front row caught in the gleam as the spotlight swept the auditorium, and when their eyes met, he did not seem in the least bit concerned that he would not receive the prize.

For the rest of the audience, there was much respite in the final announcement, which not only relieved the excruciating suspense, but also portended that the drawn-out affair held only a few more gasps of life before arriving at its long-awaited expiry.

Miles made a dapper entrance up the steps in his velvet

jacket, and slid his arm around Tiffany as he reached the podium. He took the trophy from her with his other hand, and held it in the air like a prize-fighter after fifteen rounds, as the barrage of cameras exploded on what was surely the First Couple of Porn: he, the winning director for *Wake*, and she, the Best Actress (and the biggest star) for Travis Lazar's movie, *Dreamboat*. They held all sorts of poses from romantic to ridiculous for shots that would be all over the Internet for posterity, and in all the trade papers and magazines for topical evanescence.

"Well, first of all," Miles said, leaning into the microphone, "Thanks to Tiffany, not only for handing me the award, but also for marrying me right after we finished shooting..."

He was interrupted by extemporaneous whistling and shouting, at which point the band, in the spirit of spontaneity, thought it opportune to strike up again with a short sting, although, since it was all improvised, caught the drummer off beat on the cymbal again.

"...Seriously," Miles went on, "I want to thank Selwyn Felwyn for all his support. The most supporting thing he does is that he doesn't interfere with production at all, and I am just pleased that we didn't let him down." He held the statuette in the air. "I'm so tickled to get this, thank you all."

The band started up one last time, and Summer and Storm stepped up to close the show, with the last of the scripted wise-cracks and a goodnight to all. Two skimpily dressed young women whom Tiffany had never seen before appeared to escort the winners off the stage. The house lights came up in the hall, and, after the long arduous contest, everyone seemed surprised that nobody sparkled with the same radiance they had emitted at the beginning of the evening. Looking as if they had all just woken up blinking in their pajamas, hair was disheveled, eyes were bleary, make-up was smeared. Of course, like the prover-

41

bial pair of chimney sweeps in a bathtub, nobody realized how they each looked to everybody else.

There was a scramble of confusion as they all rose to their feet and gathered their belongings and promotional souvenirs of the unforgettable evening. Items of wardrobe, cell-phones, keys, purses, and accessories were missing, and panicky hunts began for whatever was mislaid. Numbed by the proceedings, nobody seemed to know quite what to do now, or how to find the exits, and everyone tried to locate whoever it was that they were supposed to meet after the show.

There were going to be after-parties, post-mortems, drunken quarrels, throw-ups, break-ups, make-ups, trysts, celebrations, and the drowning of sorrows.

Tiffany and Miles were whisked by their two female escorts – who were joined off-stage by two of the bristly bouncers with their ear-pieces – down a long, dim hallway through a portal in the wall somewhere backstage. The floor was a concrete slab cracked with potholes, and there was a vague odor of urine and rotten vegetables. Not without some alarm, it felt to Tiffany that they were being led down a rabbit-hole, but it all happened so fast, with the girls robotically clacking ahead of them, and the security guards breathing down their necks like a wheezy air conditioner in a cheap motel room. But her spirits quickly brightened. Ahead of them were lights, music, and laughter, and she began to realize that she had not been kidnapped, but conducted into an exclusive VIP lounge for the winners.

They emerged into a private bar, a narrow, oblong-shaped room, with brick walls painted black. Beneath the dim lights, there were small, round café-style tables with spindly chairs, and everyone who was milling around was holding a statuette. Blimp Pullman and his award for Best Movie Title took up one table all by himself. Colt, who had won for Best Male

Performer in a Reverse Gangbang, had stripped down to the waist for no apparent reason other than to display his washboard stomach, and was wandering around with his tuxedo jacket and shirt slung over his muscular shoulders. Maria Blush had received an award for Best Make-Up in a Comedy, which came in handy as a prod to keep at bay the executives in the room who kept propositioning the tawny crew member as if she were an aspiring actress. Traci was giving an interview to a reporter from one of the trade magazines, coming up with answers to questions that she did not understand partly because of the noise and throbbing music, but also because of his exotic accent. Lit with photographic lights, there was a seamless J-card set up in one corner, with the logos of different studios and sponsors on a white backdrop. Everyone had his or her opportunities to pose for the press.

First things first, Tiffany had to pee, but the line for the bathroom was so long that some enterprising couples were doubling up when it was their chance to use one of the two available unisex conveniences. It was obvious that part of the delay was the time-consuming amount of fellatio that was occurring in the stalls, notwithstanding the odd ingestion of illicit substances, but, so as not to be rushed when their own opening came, everybody patiently waited their turn. Oral favors were a currency of the industry, and liberally disbursed on a night of such festivity.

Tiffany took her place at the back of the line while Miles went to get her a drink – a kamikaze with Absolut – and her bare-chested co-star, Colt, sidled up behind her, assuming a familiarity based on the number of times they had partnered up on-screen.

"Take your hand off my ass, creepo." Tiffany brushed his arm away, although she was not offended by the attention from the handsome performer.

"Just want to say congrats," said Colt, with his own prize in his grasp. "Are you coming to the after-party?"

"We have to stop by Selwyn's first. Miles has to put in an appearance."

He lowered his voice in pitch and volume to entice her with a husky purr, "Well, it's in suite 33013. Come by. It's mostly talent. Invitation only."

"It's not going to be a bunch of hairy guys with fat bellies and short cigars?"

"No." Notwithstanding her earlier admonitions, Colt squeezed his hand on her bottom again. "Big cigars. Starting with mine."

The bathroom door ahead of them opened, revealing the starlet from Kentucky and an executive from Canoga Park hastily buttoning up their clothing. Even though Tiffany was at the back of the line, her bladder was about to burst, and, as befitting a celebrity of her prominence, she dashed forward and cut into the front of the line. "I'm sorry to all of you, but the dam's fixing to gush. I got to pee so bad you're going to need umbrellas if I wait out here a minute more." She darted ahead, and, squatting as she closed the door, she reminded everyone she had circumvented, "Besides, I got the award for Best Actressing."

* * *

Travis was filled with an unaccountable sense of urgency, which had nothing to do with not gaining an award. His long odds in the pack of directors were helpful at this point because expectations had been kept low. Of course, as Billy had warned, he wondered if Duncan would keep his word and green light the new project now that Travis had succeeded in not bringing home the Best Picture. The President of AXE must have been galled that Paradise Media had taken the garland. At least, Travis was satisfied that Alec had not emerged victorious, but, other than that, he did not give the prize a second thought; there was no political stake to it now that the moment had passed, and he did not give much for the acclaim. There was no money in praise. He did not dwell on the issue, since there was not much he could do until the dust settled in the morning. Rather, as soon as he stood up from the disappointed faces at the AXE table and disappeared with all the invisibility he could conjure into the audience headed for the exits, he was seized with a sudden and inexplicable notion that he had to talk to Miles.

In his current frame of mind, the heady rush of the Best Director's momentary victory was sure to be followed by a headlong crash when Miles returned to the realities of life. There was a lot of pressure in being on top, and even given the Irishman's strong constitution, the whirl of temptations and emotions in Las Vegas on award night could prove dangerous.

Unbeknownst to Travis, of course, was the information that Miles had been spirited away by sprites into the burrows of the backstage VIP lounge.

Instead, as he followed the departing crowd, he ran right into The Duchess, who looked as if she could not survive another minute in her dress, but who, like the rest, had fortified herself by drinking through the evening, a course which only served to sharpen her wits. "How did it go at Duncan's table?"

"Uneventful," Travis said, walking alongside her, at a pace appropriate to the trundling attendees and the limitations of her wardrobe, "I spent the whole evening button-holed by Oscar Blowport."

The Duchess had already experienced the unctuous foreign sales broker's pitch. "Did he tell you how much money he was going to make for you?"

"I never have to work again," Travis informed her, "And that's without counting the big pay-off from Liechtenstein."

"You got *Lowportimized*," she explained, "If you're ever feeling down, have a conversation with him. You'll feel much better afterwards, although none of it is ever true."

"What happened at the meeting today? Did you get the spot?"

"Oh, they want me, all right. They are locked into a woman at the top. But, what they are doing, Travis, the palace intrigue, it's sick. It's diabolical." She shook her head, fanning herself with a program in the closeness of the departing crowd. "I just did not know that people operated at this level of ruthlessness."

"So, are you turning down the job?"

"Hell, no," said the petite producer.

The mob of people ahead of them ground to a standstill. Two ingénues had broken into a spontaneous love scene, swept up by the excitement of the moment and a cocktail of intoxicants, resulting in a mountain range of exposed bosoms which quaked under the flash of lights. In the interests of maintaining the decorum of the event, Billy Dallas waded into the clutch to break up the romance, like a sheriff refereeing a boxing match. The instant was over before the security guards, whose vigilance had flagged with the lateness of the hour and the enormity of the challenge, could even notice the infringement.

In the role of accomplices, the press and fans quickly assimilated the starlets back into the general population, as they all shuffled towards the exits again.

They poured out of the double-doors into the shouts of waiting fans, press and on-lookers, among them Howard, who had maintained his vigil at the front of the velvet rope throughout the evening. He played the insider, and was a king among the consumers, who considered his low rung in the hierarchy of the industry to be the pinnacle of an unattainable ascent. Stars came over to greet him. He was familiar with all the players. He was recognized.

In pursuit of this luster, Howard waved at the producers, with a cheery smile, but they both blankly ignored him because Travis had too much on his mind to deal with Howard now, and The Duchess considered him as brainless as a box of burnt-out light bulbs.

"I'll tell you the whole sordid story later," The Duchess continued, "But I have to go up to the room and put on my yoga pants before the fabric splits. Where are you off too?"

"I have to find Miles."

"You're going the wrong way. There's a private bar at the back of the stage. He's in the VIP area. With Tiffany."

* * *

Tiffany was lingering among a group of performers towards the rear of the VIP bar, where the black brick walls provided a contrasting backdrop to their dazzling ensembles.

"Listen, I don't wanna stay too long," Tiffany said when Miles came up, holding a drink for each of them pinched in one hand, "Colt is having a private party in his suite..."

"We still have to make an appearance at Paradise," the Best Director reminded her, clasping his statuesque award like a life preserver in his other hand. Paradise Media, Inc., was his home studio, so he had to stay in good graces.

"Fine," she snapped, "We'll do a drop in." She was having fun and did not want to spoil the star-studded night with the buzzkill of arguing with her spouse now, and she was on a roll with her awards, the spotlight at the podium, and being the focal point in the room full of spectators. Anyone who performed sex acts in front of a camera was an exhibitionist by definition, and there was nothing in the world that Tiffany loved more than the flattery of her adoring public.

To get away from Miles, who was on the edge of one of his moods, she decided to take the moment to pose before the J-card, where she would be pampered by the gaggle of paparazzi who wanted to ask her questions, take pictures, and capture her on video. Traci was just finishing up, and came to her concluding remarks when she saw Tiffany standing by off-camera with her arms folded.

"Tiffany West, next," said a reporter with a foreign accent, as Traci blew a kiss to the camera and extricated herself, stepping off the J-card on tip-toes so as not to puncture the paper with her pointy heels.

"Thanks," said Tiffany, making sure the reporter spelled her name correctly on the slate.

"No big, I'm done." Traci furrowed her brows. "Listen, have you talked to Howard at all? Do you know that he is starting his own movie line, and he wants to perform in sex scenes with the girls?"

"Howard? Perform? That's disgusting. Who is going to pay money to see that?"

"He thinks it will sell. He thinks fans want to see some nerdy guy getting it on with stars."

"Oh, come on," Tiffany scoffed, "It's just a way for him to get himself laid. He's a slobbering perv whose mission in life is pumping his peanut like a monkey. "

"Well, he's paying me more than my rate, and he's going to have a test proving he's physically healthy."

"He should have a test proving he's mentally healthy," said Tiffany, "Does Travis Lazar know about this?"

"I'm not the one who's going to tell him." Traci headed off to join an animated clique of long legs and high shoes dancing in the middle of the aisle. "But he'll find out."

"Ready," somebody told Tiffany, as the photographers and interviewers bunched around her.

The Best Actress stepped before the lights with her chin up and her hair back as she posed, pouted, and paraded for them. She nodded, displaying gentle smiles when she did not know what they were talking about, but she was quite sure she did not know what she was talking about either. Still, she gave an interview for a French magazine, a promo for an entertainment show on cable, five minutes for a Las Vegas newspaper, and her insights on the industry for a European film crew which was making a documentary on the adult entertainment business.

The journalistic proceedings were momentarily interrupted when Tiffany spotted Maria and demanded that the make-up artist – even though she was off the clock – check her appearance. Maria was as prompt to comply as seconds coming in for cutwork between rounds in a heavyweight title bout, since she had been on the clock for the Tiffany before the evening began, and considered the late touch-up to be part of her professional duties. She always had a few items from her kit with her, and Tiffany needed powder to take the shine off her forehead.

Colt was the next one up for an interview, and they stood under the lights together, both smelling of make-up.

"So, you're coming...?" Colt asked.

"Depends. Who else is going to be there?"

"There's this new girl, Mariana Trench."

"Mariana Trench is going to be there?"

"Yes. She's a slut." This was a high compliment from Colt.

"She's hot," Tiffany expressed more delicately, "I want to do her. I'll be there."

* * *

Travis made his way down the dank tunnel to the VIP room at the end, but found the entrance obstructed by one of the security guards.

"Sorry," intoned the beefy official, who compensated in large shoulders for what he lacked in neck, "It's for the winners only." Travis held up his all-access pass, but the guard stopped him. "Private party. I can't let you in with that."

The producer poked his head into the room, scanning for faces of friends, and also checking the room for any faces he preferred to avoid. He could not mistake the amorphous form of Blimp Pullman, offering his opinions on sundry subjects to anyone who would listen. There was a group of sparkly women all dancing together, and men dancing around them to get down the aisle. Curling four fingers, Travis beckoned to Traci.

She came over in prompt obedience, her statuette in tow. "Hey, Travis, what are you doing out there? Come on in."

"Barricade." He pointed to the diligent security guard. "Plus one me."

"Oh, for shit's sake," said Traci, sizing up the guard, who could have disarmed any intruder brandishing an automatic weapon, but who was not well-trained at confrontations with busty women in spikes and sequins, "That's Travis Lazar. You can't cock-block him."

"I was told you have to have a prize to get in," he responded, not looking her in the eyes.

With a spring like a Jack-in-the-box, Traci handed Travis her own award. "There. He's a winner. Happy now?" She took hold of the lapel of the producer's tuxedo, and pulled him into the room past the hapless sentry. "Come and have a drink."

Travis passed the trophy back to Traci. "No, I got to find Miles. Thanks for doing that."

"No big," she shrugged, before twirling her way back to the

makeshift dance floor, "It was your movie that got me the award."

He headed over to the bar, where Miles was on his second assignment to fill Tiffany's glass, as well as the fourth replenishment of his own refreshment. As soon as he noticed Travis, he put a cocktail into his rival producer's hand. "Vodka tonic, have I got it right?"

Travis toasted him. "I kept thinking about what you said to me at Duncan's party. Are you okay?"

"Top of the world." Miles brandished his statuette. "Inside the winner's circle."

"I mean besides that."

"Travis, I'm in hell," Miles confided, "And the devil's name is Tiffany."

"You have to be careful who you fall in love with..." Travis tried to be supportive.

"She is breaking my heart. It's all about the entourage. I'm not sure if I'm a husband, or a production assistant. I feel like I just orbit around her like a minor moon in the gravitational pull of Jupiter."

"Hello, Travis." Maria interrupted them. "Sorry about *Dreamboat*. You should have won." Then, with a twinkle in her eyes, she added the consolation, "Now ,you won't be able to get a blow job...."

"I'll survive just fine," said the producer, with a knowing glance towards the line to use the facilities.

"...Unless someone takes pity on you," she teased, continuing her former remarks, with a light touch on his body under the pretext of straightening his uncooperative bow tie.

"Now, now, Maria, you know that I'm a married man."

"Oh, that's right," remarked the make-up artist, "I'm sure Ginger Vitus will be devastated when she finds out."

"You ready?" Tiffany addressed Miles, as she returned

from her in-depth inquisition by the press, still smelling of face powder.

"I suppose." Miles gulped down the rest of his drink.

Tiffany turned her body towards Maria, who instinctively began to dab at her brow with a cocktail napkin where there were beads of sweat. The conscientious make-up artist tucked back a few loose strands of blonde hair, which had crept across her face, even though the luminary had completed all her work before the cameras for the night.

"Well done, Tiffany." Travis nodded at her trophies. "Two awards for two roles in two of my movies."

"I don't know what you would do without me," declared the star.

* * *

Selwyn Felwyn, the President of Paradise Media, had a grin from ear to ear. He preened about the party in his penthouse suite with his jacket off, the sleeves of his dress shirt loosely rolled with the cuffs back exposing his strong short forearms, and his bowtie hanging untied around his open collar. Trying to look relaxed, he welcomed everyone with a warm smile and an uncomfortable pat on the back with a lack of restraint that was out of his diffident character.

The newly achieved Best Picture statuette was prominently displayed. There were platters of cold *hors d'oeuvres* on cracked ice, and a full bar, although almost everyone was drinking chilled champagne.

The Paradise contract players were there, freshly made-up for the party; they wore matching gowns with plunging necklines and the golden logo of the studio dangling between the breasts. The international distributors of the Paradise brand were in attendance, with the representatives from broadcast media and internet acquisitions, mingling with those members of the sales force who specialized in providing content to those buyers. There were producers and directors and agents and the head of the marketing department and the woman in the talent department with a whisky voice who was assigned to the thankless task of being in charge of the girls.

When Miles and Tiffany arrived, Selwyn wrapped his arm around Miles, commented on the velour of his jacket, and pulled his triumphant director into a corner of the room while Tiffany went to say her hellos, drawing a buzz of starlets around her like bees to a succulent flower.

Miles and Selwyn gazed out at the lights of the Las Vegas Strip twinkling through the floor-to-ceiling windows of the suite.

"We did it," gloated the president of the studio, taking credit for directing the movie himself, "Duncan must have been seething that he got pipped to the post. Now, the marketing department is going to capitalize on the Best Picture award, with fresh packaging and heavy advertising, and the first thing I want to do is make a sequel. I'll put some money into it. I'm going to do a new gold-leaf box and a billboard on Sunset Boulevard. We might even be able to create a series out of this."

Miles was keeping his eyes on Tiffany, who kept biting her lip and looked like she was about to slip out the door.

"What do you think?" asked Selwyn, without waiting for a reply, "We'll go into production as soon as we all get back to L.A."

"It could be a good continuing vehicle for Tiffany," Miles proposed, watching her do air kisses with the Paradise actresses who did not want to smudge their fresh lipstick.

Selwyn shook his head. "I can't get another appearance out of her. Duncan will never agree to loan her out now, and she is still locked into an exclusive contract with AXE." Having ruled out the idea, he immediately reconsidered it, and then dismissed it again. "No, there's this new girl. Mariana Trench. Great look. I want to see if I can sign her before Duncan does."

* * *

They had sampled everything. Every sexual scenario or fantasy that had crossed through the imagination of some filmmaker had been realized by the performers. They had been angels with feathery wings fluttering under wind machines; demons in red body paint with horns and tails; mermaids dripping from the surf of spray bottles; superheroes defying gravity on a painted green screen; cheerleaders with pink pom-poms; college roommates with the same pink pom-poms; prisoners in lesbian jails where standards of cleanliness were so high that the inmates showered multiple times a day; cheating house-wives with homes in such constant need of household repairs that a stream of plumbers, pool-boys, and handymen were always ringing the bell; and more pizza delivery men than there were tomatoes in California.

They were versed in missionary, doggie, cowgirl, reverse cowgirl, spoon, deep-throating, skull-pounding, muff-diving, sixty-nine, seventy (which was sixty-nine plus one), finger-banging, single girl, double penetration, double-beej, dueling banjos, three-ways, Velcro, scissors, tribbing, criss-cross, ski-slope, shishkebab, pile-driver, donkey punch, daisy chain, gravy train, golden rain, drooling, spitting, spanking, wanking, jerking, twerking, squirting, flirting, hurting, choking, poking, rider, spider, astrider, stacking, racking, fudge-packing, peep-ing, sleeping, massage-creeping, pegging, motor-boating, fish-hooking, queening, kinging, jack-and-jilling – all in lying, standing, seated, and flying positions. They had participated in solos, duos, *ménages a trois*, and group sex. They had been made up, tied up, dressed up, messed up, soaped up, roped up, groped up, and upside down. They had copulated on beds, on sofas, on desktops, on tabletops, on countertops, on top of one another, in bathtubs, in hot tubs, in tubs of jello, in cars, in carriages, in spaceships, in forests, in the desert, in the heat, in the cold, in the mud, beside the pool and under the lights.

They were sexual athletes who kept their bodies in perfect shape. Their daily ritual was being attractive. They manicured and pedicured. They worked out, laid out, ate healthy, dressed sharply, groomed, trimmed, shaved, plucked, squeezed, dyed, tanned, and inspected themselves in the mirror. They knew every inch and crevice of one another's bodies, and they had viewed their own bodies from angles best reserved for proctologists, obstetricians, and practitioners of colonoscopies. They were as curious as toddlers and loved experimentation. Taboos became habits. With hardly an exception, the women were all openly bisexual; the men, with hardly an exception, were straight, or at least, discreet. In an unjust cultural double standard, the whiff of even being gay for pay could sully the reputations of professional studs.

Having tried everything, done everything, experienced everything, they only wanted more.

The orgy was in full swing by the time that Tiffany and Miles arrived, hand in hand, at Suite 33013 where Colt was encamped. He opened the door for them in a silken robe, which hung apart at the waist thus serving hardly any purpose as covering. Strewn around the suite, there were some dozen participants in various stages of undress in various stages of carnal progress. Orifices were explored, flesh was exposed, and limbs were splayed like a multi-legged, multi-headed mythological creature. Much attention was given to a blonde with a spiky punk Mohawk, riveting blue eyes, a cobweb tattoo on her shoulder, and signature large pink areolae on perfect natural breasts that dangled firmly as she leaned over a sofa.

"Mariana Trench," breathed Tiffany, "Introduce me."

"She's a little busy," said Colt.

"I don't care," said Tiffany, "I want to meet her."

"This might not be the time," Miles agreed with Colt.

"Oh, Miles, why do you always have to be such a downer?" retorted his vivacious wife, "Nobody is stopping you from having fun. Go and mingle."

She relinquished his grasp and, without waiting to be presented, strutted over to where Mariana was in a complicated embrace with another woman and two athletic gentlemen with large biceps and large erections. Mariana blinked at Tiffany, displaying an unnaturally glassy limpidity that suggested either intoxication or insanity, and extricated herself from the position.

With a formality that went beyond the protocol of the occasion, Tiffany extended her hand to the naked beauty and offered her best smile. "Hello. I'm Tiffany West. I wanted to meet you."

"I know who you are," said Mariana, by way of introduction, eschewing decorum and immediately kissing Tiffany on the mouth with such passion that she swooned.

The lady and gentlemen with whom Mariana had previously been engaged took that as a cue to return to the coitus which had been so charmingly interrupted, and not only were there now five in the group, including Tiffany, who was willingly swept away by Mariana, but, one at a time, other attendees began to gravitate towards the central action either as spectators, or joining in as additional participants.

"Take your jacket off," Colt said to Miles, who seemed unsure about his role, since the performers clearly did not require a director. "It's a party."

* * *

By the laws of the universe, the reluctant sun came up in Las Vegas, burning a golden glow across the sullen desert, with a bitter January wind whistling through the city. Debaucheries had raged on through the endless night like an out of control fire drunkenly feeding on gasoline. Most of the revelers had staggered home in the early hours; in rooms blackened by heavy drapes, some kept going past the hidden dawn. Nobody got much sleep, and nobody wanted to show up for work.

It was the last day of the convention, and business was done by now. The deals were closed, the sales were final, there were no more buyers. Junior employees manned the stands, the principals would surface late. Stars who were scheduled to appear for final autographs were sure to be no-shows. The stream of fans continued to trickle in, but these were purely the most committed stalwarts, since the fans had had a late night too. The sole tasks left for the exhibitors were to dismantle everything, like a circus tent coming down to leave an empty lot at the end of the engagement. Booths were taken apart, posters were rolled up, samples were packed away to ship home. The last stocks of the giveaways were abandoned. Trash bins were filled with debris. Fans scavenged among the remains for free souvenirs to memorialize the annual occasion.

One by one, more of the industry straggled in: those still dressed in their evening wear, doing the walk of shame with their heads down as if – by avoiding eye contact – they could affect invisibility; some, hungover, ill-rested, green at the gills; and anyone who had not won an award the night before, still smarting from defeat.

Among them, in a restricted industry lounge outside the convention hall, Travis had a much-needed cup of coffee with

The Duchess who was in equal necessity of the stimulatory properties of caffeine.

They sat in comfortable armchairs, sinking into the cocoon of pillows. In contrast to the raucous voices of the night before, there was a subdued undertone of conversation. People walked stiffly, as if there were extra gravity. Coffee was in high demand. Waiters kept bringing in fresh urns. Nobody stirred much, as if the wobble of any movement would upset the delicate equilibrium that held at bay impending headaches and unsettled stomachs.

"Somebody is going to get rich out of this," she told Travis, picking up the discussion from the previous night without making much effort into exchanging pleasantries, "They have an insider at one of the studios who is going to present the offer and try to push it through. But it's a deliberate act of sabotage. They have no intention of honoring their first proposal. It's all brinkmanship. They just want to feel out where the breaking point is."

"So, it's not going to happen overnight..."

"We have time. It's going to be a long grind."

"And we have no idea who they have on the inside or which studio they're targeting?"

"Not yet." She took a sip of coffee, looking over the rim of the cup.

Across the room, wearing a coat, Beppo the Bear lumbered towards them with a small suitcase. Well-rested after a deep, nine-hour slumber assisted by a sleep mask and nasal strip to alleviate apnea, he was the only one in the room who had made the sagacious decision to avoid the award gala. He did not care for glamour, and discretion being the better part of valor, he had not wanted to mount the public stage to accept a prize, in the highly unlikely event that one would be proffered.

"Listen," he said, sitting down with a nod at each of the producers, "If anyone asks, you didn't see me."

"You're leaving?" Travis asked.

"Yes. Heading out." He cast a furtive look around the room. " I want to beat the traffic. It's going to be dead in here today."

Travis disagreed. "There's always one more deal to be done."

"I'm getting on the road," said Beppo, without going into too many details as to the expediency of his departure.

"At least, we got the Germans in place," Travis said, trying to lift his spirits.

"How'd you make out last night?" Beppo asked, directing his question to Travis.

"We didn't win." The Duchess intercepted the question. "Neither of us."

"How'd you make out with Duncan?" clarified Beppo, whose interest was politics not prizes.

"Supposedly, we made a deal," Travis said, a little glumly, "But that was before we didn't win."

"There he is now." The Duchess motioned to where Duncan had entered the room, appearing as hungover as everyone else and more frail than anyone had ever seen the studio boss. The silver-haired mogul looked like the oldest man in the industry, with his back bent, a tremble in his fingers, and a prominence to his jowls.

"If he comes over," Travis said, without much hope, "I'll know we still have a deal."

"I'm not sure if he can make it this far across the room," The Duchess remarked sardonically.

They watched the mogul go along the line for coffee, and from clique to clique, just shaking hands without getting engaged in any discourse, and with more humility in loss than his characteristic bombast in achievement. He was popular and respected by all, although they all whispered behind him, expressing to whomever was beside them their own familiar terms with the great personage.

In the back of his mind, Travis knew that there was more than a movie at stake. He had come to Vegas with the intention of making peace with Duncan, and, if the deal fell apart, there would be sour blood between them both again. It was better to be allies. War was good, peace was better.

The mogul paused to have a word with Nicholas, who had taken refuge in a Bloody Mary with a leafy stalk of celery, and was wearing such dark glasses, notwithstanding the impediments of the foliage, that it must have been impossible for him to see a thing. Duncan made it a point to greet everyone in the room, although he omitted Oscar Lowport by mistake, and had to retrace his steps to say hello.

"He will keep his word." Beppo tried to be encouraging, but his face was grim, as they eyed Duncan running out of people to wish good morning, thus narrowing the window for their ineluctable encounter.

"You know what they say in Hollywood," cautioned The Duchess. "A verbal agreement isn't worth the paper it's written on. Nobody remembers what people negotiate at a cocktail party unless it's set down on a napkin."

Duncan approached the three of them, extending his hand first to Beppo, out of respect for his place in history, then The Duchess, and finally to Travis, the only one with whom he actually spoke.

"Can't be helped," Duncan said magnanimously, "You were robbed. You made a damn fine picture, and should have had the award. Check in with Nicholas, when you get back to L.A. We want a winner for next year."

* * *

Tiffany's lapdog, Coochie, waited forlornly in her basket which was hidden in the back of a closet in the suite, in case the maid came in, although the closet door had been left open or the animal would howl. Her mistress had not returned all night, but, as the day was breaking, Miles came back to the suite alone.

In plastic wrappers, and still on metal hangers, a selection of the star's wardrobe lay strewn over the sofas. Her bags – and there were six (two for wardrobe, one for lingerie, one for shoes, one for cosmetics, and one for sex toys) – splayed open everywhere. Nothing was folded, everything looked as if it had just been stuffed in a sack instead of being packed in a suitcase. She had lined up all of her shoes against one wall. There were unfinished drinks with her lipstick stains around the glass rims on the coffee table, and the ashtray was filled with half-smoked cigarettes with the same lipstick stains. The TV was flickering in the living room, set to a local station with local commercials. The heavy blackout drapes were closed, but all the lamps were on, and there were damp towels bunched on the floor.

When Tiffany finally returned a good two hours later, she found, in varying degrees of dismay, that housekeeping had not tidied the room, the dog had left a smelly deposit on the carpet, and Miles was sitting on the edge of the unmade bed in his underwear, staring at a pistol in his hand.

"What the hell are you doing?" she gasped, "I didn't even see you leave."

Coochie came running up to her, and she scooped the dog up, holding her pet across her chest, like a shield.

"I can't do it anymore, Tiffany," her husband said quietly.

"Oh, come on, Miles," she said, keeping her distance so as not to provoke him while he was cradling the weapon, "Don't be such a drama queen."

"You had sex with everyone at that party, except me."

Coochie gave a little growl, a wriggle, and a few short yaps, clearly uncomfortable at the prospect of being used as a potential buffer.

"I came home to you," the star protested, "I can have sex with you anytime. Do you want to do it right now? Just take it slow because my cookie is tender."

Turning away, she put down the dog, and turned back to face him, but then, she was shocked by the sound of a thunderclap, and a sudden pink mist of blood and tissue, because, with his eyes full of tears, the Best Director of the Year put the barrel of the pistol into his mouth, and squeezed the trigger.

CHAPTER THREE

SUNBEAM

M otti Sunbeam struck terror into the hearts of everyone in the adult industry. There was nothing sinister about him, even though he was also sometimes known as The Destroyer. He was not a violent man, as the sobriquet implies, and, as a matter of fact, someone once broke his windows. What he destroyed, however, were markets, laying waste to territories, media, whole countries, like the invasion of a plague of whirring locusts, by cutting prices so viciously and unloading so much cheap product against the target of his choice that he drove prices down for the entire sector.

It was a common complaint in the San Fernando Valley that nobody could compete with him. One baking hot summer, during a sluggish economy, when Sunbeam started selling DVDs for fifty cents apiece, a cigar-champing mogul from one of the other studios had a nervous breakdown, fired ten employees in one afternoon, and sent his Lexus back to the dealership.

Mister Sunbeam smiled all the way to the bank.

His strategy was brilliant.

On the surface, it was about taking out the competition, saturating the market, and devouring market share. Once, in a while, he used his business model as a weapon against his enemies, damaging the Brazilian market because of a Sao Paulo producer who had cheated him by double - make that triple - selling his copyrights. The South American sold Sunbeam the exclusive worldwide rights on a line of transgender titles, and then sold the same movies and the same exclusive rights to a company in Europe. Sunbeam took his revenge by flooding the Brazilian market with such low-priced product that it probably lost him money.

Sometimes, it was worth absorbing a loss by dumping goods into a market so cheaply that it left your competitors baffled and obliterated. You could always make up the losses later, when the opposition had been eliminated.

But, the way that Travis saw it, Sunbeam's system was really about generating a huge revenue base. First of all, he generally made a profit on everything that went out of the door, even right on the margin. He cut costs as much as possible, sacrificing quality not because his budgets were low, but because of the enormous quantity of product that he produced. It was hard to keep track of every droplet in such an ocean. To trim expenses further, he controlled all aspects of production under his own roof, instead of outsourcing to independent contractors, which was more common. He had the resources to invest in his own infrastructure. He owned his own editing equipment, conversion systems, printing presses, shrink-wrap machines, duplication, DVD authoring, and replication. But, even Mister Sunbeam the manufacturer could not compete with Mister Sunbeam the distributor running rampant through the marketplace, and so his profits per item were extremely low. It did not matter. His unit sales figures were enormous, and his philosophy was simple: any profit is all profit.

Because his product was so inexpensive, he was beloved by his buyers, and his customers stayed loyal. Because his volumes were so large, he generated very healthy cash flow. He loved money and he always had money, and, except for the fact that he was a compulsive gambler on the rare occasions when he was confronted with a roulette table, he was unassuming in the highest degree.

Wealthy, but without even the sophistication to be pretentious, he wore the same blue check shirt and saggy jeans for twenty years, even though his clothing never quite seemed to fit. In the California winter, he put on a blue sweater.

He was an affable, wiry-haired man, dumpy in the legs, with a cherubic face that made people want to pinch his cheeks. A Middle Easterner, his accent was slight, but he barked out English, which was his third language, in staccato sentences that were hard to understand. A bad temper never lasted long with him, but he sometimes ranted in a burst of anger, and when it was hard for anyone to comprehend him, he would finally punctuate his remarks, as if his meaning would become crystal clear, by exclaiming, "I am Sunbeam!"

* * *

When Travis got to McCarran Airport – as the sun was going down – for the one-hour flight from Las Vegas back to Burbank, he had his eagle eyes peeled for anyone he might have missed during the convention. He scanned the crowd as the taxi pulled up at the curbside, and spotted a few familiar faces lining up to check baggage. There was often a deal to be closed on the way home when the executives had their guards down allowing opportunity to strike. More often than not, the chance was that they were all traveling on the same flight, since the convenient

Burbank airport was the preferred destination rather than Los Angeles International.

Everyone was trying to get out of town, now that the weekend was over, the convention was behind them, sales were made, accounts were settled, and peace – or what passed as peace – was declared.

With all the cars, shuttle vans, and limousines pulling up outside, it was hard to even get inside the crowded airport. There were not enough luggage carts to go around, and baggage blocked the thoroughfares. Ticket kiosks and counters were jammed. Uniformed officials strutted about like soldiers. Announcements were made in strict and formal terms. Ubiquitous cameras surveyed everything, just like the eye-in-the-sky over the gambling tables, and it was not the only way in which the airport resembled the casinos. The last of the slot machines jingled, as travelers wagered one last dime, and the carnival smell of popcorn and caramel wafted through the terminal.

The line for the security checkpoint stretched past the brightly-lit retail chains selling candy, velvet jackets, and Las Vegas memorabilia. Even though McCarran felt less like an airport and more like a shopping mall, the authorities took their jobs as seriously as the gatekeepers at the convention halls and made an indefatigable inspection of every piece of luggage going through the x-ray machines. Men and women, elderly or under-age, were all searched without exception.

Most passengers were traveling to the East Coast, and were bundled up in heavy coats, which were not of immediate necessity given the efficiency of the heating system with which the airport withstood the desert winter, but even in the stifling line, they shuffled along compliantly. They had all over-indulged their appetites. They had been intoxicated by the bright lights and the whirling distractions of the town. Almost everyone had lost some money gambling. The excess of stimulants in Las Vegas, and the sobering reality of an expensive spree, bombarded the herds into numb submission.

But Travis had his wits about him. His mind was racing with the review of everything that had occurred in the last few days – the intensity of deal making, of the awards, of all the politics and personalities, and the sexual axis around which it all kept spinning.

He had closed the German deal for Majestic – totally under the radar – and heroically shared the cash with Beppo. He had solidified his ongoing deal with Sylvia Bern, and there would be work ahead as they began preparations on a new release for New York Pictures. But the cherry on the top, of course, was the deal with Duncan. The President of AXE had acted like a nobleman, but Travis was satisfied that he had done well to close him.

Standing in the line, among the weary and the enduring, he felt restless and impatient. He began wondering if he might be late for his flight, and he started thinking about going home, and seeing his wife and children. They had been counting the moments till his return. He did not want to disappoint them. He imagined his house behind the white picket fence, and sleeping in his own bed.

The line behind him grew longer, but it did not seem to be moving very steadily ahead of him.

"I with you," someone said, stepping beside Travis, with a bulky carry-on bag.

He turned to recognize Motti Sunbeam. "Hello, Motti."

"I standing with you," he clarified, sheepishly cutting into the line.

"Of course." Travis shifted over, ignoring the grumbles of the couple behind him. "I've been holding your place."

Sunbeam's round pink cheeks lit up, as he smiled. "You see

this line? This much people. I afraid I miss my plane. You go to Burbank?"

"We'll make it," said the producer, always projecting confidence, "So, how's business?"

Sunbeam gave a humble shrug. "I making a living."

They had first met years before when Sunbeam was working the street, peddling movies from the trunk of his car to mom-and-pop stores all over Southern California. They were both employed by the same company; Travis was already directing pictures, and Sunbeam sold them. Sunbeam soon left to start his own business with a partner, also a mercurial character from the Middle East, who found it impossible to work with him because he went wild with impulsive decisions and volatile risks. That recklessness brought him the occasional loss, but more often with a little luck, he succeeded through bold, original moves, and became his own force in the industry.

They sat together on the airplane, (after Travis had negotiated a middle seat for Sunbeam from another passenger in exchange for his position on the aisle). They talked about old times and current developments, sharing their opinions on the prevailing state of the industry, and each silently mulling if there was any way that they could make a deal on something.

Sunbeam broached it. "So, why you don't come and shoot movies for me?"

This stopped Travis in his tracks. Sunbeam Video was an entry-level studio for directors, and there was not much prestige for the established filmmaker in taking the position. In addition, it was a chaotic company, lurching and swerving from decision to decision under an erratic helm. But, especially with a new big-budget production coming up for AXE, Travis liked to counter-balance himself politically so that he was not over-reliant on one avenue of financing, and it was not so easy to say no to more revenue. When he worked, everybody worked;

there would be thankful crew members who needed the paychecks, and there would be roles to cast.

"You make what you want. I give you what you like. Just give me budget. I put the money." Sunbeam licked his fingertips, which were salty from peanuts, and clapped his hands together. He looked over at the flight attendant, who was dispensing sodas, then looked back with his fist at his mouth, alarmed that in his haste to secure the director's services, he might have promised too much. "You make me good price. We do a lot." Lacking a more extensive vocabulary, he raised his voice to emphasize his point. "A lot!"

That was true, there was no doubt that Sunbeam was capable of quantity. His demand was infinite. He was never going to have enough movies. Most of his inventory consisted of cheap one-day-wonders from the bottom of the barrel; compilations that had been chopped up and re-chopped into dozens of different versions; his Brazilian stock which had been devalued through more rampant piracy than when buccaneers commanded the waves; and a catalog range range so vast that he always needed some showcase pieces, which was where Travis came in.

The airplane began its descent into Burbank, and the lights of the sprawling San Fernando Valley shimmered beneath them. There were rows of suburban houses, luminous swimming pools and dark, amorphous shapes where there was greenery. He could recognize the neon signs of convenience stores, theaters and strip clubs in North Hollywood, and the endless snaking of the freeway dotted with lights, and then Burbank airport and the runway beneath them.

"We should do a series," Travis said, trying to figure out the most profitable approach against the savvy Middle Easterner, who was helpless against a discount, "Let's do a three picture package."

The airplane touched down on the flat valley floor.

Sunbeam wiped his fingers on his pants and shook the director's hand. "Deal."

* * *

The funeral for Miles Patrick Flannigan took place on a wintry afternoon in the San Fernando Valley at Forest Lawn Cemetery, on a hillside overlooking the backlots of Warner Bros. and Columbia, an idyllic site for the departed director. In the distance, across the valley, snow-capped mountains hulked on the horizon. There was not a cloud in the spotless blue sky, but the breeze took on a cold bite in the sunshine.

A ceremony proceeded in the chapel, an airy, white-steepled place which looked like a small-town set belonging on one of the neighboring studio lots. There was a shiny, brass-handled, closed casket, wreathed with flowers, and a large framed picture of Miles placed on an easel beside it. In the photograph, he was perched on a camera dolly in military fatigues, with a gruff smile on his face, the way that everyone remembered him.

Tiffany sat in the front pew, dressed in a black dress, black, elbow-length gloves, a black, wide-brimmed hat and a black veil, which covered her like a burqa. The grieving widow had Coochie in her lap, who hardly simpered, and clutched a handful of soggy Kleenex tissues in her fist. On her left, Traci sat beside her, providing emotional support to her frequent co-star in the form of an occasional squeeze on her thigh, thus provoking the occasional growl from the dog. Maria sat on the other side, watching the make-up – which she had administered for an hour before the event – trickle down Tiffany's face, quite conflicted about whether or not it was appropriate to do a touch-up. She decided against it given the decorum of the ceremony and limitations imposed by the veil.

There were so many members of the industry in attendance that those who were not present were conspicuous by their absence, most prominently the moguls, Duncan and Selwyn, whose tight schedules had prevented their participation. Billy looked as out of place in a suit as a scarecrow in a subway. Oscar, sitting in the back, had brought his Swedish buyer, which accounted for the pervasive smell of Aquavit. The scent of strong liquor was matched only by Howard's cologne. Freshly shaved for the first time in a week, the production manager sat with Jack Limo, Travis' grizzled cinematographer, and Tommy Hargis, the burly gaffer who was in charge of lighting and who had assisted with the set-up of the easel. Male and female, all of the performers were dressed up, as if they had been cast in a soap opera. Many of the female stars were sobbing, streaking their immaculate faces with sooty trails of mascara. They were all on their best behavior – there were not going to be oral favors dispensed at the back of the hall – and were all the image of sedate elegance. Everyone grouped in little factions, based on studio affiliation, or professional association; executives did not sit with technicians; the performers all huddled together; producers found their natural packs.

Travis sat with The Duchess, each wearing dark glasses to match their dark attire. The conversation between them consisted of nothing but grimaces. There was a printed program, listing the chosen readings, musical selection, and speeches. Tiffany was too overwhelmed to take the podium, some blood relatives spoke, and the pastor opened the microphone to anyone else in the congregation who wished to say a word.

Taking their cue from the widow herself, and without the benefit of scripted dialog, all of the artists prudently decided to remain in their pews. This was not the context in which to make a spectacle of oneself. In acceptance of that challenge, the only person who lumbered up the steps was Blimp Pullman.

"Miles was just about my best friend in the industry," intoned Blimp, who was so much detested by the deceased that half the industry wondered if the casket would start revolving. "We worked together at Paradise when I was making *Titanus*, and he was very supportive." He rested his large palms on the pulpit, as if he were about to offer a regular Sunday reading. "Even though we were competitors. But his talent as a director only made me sharpen my own skills so that I could compete with him. I will always be grateful to him for making me a better director." This did not draw much response from the mourners, who had little at stake in Blimp's professional advancement, and were not impressed with his ecclesiastical impersonation. "And a better human being."

There was no applause, but the silence was broken by some solemn music from an invisible organ, like the underscore of a horror movie, then the pastor said a few more words, and people got to their feet with heavy hearts.

After the service, they stood in a receiving line to offer their condolences to Tiffany, and Miles' brother, who bore such an uncanny fraternal resemblance to his late sibling that it was morbid, and Tiffany could not look at him.

"I am sorry for your loss," Travis said to the star, "How are you doing?"

She peered at him through the veil which, coupled with the hat and gloves, made her look like a beekeeper. "Not as well as you."

"I know how you are, Tiffany. You're a trouper. You're a survivor. You'll be back on your feet in no time."

They all streamed out of the chapel, climbed into their cars, and drove in a slow file behind a hearse to the burial site on the other side of the cemetery. From the hillside, they could see the major movie studios and the cars rushing by on the 134 freeway, in an apparent haste to get to Pasadena. But among the graves, where the headstones stood duty like patient sentries, time seemed to stand still, and the hustle and bustle of the outside world was devoid of any meaning.

The mourners parked bumper to bumper all along the access road and walked across the lawn in formal shoes that were not meant for outdoors and pointed heels that made divots in the turf. They chose their paths so as not to walk over the population who had already been buried.

A freshly dug hole lay gaping in the ground beside a mound of dirt. Three gravediggers in overalls stood off to one side leaning on ready shovels with muddy blades. The wind screeched over the distant whoosh of the freeway.

None of the mourners spoke a word. The raw shock of truth hit them all in the marrow. For a group who made a living out of make-believe, it was all too real now; even on such a flawless day in the flux of life, nobody could ignore what ending came to all. This was not a community for sorrow. Each of the ladies held onto a gentleman for bracing, sometimes linking arms with others. Many held hands, fingers twisting together. The weeping and whimpering increased as the stiff coffin was lowered into the mouth of the earth.

Travis watched his friend committed to eternity, trying to come to some conclusion that would give him solace. He wished he could have done something to prevent this outcome.

The sharp wind combed each blade of grass and rattled the leaves on the trees.

"This is a fucking tragedy," Billy muttered, summing up everyone's feelings.

There seemed to be nothing to add. Travis nodded at The

Duchess, and they turned their backs on the interment, heading back across the lawn to where they were parked.

"So long, Miles," Travis said, "You're wrapped."

"You can say he killed himself," commented The Duchess, "But the way I heard it, this was a murder."

Travis shook his head. "You can't blame her. We are all responsible for ourselves."

"All right," she accepted, "Life goes on."

"Yes. Let's get back to it."

They were almost at their vehicles, The Duchess in her SUV and Travis in his black Mercedes, away from the rest of the congregants. On a nearby grave, someone had placed a bunch of fresh flowers in a cellophane wrapper – which seemed to give Travis an idea.

"I don't suppose..." He glanced about, and with no other witness than his longtime accomplice, he scooped the flowers off the plot. "I'm sure nobody will mind."

"Not *Marion Shaughnessy, Beloved Mother*," she said, reading the marble lettering engraved on the stone, "Where are you headed?"

"Chatsworth," said the producer, cradling the bouquet, "Pitching."

* * *

Howard was working on a pitch of his own. As the falling clods of dirt drummed on the wooden coffin, the mourners began to disperse, some taking a moment to pay their last respects, and others straggling away with their heads down or their hands to their faces. The production manager made sure that he ditched Tommy, who wanted to talk but never made sense, and kept up with Jack, so that he could have a private word with the cinematographer.

"You want me to do *what*?" Jack reacted.

Jack had a longer stride, and was racing to get out of the graveyard, which he found spooky, so Howard had to keep up to his pace. There was a group of cute porn stars ahead of them, dressed up in their formal wear, but, given the occasion, they were all extra untouchable now, which to Howard just made them hotter.

"I want you to shoot a scene," Howard explained, "I'm producing something and I want to know what it will cost me."

"Does Travis know about this?" asked the cinematographer. "Because I can't afford to do anything behind his back. We all know how he is. Don't get me wrong, I love the guy and all, but he can be a throbbing asshole."

Howard kept his voice down and his eyes on the swishing black chiffon swaying ahead of him in the departing group. "The hell with Travis. This is coming out of my pocket."

Jack did not think that Howard should be left to his own devices in the best of circumstances. "Yeah, well, who's the talent?"

"I think it's going to be Traci."

"Who's the guy?" Jack asked, for one reason only, namely to be assured that the male performer would be able to fulfill his professional obligations by raising an erection.

"I'm going to do the scene. As a performer."

"With Traci?"

"Yes."

"Where is this supposed to take place? Is Traci even aware of it?"

They glanced over at where Traci was helping Tiffany into a polished black limousine. Traci cradled the dog, while a chauffeur in uniform held open the door, and raised a black umbrella over the widow, purely for ornamentation since it was a cloudless day.

Howard spoke to Jack slowly like he was a moron, the way that people usually spoke to him. "We're going to do it in my apartment. I'm going to do a scene with Traci. She's already agreed. And I want you to shoot it. And I want to know how much you'll charge me."

One of the women in the group ahead of them broke down in spontaneous sobs and had to be consoled by her companions.

Jack had to think this one over. "Come on, Howard, we're at a funeral."

* * *

Off the 118 freeway right after the De Soto Avenue exit, pulled over onto the gravel shoulder, there were always one or two old trucks which had driven in from the farmlands in Ventura County, laden with fruit for sale. There were iced coconuts, fresh tomatoes, plump grapes, ripe avocados, and juicy berries, which were listed on handwritten boards. Right on the edge of the Los Angeles County line, the blue hills of Chatsworth, with their serrated tops against the cloudless skies, enclosed the San Fernando Valley. The next valley – Simi Valley – lay beyond the ridge. The intersection of Hollywood and Vine, the traditional epicenter of the legitimate movie industry, was situated about twenty miles away in the heart of Hollywood, as if the X-rated sector was a black sheep kept paddocked as distantly as geography allowed within the county limits.

Travis headed south into Chatsworth, past the strip malls, apartment blocks, suburban homes, and schools to where it became more commercial and industrial. He drove past the anonymous boxy office complexes squatting up and down Nordhoff Avenue where most of the world's pornography had its origins.

His first stop was at AXE, where he was meeting with

Nicholas. Supposedly, it was a done deal, but Travis knew how those things went. The devil was always in the details. And there was one devilish detail that was bothering him the most.

He entered the grand lobby of the sprawling black glass building, carrying the bouquet, which he had taken from the cemetery.

"Those are beautiful," remarked the receptionist, who sat at a sleek counter like the concierge in a hotel.

"Can you see that Evelyn gets them?" The producer laid the flowers on the countertop, making sure that the patronage of the boss's wife was acknowledged. "I'm Travis Lazar. I have a meeting with Nicholas."

Nicholas was paged, and Travis watched the vermilion-hued Koi gliding in the fishpond, under the splash of the water-fall in the lobby, oblivious to the fact that they were at the center of the X-rated industry. Classical piano music was being piped through the speakers into the immaculate spaces. There was an illuminated display case full of awards, where the *Dreamboat* trophy would have been enshrined, if Travis had won.

Within minutes, the Head of Production responded to the summons. The producer and the executive shook hands, doing a long reach towards each other for the handshake.

"So, Duncan gave you a green light," Nicholas acknowledged, as he walked Travis from the lobby through the bullpen of the art department to his office.

"You were right." Travis was quick to give Nicholas the credit, and even quicker to reaffirm the color of the light.

They sat down in the candlelit gloom in the office of the Head of Production and Creative Affairs. His mystique as an *artiste* was encouraged. A stick of incense trailed smoke, leaving the perfume of Jungle Rain hovering over the desk. A bank of monitors showed eclectic images: news, stocks, the latest X-rated releases, a documentary on Mozart, a logic game, and the closed-circuit security cameras that were posted through the building.

Nicholas leaned forward, with his elbows on the desk. "Duncan says you can do whatever you like. The contract is already done. Just get me a script, and I'll push it through. Something big, but not like *Dreamboat*. He doesn't want to spend that much on anything at the moment."

"I have a title..." the producer began, completely ignoring any admonitions about spending, "*Fireworks*...about a female firefighter...we could do some effects..."

"I like that. For the box, we can have her dressed in the uniform...dirty her up...coming out of a burning building..."

Travis got straight to the elephant in the room. "Now, as to the lead girl..." The one thing that he did not want was to have Tiffany assigned to him again.

Nicholas offered a hasty reassurance. "Well, Tiffany's out of commission," he said, shaking his head and stroking his goatee, "Terrible thing. Terrible. Poor girl. What she's been through. Although, there might be something in it for you..."

"How's that?"

"The award. They want to re-assign it."

Travis had no interest in this unexpected stroke of fortune. "They can't do that. Miles won it. We were all there."

"The critics all feel insulted that he killed himself right after they honored him. The argument is that it gives the award a stigma. What happens if it becomes an annual tradition?"

"What's Selwyn going to say?" asked Travis, starting to get the idea, "He's putting up a billboard on Sunset Boulevard, trumpeting that Paradise Media got Best Picture."

"Selwyn's not happy, but Duncan is behind it."

Travis understood. "This is just about Duncan retaliating against Selwyn."

"Duncan figures that if they are going to re-award the Best Picture, the chances are that it will go to either you or Alec Zig. He's behind it."

It was obviously all rigged for Alec Zig. The producer veered away from the politics and kept the focus on the pitch. "So, what do you want to do about the starring role? The female firefighter." Travis had his own agenda. "I was thinking a redhead would be good because of the theme. Maybe Ginger."

"There's this new girl," Nicholas said, "Mariana Trench. And we could always put a wig on her."

A wig would be a challenge on her signature Mohawk, but the producer embraced the executive's casting suggestion with no hint of demurral, and as a reciprocative courtesy, Nicholas accepted that there could definitely be a supporting role for the performer towards whom Travis was inclined.

As he returned down the hallway towards the lobby, Travis deliberately took the long way around the bullpen so that he would pass Duncan's office. The door was wide open, and Duncan was swiveling idly behind his large desk, dressed in a Hawaiian shirt, and cream trousers, with one eye on the golf channel. This essential responsibility, notwithstanding his sartorial choices, had regrettably precluded him from attending the burial.

"Hey, boss," Travis put his head through the doorway.

"Lazar..." The mogul motioned for him to come in, turning down the television volume with the remote control.

They shook hands, stretched over the broad desk, although Duncan did not rise.

"Just wanted to say hello, and thanks again for the opportunity," said Travis, who did not sit.

"You work everything out with Nicholas?"

"We're all up to speed. We're going to try to get Mariana Trench."

"Go make a good picture," Duncan said, turning up the volume again which indicated that the meeting was over. Brevity was a welcome tactic to each personality, not only for the sake of palatability, but also, in the fact that the least amount of time spent with each other lowered the possibility of any reason for unnecessary discord.

Evelyn's small office – directly across from her husband's – was scarcely large enough to hold her chair and table. Proximity was paramount. To her, the closet across the hall from Duncan's office was preferable to the large corner suite on the other side of the building. She was coming towards the office as Travis walked by it.

Evelyn stopped him, her palm raised, almost touching his chest. "Mr. Lazar." Her voice was warm. "I want to thank you for the flowers."

"I know you took an interest."

"And the card..." she continued.

Travis had written no card. "The card?"

"It was so..." She made sure to find the correct word. "Eloquent. The way that you expressed your sentiments." The mogul's wife took his hands in hers, holding them in dangerous propinquity to her matronly bosom. "You really are a gentleman. You're not like everybody says."

* * *

Sunbeam wanted to meet Travis after hours, because he spent all day as a nervous wreck, dreading the looming deadline when the brown UPS delivery trucks arrived. Everything had to be ready to load. Every day was a sprint against the clock. He could only unwind after the daily shipments had gone out crate by crate to an infinite assortment of liquor stores, truck stops, gas stations, magazine kiosks, convenience stores, bodegas, swap meets, adult stores, and his loyal mom-and-pop shops all across the country. His favorite moment of the workday was watching the red taillights of the trucks disappear.

He had a gargantuan warehouse, with packages, pallets, and pornography all over the place. Each afternoon, he would take artless satisfaction in marching through the cavernous area with a tall stack of DVDs balanced in his arms like a jolly circus act, and personally load up the cartons to be shipped. The stack was so high that it obscured his vision and he had to peep around it to grope along the floor with his feet, like an animal pawing an uncertain terrain. Open boxes obstructed the aisles between the metal racks of shelving. It was a skill to find a step between them, especially while balancing a column of merchandise, thus adding drama to the spectacle, but one by one, he managed to slide DVDs out from the tower to fall into waiting receptacles.

Every time he dropped an item, he made money. He made money penny by penny, and there were a lot of pennies. He made money on every disc, and every carton, and every pallet, and every truckload, and it was a daily routine. The machine worked. Hundreds of invoices were generated. Boxes went out, money came in, the wheels turned. He knew his customers, understood their needs and idiosyncrasies, and had his own system of selecting every single DVD, which went to which-ever buyer. The method to the madness seemed to be compre-hensible only to Sunbeam himself. There was no order to anything in the place, only a few low-wage employees, and lots of shouting.

Most of the shouting came in a loud, raspy voice from Motti's older sister, Maya, who was a dragon.

"What you want?" she snarled at Travis, through a sliding

window in the cramped hallway that looked into her office, which did double duty as a reception area. She wore little make-up, and dressed as if she were never expecting visitors.

Travis did not waste his breath on pleasantries with the dragon, who continued to stand sentinel at the gateway to the enchanted kingdom. "I'm here to see Motti."

"In the back." The fiery creature pressed the buzzer to allow him access, snarled again, and returned to her office, messy with papers, bags of coins, fast-food menus, and a tray of miniature bottles of hot sauce.

Travis found Motti in the warehouse, pirouetting through an obstacle course of cardboard boxes while steadying a stack of DVDs held in place by his chin.

"Not now, not now." Sunbeam spun from one box to another, letting DVDs tumble into the assorted packs.

"I brought you some ideas," Travis began his pitch, fresh from his victory with AXE, "I know you don't want to pay Duncan's price, but I still want to be able to give you something on the screen. So, I think the most cost-effective way we do it is to shoot all three pictures at once."

"Not now," he pleaded, "You confusing me."

"Motti!" There was a roar from the dragon.

"My sister," he said meekly, apologizing for the clamor.

"Motti!" The dragon charged towards them. "UPS is here."

"I no ready," he confessed.

At this admission, the dragon breathed a streak of fire in the form of a string of flaming words in a language that Travis was fortunate enough not to understand. The blaze went on for quite some time, intensified on its own fervor, and clearly singed the target, since Motti grew redder in the face, until he could take the abuse no longer and erupted with his own furious response in the same indecipherable tongue. The hostile siblings went back and forth in heated verbal combat, until they both turned to glare in unison at Travis, apparently coming to the joint conclusion that whatever the issue, he must be to blame.

Sunbeam switched back to English, or his version of it, with a scowl. "He confusing me!"

"Maybe you should go," suggested Maya, her nostrils widening as if she were about to exhale smoke.

"We had an appointment," protested the producer.

"Better if you come back," Sunbeam advised.

Another explosion of untranslatable ire spewed from the dragon, and Sunbeam spat his own angry version back to her. His rage culminated when with both arms and all his might, he tossed his tower of DVDs straight up into the air. The pieces scattered all across the warehouse, and he turned to Travis, yelling.

"Go!"

* * *

Travis Lazar had skin as thick as armor, and, because all producers were salesmen at heart, he never took no for an answer.

The next morning, the producer sat at his desk in the production office at Sound Stage B in a compound of industrial buildings deep in the northwest corner of the San Fernando Valley. Travis had already formed his plan. Across from him, at his own, smaller desk, sat Howard, chewing on the plastic cap of a pen. There was a window all along one wall with a view of the parking lot, but both men were staring at the white board on the opposite wall, which contained the roster of their production schedule.

In black dry-erase marker, Howard had placed a large question mark in the square on the grid beside the name of the client, Sunbeam Video. The other two items in the list read AXE: *Fireworks*, and New York Pictures: TBA.

"We don't have to worry about New York yet," the producer said, "Because The Duchess is going to go first, and we'll alternate with her after that. Let's begin preparations for *Fireworks*. We're doing pyro, so we are going to have to deal with insurance, fire department, and effects. Get an early start."

The logistics of arranging for explosions in downtown Los Angeles always took a little extra time.

"What are you going to do about Sunbeam?" asked Howard, examining the roster in which Sunbeam was scheduled for their initial production. "Is that off?"

"No, I will close him. He needs my movies because, with my name all over the box, he can list them for a much higher price than any of his other garbage."

Howard shared his opinions on the general quality of their customer's taste, but even he knew that Sunbeam lived on low pricing. "I give it two weeks until he drops the price to the same as everything else he shits out."

"Doesn't matter," Travis surmised, " Nobody in their right mind expects Sunbeam not to make deals. He will list it high so he can trade it with the other studios for their high-priced product, and they will have to keep the price up."

"Yes, trading, but it's still going to get dumped...the..." Howard could not remember what the practice was called. "What do you call it...?"

Travis knew what Howard was trying to say. "Bundling. Trading and bundling. Bundling and trading. He's going to bundle it. Sell it in a grab bag with his other cheap product at the same price. He doesn't care. He's making the same amount on every disc."

"No. Your budget is much higher than any of the other stuff, so it costs more to make."

"He'll make all the production money back out of broadcast deals and international licenses. The discs are his profit."

Since he had it all figured out so well, Howard could not help wondering about Travis' profit. "What about Travis Lazar Productions?"

The producer had done the calculations a hundred times. "Three medium-budget pictures with Sunbeam are worth more than one big-budget production with Duncan. Everybody is going to make money. It's a good deal for us and a good deal for Motti."

Howard understood that when a producer said "us" he meant "me." He drew a second and third question mark on the white board against the Sunbeam entry. "I thought he threw you out of his warehouse," the production manager said coolly.

"That was yesterday," said the dauntless producer, "I will go and see him again this afternoon, and close him."

"Why is today going to be different? Because you're bringing reinforcements?"

"Timing..." Travis paused for the effect. "...is everything."

* * *

At precisely 5:05 p.m., Travis pulled into the front parking lot of Sunbeam Video, just as the last of the brown UPS trucks was rumbling out of the rear parking lot. His timing was impeccable.

He was accompanied by an impeccably made-up Ginger Vitus, who stepped out of the Mercedes as he opened the door for her wearing a short dress in a red to match her hair, a waist-length leather jacket, and stockings reaching down her long legs to spiked heels.

She walked into the lobby of Sunbeam Video on Travis' arm.

STUART CANTERBURY

The dragon slid open the window, and, like a mythical beast confronted with magic, Maya froze in dumbstruck awe.

"This is Ginger Vitus," Travis said.

Ginger batted her eyelids and pouted her lips.

"Yes, of course." The dragon blushed. "I know Ginger. How are you, dahling?"

"How are you, my little bitch?" Ginger teased in her most coquettish delivery, provoking the same jolt in Travis as her impromptu turn on the red carpet in Las Vegas.

"No, no..." The dragon waved her hand in a flustered, dismissive way. "Please, dear, not now, you are too much." She pressed the buzzer to open the door, and tittered. "You go see Motti."

Travis and Ginger entered the warehouse and started down the length of it towards the loading dock where Motti was standing in satisfaction, staring away from them into the alleyway which had just engulfed the trucks and his merchandise.

Travis murmured, "I've never seen Maya like that before."

"That's what she likes," Ginger explained, as her heels clacked on the concrete floor.

Motti turned to face them. "You come? Good."

"This is Ginger," Travis said, "I would like to use her as our star."

"Yes," Motti said bashfully, "We know Ginger. Ginger very good. My sister like Ginger very much."

"She's a bad girl, your sister," Ginger said provocatively.

"No, she good." Motti gave a pink grin. "I. I am the bad one."

He started chuckling shyly, and Ginger gave a little laugh too, and Travis did not miss the opportunity to join in on the joke, since everyone was in such an agreeable mood.

In Ginger's honor, Motti broke out a bottle of vodka, and

86

three tumblers, and, using a crate as a tabletop, they shared a single toast.

They finalized the deal in the parking lot after nightfall, as the rolling doors on the warehouse clattered shut behind them. Cars headed out into the rush-hour traffic where the UPS trucks with cargoes full of merchandise were on their way across America. A few brave stars appeared in the dark sky. The night chill descended over the valley. They had the clean smell of vodka on their breath. They were in accord on all terms. They shook hands like gentlemen.

Nothing was written down, but they would both honor the agreement, if only they could remember what it was that they had agreed.

CHAPTER FOUR

HEADS-UP

B eppo the Bear peered through the venetian blinds on the
window of his ground-floor office at the front of the warehouse of Majestic Movies worldwide headquarters in
Chatsworth.

He was looking across the parking lot and across the street
at a white van which was parked fifty yards down the block
parallel with the railway tracks. He was perturbed by the sight
of it. The van had been there the day before, parked in the
same spot under a leafy tree, and the week before that. There
were no markings upon it. The windows were tinted. No
matter how long he watched it, nobody came towards it or went
from it. He had become obsessed with it and could not sit
behind the stacks of paper at his desk for more than five
minutes before rising from his well-worn seat to continue his
observation of the vehicle. He had half a mind to wander over
there himself and get a closer look, but he could not summon
up the nerve, especially under the consideration of what he
suspected was inside it. He was so transfixed that he could

barely tear his eyes away from it, so he was reluctant to go tell the girl in the front office what to do.

Whatever you do, Beppo thought, you got to do the right thing.

Breaking his gaze, he went across the hall to where the receptionist-slash-secretary was sitting at her desk, playing with a long strand of her purple hair and giving too much attention to a game of solitaire on the computer, though it was at least a productive use of her downtime.

"Hey," said Beppo, in a low voice, "When you have a minute..."

She had many minutes to spare, and was full of hope for something industrious to occupy her agenda. "Oh, sure. Do you need something?"

"Uh...yeah..." said Beppo, keeping it low, "Tell Travis Lazar to don't come in today."

She reached for the telephone. "To don't come in?"

"Yeah. Cancel. We got company."

He put his head into the warehouse, startling the warehouse manager who had nodded off on a folding chair. Beppo indicated that he had not meant to disturb him during what was obviously his allocated break in the cozy den that he had improvised for himself. A plug-in heater was glowing. The rolling doors to the loading dock were shut to keep out the cold. Taped to the wall were graphic posters advertising X-rated movies, which would be frowned upon in any other workplace environment, other than, perhaps, a mechanic's garage. There was a coffee pot with a rich, aromatic brew. There were porcelain cups, branded with the logo of a rival studio, one of which contained box cutters, markers, and a nest of paper clips. Clipboards hung on flat-topped nails. There was a stack of labels and inventory slips in a flat wire basket on a large table. A pallet stood empty of merchandise. Beppo scanned the metal racks that held the outbound shipping orders, checking for a package.

Beppo was planning to deliver to Travis the materials for the German deal, and, even sweeter to Beppo, Travis was to provide a payment to him upon the occasion of the delivery. There were two boxes in the warehouse, labeled for international freight, filled with Styrofoam popcorn to protect the contents and sealed with packing tape, ready to ship. Regrettably, that would have to wait. He shuffled back to his own office and took up his post, squinting through the venetian blinds while he weighed his next moves. The white van had not budged. Not a leaf rustled in the valley. He was not yet sure what to do.

But whatever you do, Beppo thought, you got to do the right thing.

* * *

Howard was on the telephone with Majestic Movies when Travis walked into the production office at Sound Stage B.

There were already messages for him from Billy in regard to a booking conflict with one of the performers on the new project for Sunbeam Video; another from Fire Officer James Fleet of the Los Angeles Fire Department in regard to the pyrotechnical requirements of the new big budget feature for AXE; and one from Ginger in regard to a crisis which was only comprehensible to Ginger, her psychic, and her manicurist. But, more dire than all these was a call from Motti Sunbeam, The Destroyer himself.

"You'd better call Sunbeam." Howard hung up the telephone.

"That was him?"

"No, that was Beppo's half-witted secretary," said Howard, "He's canceling today's meeting."

Travis was puzzled. "He never cancels on money."

"I think they had a visitation," said the production manager, "The way she talked, or she's just a dim-wit."

"Well, we need to ship those materials to Germany," Travis noted.

"Not today," Howard shrugged, "Meanwhile, you'd better call Sunbeam. He's pissed."

"About what?"

"I don't know," Howard said, "I don't speak Middle Eastern."

Travis would try to get hold of Beppo after hours so as not to disturb him while he was dealing with business at hand and the possibility of incarceration. He was in no hurry to confront his volatile financier, so instead, he directly addressed the conflict with Billy then took his time to reply to the questions from the fire department with respect to a planned explosion in downtown Los Angeles. When Travis got hold of Sunbeam on the telephone, he kept it on speaker for Howard to listen in so that they could collectively decipher what was said afterwards.

"I very mad," Sunbeam said, "I don't put money. I get my money back. I go to sue you. I mad. My sister she mad. She very mad my sister."

Travis found that he did not speak Middle Eastern either. "Motti, what is this about?"

"Wait. You talk with my sister."

There was a string of foreign words between the siblings, then Maya came on the line.

"Travis." She restrained her emotions, highly sensitive to the fact that the producer had already accepted a sizable monetary deposit on the production "What I hear from Motti. We pay you for three movies, and you only make one."

"No. We are going to give you three movies. We are shooting them all at the same time."

Maya Sunbeam was unaware that the process of film production commonly involved shooting out of chronological sequence. "You can do that?"

He knew that the Sunbeams were unable to resist a bargain. "That is why you have such a good price."

"But you have Ginger as the star in all three movies, and she only doing girl-girl?"

"That's her new policy."

"She must to do at least one boy-girl scene," ruled the dragon.

"One per movie!" Motti yelled over his sister.

"One of the movies is all-girl," Howard reminded everyone.

Another heated exchange in an alien tongue was heard over the speaker.

"At least one boy-girl," insisted Maya, returning to English.

"I'll talk to Ginger," said Travis.

"Or we get someone else!" shouted The Destroyer.

* * *

Without delving into details, Travis arranged a late lunch with Ginger at a one-room Thai restaurant on Ventura Boulevard, where the waitresses always made him think of pixies. A golden Buddha with an open smile sat against a red wall. There was a string of perennial Christmas lights decorating the windows, even though the season had long passed, a fountain, and a framed photograph of the King of Siam with his extended family. The aroma of lemon grass steamed from the kitchen, and, at that hour of the afternoon, they were practically alone in the restaurant.

"So, they're saying that they want a boy-girl scene on the

Sunbeam movies..." Travis explained after they had received their food.

"I'm not doing boy-girl anymore," Ginger said, so unnerved by the request that she put down her chopsticks.

"Don't blame me," said Travis, laying his own chopsticks aside, and resting his hand over hers to be supportive, "I'm just the messenger. I'm against it. But I'm telling you what they said."

"Maya," said Ginger, with a quiver, "She's doing it to mess with me because I won't play her game."

"Look, they have a point," said the producer, removing his comforting touch so that he could return to eating, "You're the lead in three movies for them. The lead is supposed to do at least one boy-girl."

There was, of course, no rulebook, but the producer was correct about the standard convention in the industry.

"I don't want to do it." Ginger looked down into her noodles. "I don't want to get hammered any more. Most of the time I don't really like the guy." She picked at her dish of food with no appetite. "What do you think?"

"They're saying if not then I should replace you," he said, allowing a big crown of stir

fried broccoli into his mouth.

"Everybody wants Mariana Trench," complained Ginger, "But she's a trainwreck. She flaked on a shoot last week after confirming that she was two blocks away at a stop light."

"So, what do you want to do?" asked Travis, deferring to the decision of the performer.

She pushed her plate away, unable to finish the meal. "Tell Maya to go to hell. She's disgusting. I'm not going to do a boy-girl scene."

* * *

Night fell early in winter. The headlights of the Mercedes cut through breaths of fog and the low fumes from the traffic as the producer pulled out of the parking lot of Sound Stage B. Travis called his wife from the car to let her know that he would be home late, and she promised to keep dinner warm for him and put the children to bed, but he was the only one who could sing them their songs.

He did not have any appointments for the night – at least, not formally – but the producer figured that he had better be on call. He headed in the direction of the freeway, the streets clogged with rush-hour commuters returning home. There was a stream of cars in his rear-view mirror.

He dialed the number to Beppo the Bear. "Everything all right?"

"Nah, there's a whatdoyoucallit..." he muttered, always keeping it vague.

"Right." Travis understood perfectly.

"It was better you didn't come in," said the acting President of Majestic Movies.

"So, you got the stuff?"

"For the Germans. In my car. You got the money?"

"I'll meet you at The Chatsworth Diner," Travis proposed, although they both already knew where they were going.

The Chatsworth Diner was neutral ground, right in the heart of the industry, at the cross street of Nordhoff and De Soto, the epicenter where the great Northridge earthquake struck. For the industry, the diner was a classic meeting place where a discreet conversation could be held in its crimson leatherette booths. Rips in the upholstery that had worn over the years exposed where the leatherette was peeling, and the Formica tabletops were chipped and faded. There was a private hall that stood empty and was seldom used, an adjoining bar with a separate entrance which was used frequently, together with a long counter and a row of booths along the full-length window.

Whenever there was an argument, the Chatsworth Diner was often where it was resolved. Salesmen, looking to jump ship to a different company, were interviewed there. Trysts were begun. Conspiracies were hatched. When there was somebody to meet outside the office, when there was information to be confidentially divulged, when someone needed to be anonymous, or when there was trouble, it was the automatic and unspoken place to rendezvous.

Travis circled the parking lot once, looking for Beppo's car, and saw the mint condition Cadillac in a lonely spot with Beppo looming inside it. Under the circumstances of his apparent surveillance, the acting President of Majestic Movies thought it more prudent to wait in the shadows. Travis flashed his lights and pulled up alongside the parked Cadillac. Beppo climbed out of the car, with his collars up, and without saying anything between them, they made what seemed to be a long, silent journey across the parking lot into the diner.

They sat at a booth along the window, so they could see outside, and both ordered coffees from the uniformed waitress who had been employed by the loyal establishment since it first opened decades before.

"On the QT..." said Beppo, "I just want to give you a heads-up."

"I have nothing to say." Travis put his hands in the air to express his innocence, but he already was not sure if he wanted to be one of the parties in this conversation.

"There's a white van that's been parked outside the office for two weeks. I seen a few other things too."

"Vice?"

"There's that task force. It's the Feds."

The waitress brought their coffees and a toasted sandwich,

which neither of them had ordered – the cuisine at the Chatsworth Diner was famous for being as bland as the décor. The establishment owed its success purely to a fortunate accident of geographical placement rather than its culinary excellence. She blinked at the sandwich in confusion, as if the bread itself would divulge the identity of its rightful owner. Travis waited until she doddered away – unclaimed sandwich plate in hand – partly because of the extraordinary discretion required by their exchange but also so that Beppo's words could sink into his brain.

"Everything is on the up and up," Travis said, "People are making money legitimately in this business, nobody needs the headaches."

"It's not that." Beppo slowly stirred a spoon around in his cup. "I'm not even supposed to be involved in the first place. With my background." Then, deftly changing the subject, as an elderly couple, enticed by the senior discount passed their table, he asked, "How's it going with Motti? Sunbeam treating you all right?"

"Piece of cake," said the producer, circling back, "You're sure about the van?"

"Hundred per cent. They're building their case." He took a sip of coffee, put down the cup, added sugar, and stirred it again. "And then, they're coming."

He waved at the waitress to bring the check, but she walked right by without acknowledgement.

Beppo asked, "So, you got the...uh...?"

"Sure." Travis patted his breast pocket. "You have the materials?"

"In my trunk," Beppo said.

"Where do you want to do this? Here?"

To Beppo, there was no spot on the surface of the planet that was not suitable for the acceptance of cash. "Here's fine."

Without the slightest hesitation, Travis reached into the pocket of his leather jacket, and slid an envelope across the table towards Beppo, which he seized so rapidly it disappeared, like it had never even existed. In support of this vanishing, the two men blinked at each other across the table, as if the transaction in which they had both participated had not even occurred.

They left the diner as soon as they finished their coffee, without waiting to receive the check. Beppo, the beneficiary of the hefty envelope, generously left ten dollars on the table.

They went across to the far side of the parking lot where their cars were parked side-by-side. They waited while a patrol car cruised along De Soto Avenue, not because they were doing anything illegal, but to avoid arousing suspicions based on appearance. From the trunk of the Cadillac, Beppo and Travis transferred two 20-pound cardboard boxes into the trunk of the Mercedes. They shook hands and, checking their rear-view mirrors, drove off in different directions, as the shipment of goods in the trunk began its long voyage across land and sea to Hamburg and to the gratification of the European consumers.

* * *

There was no way to make a movie without a star, so, after a coffee with a Pepto-Bismol chaser in the production office the next morning, Howard began running through the Rolodex with Billy Dallas to see who was available on the Sunbeam dates to replace Ginger. Howard wanted to hire Traci, for his own political reasons, but she was booked with The Duchess on her new project for New York Pictures. Nobody suggested Tiffany who was unavailable not only because of her exclusive contract with Duncan, but because she was still in mourning for her late husband, a sorrow equally shared by the sympathetic mogul who was duty-bound to keep her on the payroll while she was indefinitely indisposed.

Travis liked the idea of Summer Rainfall, but she was on her annual North American tour, where she made good money by selling autographed copies of her DVDs at various strip clubs, adult bookstores, and fan conventions across the country. (For an extra fee, the star would pose in a photograph with her fans, and some of them would spend money on her used clothing, most particularly the intimate undergarments, with premiums for memorabilia which had been seen in movie scenes, or even more, if the items were unlaundered.) They went through a few other names on the list of stars. But Motti and Maya Sunbeam insisted on Mariana Trench. Before Howard could finalize the booking, however, Billy insisted on talking to Travis.

"So, we have Mariana?" confirmed Travis, coming to the telephone.

"Now, y'all are a friend of mine," Billy began, "So I'm going to shoot straight. She is available on your dates, and I can confirm the booking, but that doesn't mean I am confirming that she will show up. If I was in your saddle, I would go with Ginger."

"Ginger won't do the boy-girl..."

"Ginger was doing gang-bangs a month ago," said the agent, "But, I know, she has a new policy. Only does scenes with other girls. This always happens when the girls get involved in off-camera relationships with men. Very hard on the male to see her going off to work in the morning to swallow an anaconda."

Travis did not want to get into such serpentine details. "Understood. You have to respect the girl's feelings. Especially given the proportions."

"Oh, of course," affirmed Billy, "But all three of us are losing money."

"Well, you and I can make the money on Mariana."

"If she shows up to work," cautioned Billy, "But I'm not making any guarantees. Just ask Blimp, he did her last picture. She was already established in the movie. In the scene, she goes to sleep after having sex, and the next morning, when she wakes up, they had to use a different girl."

"Thanks for the heads-up, Billy. I will book her on one condition."

"At your own peril."

"I want you to contact Sunbeam Video, and let them know we have Mariana. Give them the same heads-up."

"You want me to contact your client?" inquired the agent, "Sure, but why?"

"We're not really on speaking terms."

* * *

Travis hung up the telephone in the production office, and sat staring at it with his brows furrowed for ten minutes, while Howard, at his own desk, repeated his superior's faraway contemplation until the instrument rang, startling them both.

The spell broken, Travis thrust his chin at Howard. "Answer him."

"Travis Lazar Productions," Howard picked up the receiver, as instructed, and nodded in acknowledgement of his captain's predictive powers. "Sunbeam."

"I love you!" the Middle Easterner declared, as soon as Travis came to the phone. "You are the best producer in the industry! We have Mariana Trench."

"You spoke to Billy Dallas?"

"He confirm." He spoke more rapidly as he became more excited. "Beely call me himself. My customers ask me for

Mariana Trench. Everyone want Mariana Trench. Now, we will have three movies with her. We give them."

"Did Billy tell you that there is a good chance she won't show up?"

"He tell," he said glumly, then broke into a chuckle. "But we take a chance." He was, of course, a reckless gambler to whom taking a chance only enlivened the matter.

"You could lose your star," Travis warned, "You already lost Ginger."

"Ginger is gone," he said, as if she had evaporated from the planet, "But we have Mariana." There was a loud disagreement in the background, and more unintelligible dialogue, then Motti said, "Wait. You talk with my sister."

"Travis." Maya came to the telephone, her scratchy voice rising in pitch. "Ginger is gone?"

"Off the project. You said get someone else. You wanted her to do a boy-girl. She won't, and nobody should think of trying to force her."

"I see." Maya did not argue. "Nobody make her do nothing."

Then there was more raucous debate between the siblings and Motti came back to the telephone, and asked sheepishly. "Maybe we keep Ginger as the star in the girl-girl movie. Find for her something." He hung up abruptly, the protocol of farewell greetings beyond his linguistic and cultural frame of reference.

Howard, who had noted the whole conversation, scratched the back of his neck with a pencil. "So, what do I do about Ginger? Do I cancel your girlfriend?"

"First of all," said Travis, "I am a married man."

"That never stopped anyone in all of history," Howard observed, but he understood the importance to the producer of maintaining close relationships with members of the performing community. "So, it's all just politics?"

"It's about leverage with talent, about publicity, and about making connections in this business," replied the producer. "We can't make movies without stars."

"Well, if you can't make a movie without a star, then you definitely can't make a movie with two stars in the same role. Who do I cancel – Mariana or Ginger?"

"Just count to ten," said the producer, which meant that the decision was delayed, "In production, we call that plan A and plan B."

He gazed at the telephone again, and even Howard did not require clairvoyance to divine the object of his anticipation.

When Ginger called, Travis could tell that she had been crying. She seemed so crushed, and spoke in a humble voice. "Okay. I'll do it."

"Your body, your rules."

"I'll do the boy-girl. Just please let me pick the boy, or at least, have a choice. No Chuck. And no Sebastian, please. I don't care that he's black, he's just so big that he could fill me from the next room. But I'll do a boy-girl if that's what they want. I thought about it, and it's not like I haven't done them before, so I'm okay."

"You don't need to compromise..."

"It's Mariana Trench, isn't it? That's what they're saying on the grapevine, that she got the part. I saw Traci at the clinic getting her test for The Duchess. She just came from Billy, and that's what she said."

"This is my movie," said the producer, "And I will cast it how I choose. Which is with you. And you absolutely do not have to do anything you don't want to do."

They hung up, and Travis looked at Howard for validation. "Right?"

"Right," agreed Howard, who was in support of even the slightest hint of ethics in the producer.

"You got to do the right thing," Travis affirmed.

* * *

Beppo dreaded going into the office in the mornings, but he had to keep up appearances. He had to go through all the motions, to prevent anything out of the ordinary, and restrain himself from doing something stupid, like overshoot the off-ramp and keep driving all the way to Mexico. Every morning, he turned the Cadillac into the parking lot, and the white van was already in place along the train tracks. No matter what time of the day he left the office, the white van was still there like the familiar annoyance of a numb tooth pulsating in the back of his mouth.

He got used to checking his rear-view mirror, glancing over his shoulder, and limiting his movements between home and work. In the evenings, he stayed indoors under a quilt on the sofa, and went to bed early, only venturing out to walk the dogs in the quiet neighborhood streets. He did not feel like he was being followed, but for weeks the white van outside the office was a continual presence.

But now, the white van was gone.

This absence did not provide Beppo with any relief. Rather, he was filled with even more unease. He did not believe that the van had been an innocuous vehicle; he had no doubt that he was under surveillance. He was sure that he had been watched since the convention in Las Vegas. The disappearance of the FBI squad did not bode well. He was convinced they had built their case, and now they would be coming.

He stood in the desolate parking lot, his back towards the building, facing the empty spot where the ominous vehicle used to be. He wanted to walk over and examine the terrain, but he did not know what he might discover. He half-expected agents to screech to a halt at any moment, either to resume their clandestine post, after a late start to the morning, or to storm in with guns and shields, and cart him away to oblivion.

All he was trying to do was earn a living. He was not trying to do anyone any harm. He was only guilty of participating in his own life. He was a simple merchant, a supplier, a cog in a rotating wheel.

A train shunted sluggishly along the tracks, making its way north beyond the valley.

Everyone had a history, and he had his share of experiences, the kind of stories that cellmates spin. He did not feel like a tough guy now. The old bear was less of a wild grizzly and more of a stuffed animal.

It was probably time to call for help.

He went into the office at the worldwide headquarters of Majestic Movies, and told the girl at reception to get his lawyer on the line. He felt an instant sense of relief. The criminal defense attorney was not a barracuda; she was compassionate and cared about the welfare of her clients, notwithstanding ensuring their prolonged liberty. He could use the windfall from Germany to pay her fees.

It was a smart move to give her a heads-up.

* * *

Production began on Sound Stage B on a Tuesday morning in Chatsworth. Ginger was the first one to arrive. She was followed by Tommy, the chief electrician, whose enthusiasm to get to work was galvanized by the prospect of receiving a paycheck, a welcome novelty which had eluded him as a result of the entire industry being away in the glitter of Las Vegas while he was left unemployed in Pacoima. As the Sunbeams had requested, Ginger was to perform the lead role in the lesbian movie, but her roles in the other two movies on the production schedule had been re-written as boy-girl scenes to accommodate the new star, Mariana Trench. The schedule was confusing to everyone, with the scenes all checker-boarded together, since they were shooting all three movies at once, so that Travis could make use of the variety of available sets, for creative reasons, not to mention to drastically cut costs.

The series of movies which Travis had conceived for his capricious executive producer was called *High Risqué Parts One, Two and Three* (all-girl). The central conceit was a group of extravagant gamblers who risked their spouses in various wagers, the thematic choice of gaming being a subject matter that could be easily grasped by the giddy financier. The production had rented a craps table, a roulette wheel, and a slot machine from a specialty prop house, which they staged on a set that they sometimes used for a bar, but was now a private room in a casino.

The casino set would be the centerpiece in all three movies, and, rather than go back and forth, they planned to shoot it out completely before moving to the next set-up.

Jack and Tommy began work on lighting the set, while Maria started work on Ginger. Travis had scheduled her first for a number of reasons, some of which had to do with the logistics of the shooting breakdown, but politically, because he wanted to establish her in the movie before the Sunbeams had any other contributions with respect to casting. In addition to which, he knew that Ginger would be prompt and reliable so they could get started before the inevitable delay in the entrance of Mariana Trench.

Motti Sunbeam himself showed up about an hour and a half after the call time. As the backer of the project, he was hospitably welcomed. He was too excited to even sample any of the delicious pastries on the craft service table and spent most of the time fielding calls on his cell phone while writing notes on the back of his hand in indecipherable scrawls that were somehow linked to his daily tightrope walk through his warehouse dispensing DVDs. Like all guests, he hovered back and forth between the green room where the refreshments were served and the warm comforts of the make-up area, where Maria was applying lipstick to Ginger.

"I not interfere," he affirmed, accepting that creative and technical suggestions were beyond his expertise.

Howard had been sage enough to give Mariana Trench a call time which was a good hour before she was needed to appear, so there was no reason to panic when she did not present herself punctually, but he mentioned the matter to Travis when he checked in at the production office.

"Don't worry about it." The producer dismissed the warning with uncharacteristic indifference. "But thanks for the heads-up."

Maria came into the production office, looking for Travis. "Just want to let you know that Ginger's ready. And I have no eleven o'clock girl."

"Howard's working on it," said the producer, with unaccustomed confidence in his production manager.

"She'll be a two o'clock girl by the time I get her," concluded Maria, putting herself on a break.

Travis headed down the corridor to the make-up room where Ginger, dressed in a sparkly evening gown, was frowning at herself in the mirror.

"You look great," he said, taking her by the hand to lead her to work, making sure she did not trip up in her heels over the mop of Tommy's cables and the struts of the flats.

"They always find something to complain about." She was referring to the principals at Sunbeam Video.

"Yes, because if they don't, they think you might raise your price."

They both laughed at these true words and Ginger felt much more at ease, as they stepped onto the set, and she assumed her position laying on her back in a sea of colored casino chips on top of the roulette table.

Tommy re-adjusted the lights, dropping in a mesh scrim to soften the glare on the supine redhead.

Travis took his place in the director's chair. "We're starting with the solo, softcore first, and then we'll come in for the money." Everyone nodded in understanding. "We will do Ginger's voice-overs after that, where she's telling the story that introduces the other scenes."

Ginger's appearance before the camera was flawless, and Travis allotted so much time to achieving perfection, partly because of his pursuit of artistic excellence, but also in response, as it seemed to everyone on the set, to the eleven o'clock girl not yet being available.

Marianna Trench was a no-show.

An hour after her call time, Howard brought the matter to Travis' attention again.

"She's now officially late," said the production manager, "I tried Billy. Nobody knows where to reach her. She's not picking up. After an hour, we're supposed to replace her. What do you want to do?"

"Let's find out," Travis said, with a wry grin, marching down the hallway to the green room.

Howard chased after him with the strange sensation that they were going in the wrong direction to the problem.

In the green room, Sunbeam was sitting in an easy chair, enjoying a donut in anticipation of a short nap.

Travis said, "Well. We don't have Mariana Trench."

"She has disappeared like she went into witness protection," Howard added.

"No." Motti Sunbeam looked crushed. "Beely said this could happen. You warn me. This not your fault." His appetite gone, he forlornly laid the half-eaten donut in his lap to better contemplate the hand which fate had dealt him. "My movie. No star."

Howard tried to offer the crestfallen investor some support. "We tried everything. She's done this to a lot of people."

"What we do? My sister she go to kill me."

"We could wait," Howard suggested, "See if Mariana shows up."

"She no come," Sunbeam shook his head, accepting the facts over which he had no control, and wistfully examined the pastry, "We no can continue."

"I have an idea," Travis proposed, "Ginger is already on set. Let's go back to the old scripts, and put Ginger back in the lead."

It took actual physical exertion at that moment for Howard to restrain his reaction to the masterful skills of the resourceful producer, and he stared at a doodle on the back of his clipboard, as if it were a masterpiece of fine art.

"You are a genius," Sunbeam glowed, "My sister she will be very happy."

Mariana Trench, it was later discovered, had been out celebrating without any particular occasion at the Rainbow Bar on the Sunset Strip the night before, and even if she had remembered she was scheduled for a shoot in the morning, she would not have been able to make it, on account of the fact that she passed out and slumbered until an hour before Travis proclaimed wrap, and only woke up because she urinated in the bed.

* * *

Ginger did a capable job as the lead in all three movies, without performing in any commercial scenes with male partners. Sunbeam stayed out of the way for the rest of the production, although he often had to be silenced for answering his cell phone during a take, and from time to time fell into a distraction, staring longingly at the rented roulette table. Morale was high and the shoot progressed along the crooked paths of the confusing schedule with as little chaos as possible.

The culmination of the project was the all-girl orgy for *High Risqué Part Three*. Maria was allowed an assistant to help prepare six girls for the extravagant finale, and the players started prancing into the green room a good three hours beforehand to get ready. There were one or two stalwarts in the group, but they were mostly nubile newcomers who were prepared to work at a reasonable rate in a scene in which everyone wanted to participate. They all enjoyed having sex with other women. They helped one another with wardrobe, offering to share garments and shoes, so that they would all look their best. Some had brought their own vibrators and dildoes, which they were also willing to share, and they all excitedly discussed their comfort levels with different activities to perform and items to insert. Everyone was in an upbeat mood, and they lounged around half-clothed, chatting about all the current affairs, as they each waited for their turn in the make-up chairs.

The co-president of Sunbeam Video pulled Travis to one side.

"You fix for me something?" the financier asked, with a sense of urgency.

"What do you need?"

"All these girls we have," he gave a sheepish grin, waving to where the roomful of semi-naked starlets were getting ready, "Somebody to give me blow job."

"Really?"

"Why not?" he chuckled. "I take one blow job."

Travis nodded. "I'll see what I can do." At the top of his voice, in front of the roomful of people, he announced, "Head's up, everybody! Is there anyone here who will blow Motti?"

In various stages of undress, the women stopped what they were doing to look the dumpy executive up and down, and Motti's famous round cheeks turned as pink as Cupid, since he had anticipated a more discreet solicitation on his behalf.

"I will," volunteered Ginger, turning from the mirror, and walking towards him in her stilettos, with a gimlet gaze and a seductive sway in her hips, while the rest of the room watched.

The tall redhead got close to him, leaned her mouth towards his ear, and murmured, "So, you want me to blow you?"

The pudgy president was too embarrassed to answer.

With the heel of her palm beneath her chin, Ginger took a deep breath, pursed her lips and blew.

* * *

Final payment to the producer was made on the occasion of the delivery of the materials, and Travis thought that the whole thing had gone rather well, and was looking forward to the next project with Sunbeam Video, when he received an unexpected call from Maya.

"Travis," the dragon began, with a rasp, "We missing one movie."

"No, that's not possible. We delivered everything."

"You don't have copy?"

"I can't keep a copy," the producer explained, "You own the rights. It wouldn't be appropriate if I held onto any materials."

"We missing one movie," she repeated, "But, if you can find for us something, we give you reward. One thousand dollars."

"No questions asked!" her brother shouted in the background, then after a moment of fumbling, he came to the telephone himself. "Look, just bring back the movie. We pay."

"I am not in business to steal masters of my own movies," bristled the producer.

"I warn you. I am Sunbeam. I go to destroy you. "

"I delivered the movie to you. You lost it. And I don't like being called a thief."

It was a ludicrous accusation because if Travis had wanted to steal the materials, he would have had ample opportunity to make copies before he made delivery. Once trust had been questioned, it was gone. They would not trust him now, which made business impossible.

The Sunbeam empire did not collapse without Travis Lazar on their roster. In fact, the company expanded so much that even their sprawling warehouse became too small for them, and, a few months later, they were forced to change premises. They packed up all their wares and moved into a behemoth of a space on the other side of the valley near Van Nuys airport. During the transition, the missing movie was discovered where it had been mislabeled and misplaced.

At least, Travis received a telephone call.

"We found the movie," Maya said tamely, "You didn't take it. We want to apologize."

"I don't want an apology," said Travis, "But I do want the thousand dollar reward."

CHAPTER FIVE

FIREWORKS

Howard's morning toilet ritual did not include daily shaving, which seemed like a waste of valuable time and energy, if he were not going to leave his one-bedroom apartment on the first floor of a low-rent block in North Hollywood. He did not need to be presentable to watch the Cartoon Network and eat a bowl of cereal without company. He only shaved and cleaned himself up for special occasions. Today, his cheeks were smooth and pink, but, beneath his left earlobe, where there was a hard, stubborn pimple spawned from an ingrown whisker, he had nicked himself with the razor blade. He had to tear off a piece of Kleenex to staunch the dot of blood, which oozed obstinately from the wound.

He smelled of soap and cologne. He was wearing a new checkered shirt, buttoned up to the collar and squarely folded at the sleeves, and a clean pair of blue jeans. He had made his bed, and straightened up the bedroom and the living room. He had washed the dishes and taken out the trash, although there was a faint, lingering odor of fried chicken. His bong and his personal collection of pornography were stashed away in a cardboard box under the bed. He had opened the windows to let in some air, but kept the drapes shut. He did not want his neighbors to know what he was up to, even though he was on good terms with the Mexican couple across the hall. In the complex, there was a swimming pool, which took up most of the courtyard, and he had fished out their keys with the pool net when he had been involved in a small incident to do with a bad toss and a missed catch. Still, with what he was planning, it was better to keep things discreet.

As hospitality for his anticipated guests, there was a pre-packaged tray of warm cheese and salami on the kitchen table, and a few bottles of water. The kitchen was narrow, with wooden cabinets across from one another, a tile counter, and a clock on the kitchen wall, which he had bought at a souvenir shop in Hollywood; it was a figure of Charlie Chaplin, and the pendulum was the tramp's legs swinging back and forth in his signature walk, which Howard found oddly provocative.

The ever-punctual Traci would be arriving at any minute, but, in all the anticipation, he was nevertheless startled when the doorbell buzzed.He opened the door, ready with a well-prepared greeting, but it was Jack and Tommy, each carrying equipment, stuffed into black canvas bags as if they were burglars smuggling loot.

Jack said, "So, this is happening?"

Howard checked around to make sure that nobody had seen them, as he allowed the two-man crew into his residence. "Yes. It's happening. Traci's coming."

"You on your period?" asked Jack, noticing the blood-soaked Kleenex pasted to his face, although Howard did not dignify such sarcasm with a response.

"Nice place," said Tommy, examining the cramped living room as if he were a tourist on a guided tour through an ancestral estate.

"Where are we setting up?" inquired the cameraman, also allowing a grander scale to the limited options in the one-bedroom place. "Bedroom?"

"That would probably be the best," said Howard, in the voice he reserved for addressing morons.

Then the doorbell buzzed loudly again.

Jack said, "That'll be Traci."

Hastily peeling off the curative strip of Kleenex in blind hope that the spiteful nick had congealed, Howard opened the door, and there was the star on his doorstep. She was already painted in make-up, with long eyelashes, mascara, and shiny red lips, but she was incongruously dressed in old gray sweats and flip-flops, and wheeling a large suitcase, which contained various wardrobe choices, particularly if the role to be cast was that of a stripper.

"Hi Howard," she said, "I didn't know what you wanted me to wear, so you can pick through my stuff."

He completely forgot what he was going to say and mumbled something about lingerie being just fine, momentarily star-struck by her presence now that the moment was upon him.

"You're sure you are going to be up to this, Howard?" asked Jack, who did not want to spend the afternoon waiting for the uncomfortable thespian to achieve an erection.

"With Traci?" Howard snorted. "Please." He had spent weeks in mental rehearsal for the occasion.

Traci walked around the apartment, as Tommy had done, inspecting it as if there were much more to the humble abode than met the eye, while Howard addressed the pleasing task of rummaging through her underwear to make a selection from her varied assortment.

Between supplements of sharp cheese and salami, Tommy and Jack set up the equipment in the bedroom. It was a very basic lighting scheme, with a key light, a back light, and the natural light bouncing off the white walls of the apartment filling in the rest, so it did not take them much time. They rigged a microphone on a stand right over the center of the bed.

Traci said to Howard, "So. Before we get diddling, (a) do you have your test, and (b) do you have my money?"

He had everything ready. "Of course."

"It's going to be mostly doggystyle, so I don't have to look at your face," she informed him in a matter-of-fact way, which was well within the prerogative of the comfort levels of the performer. She glanced at the printed test results, certifying his physical health, and looked her prospective partner up and down. "And, that better be a shaving cut and not herpes."

She slid out of her sweats, and, after marching around naked to get a bottle of water, to use the bathroom, and to examine the bedroom, where the action was to take place, she dressed in the lingerie that Howard had selected, namely a pink lace bra-and-panties set, accented with a schoolgirl skirt, and, of course, stripper heels.

She sat at his kitchen table in her wardrobe for the scene, and filled out the paperwork, while the tramp's legs swayed back and forth on the wall clock. Her perfume and body lotion mingled together to evoke a fragrance of peaches. To Howard, just her angelic presence in the chair he usually occupied for a lonely fast-food dinner would transform the place forever.

The freight train rumbled through the valley, rattling the building, and Jack shut the windows for the sake of sound. The noise of traffic would spoil the soundtrack, and, also conscious of the neighborhood, it was prudent to prevent any potential for disturbing the locals with the hazards of audible nudity, which was forbidden by the City of Los Angeles.

Traci lay down on the bed, in a coquettish pose, as Jack, hoping to elevate the aesthetics of the challenging scene, panned the camera across her body. Howard made his entrance, and joined her on the bed. There was some improvised dialog between them, which even Tommy, who generally held no opinion on dramatic content, thought was inane, and then, as the electrician crept in closer with his handheld light, Traci removed what little clothing she wore, and began to help her fellow performer undress.

Howard hated the idea of taking off his clothes in front of Jack and Tommy and exposing himself to his crewmates in all his naked glory, but he had already accepted that this minor indignity was the price he would have to pay to fulfill his desires with Traci, notwithstanding the price he had to pay Traci for the deed itself.

To Jack's relief, after a few gingerly caresses from her soft fingers on his reedy body, Howard was quick to achieve a state of arousal, and now the only thing that the cinematographer had to worry about was if the novice before the camera would become too aroused too quickly so that the scene would end prematurely. But, clearly, all of Howard's mental preparation paid off, and, as a matter of fact, and to his credit, he managed to prolong the performance, by thinking of advertising jingles, firstly to rack up the appropriate running time, but also to savor every possible moment of his debut appearance.

Even so, it all seemed to be over quite briskly, although the whole thing took over an hour to complete. Now that they had passed the point of no return, the only problem that they all had to confront was how they were going to break the news to Travis Lazar.

* * *

The trucks rolled in, as principal photography began for *Fireworks*, Travis Lazar's new big-budget feature production for American X-Rated Entertainment. Shooting was to take place in downtown Los Angeles, on a backlot, which had previously been the home of old television cop shows. With red-brick walls, flat rooftops, and a maze of sets, stages, and locations, the place was so spread out that more than one company was working on the premises, including a music video, an infomercial, and two horror movies, although Travis swiftly became notorious as the only producer on the lot shooting a sex film. Nobody cared, but there was always some jostling when different productions rubbed up against each other. Travis was not intimidated.

Starring in the blockbuster were Mariana Trench, Ginger Vitus, and Traci Gold, among a stellar cast of the most attractive first responders who ever handled a hose. *Fireworks* was the costliest X-rated production of the season, so Nicholas was on set, as Duncan's eyes and ears, in addition to accepting the responsibility for managing the volatile leading lady, thus bypassing Howard to avoid overtaxing his acumen. Everyone had agreed that Mariana should have a late call, but given her reputation for tardiness, that information had not been shared with Mariana who had been told to report at 8 am sharp, which she had not.

Wisely, the reliable Traci, partnered with Colt – equally reliable in more ways than one – was scheduled for the first scene.

The former precinct station had been redressed as a firehouse. The art department had brought in props and set decorations, consisting of extinguishers, axes, and cork boards with official notices, and erected a fireman's pole, which would also serve handily as a stripper pole in one of the sequences. All the performers wore authentic firefighter's uniforms from a costume rental house in Hollywood, and a seamstress had created custom pieces for some of the women, which made it easy for them to remove. At nightfall, Travis had ordered a fire truck which was to be the centerpiece of the movie, and, as an additional touch, there was also a spotted firedog, from an animal rental house, accompanied by an animal wrangler and a member of the humane society. There was a lot of humor bandied about over whether the dog would have sex on-screen, and what kind of positions that would involve – dark comedy that alarmed the lady from the humane society so much that she sought solace in the comfort food of five frosted donuts from the box on the craft service table.

The opening scene with Colt and Traci developed as planned with no issues whatsoever: Traci slid down the pole, and, working the brass buttons and the hidden Velcro strips, she seductively peeled off her entire uniform, with the exception of her firefighter's hat, which stayed on for the duration of the sex scene. Colt retained his boots. Except for some extemporaneous yelping from the off-screen Dalmatian in concert with the moans and groans of the performers, the scene shunted along as smoothly as pistons smeared with lubrication, but, hanging over the production, as usual, was the concern about the timeliness of the timeless Mariana Trench.

Around 11 a.m., Nicholas received a message from Mariana, assuring them that she was on the way, which soothed nobody since, as they were all aware, it warranted absolutely nothing.

The spiky blonde with the 8 a.m. call made her entrance, just as they were breaking for lunch, breathless, anxious, and pale.

"I'm sorry, I'm sorry, I'm sorry," said the flustered star, dragging her suitcase into the green room with two hands, "I never knew there would be so much traffic. Now everyone hates me."

Nicholas assured her that she had no cause to apologize, and that not only was she much beloved but that everyone was thrilled that she had made it to the set at last.

Travis asked Maria to skip lunch, so that Mariana could go right into the make-up chair because he wanted to be able to shoot her scene without any additional delay as soon as lunch was consumed. For American X-rated Entertainment, the catering budget allowed more than the standard fare of the affectionately-named Porno Loco, and there was a delectable choice of entrees, including prime rib and lasagna, from the on-set caterer. Maria, being a consummate professional, took her plate back to her station, so that she could pick at it while she was working on Mariana, and while they had a chat. The conversation was always friendly, and it made it easy to work, and, even though idle chatter added time and Howard always complained, it was Travis-approved, because the producer wanted the make-up artist, as his eyes and ears, to notify him if there was going to be a problem.

Mariana had no qualms about the sex scene, in which she was partnered with Sebastian Barge, a tall, urbane black man with broad shoulders, large arms, large legs, and, in fact, as the industry rhyme went, Sebastian Barge, everything large. Mariana had been looking forward to their encounter. She had been pleasured by gangbangs, multiple penetrations, orgies, and an assortment of household objects. Her sex scenes were already legendary; the nastier, the better; she could take it.

They had to get through the pages of firehouse dialog first. Mariana had not learned her lines prior to coming onto the set, but she memorized them quickly, for the most part, and her delivery could not have been better. She was well-practiced at hitting her marks, following direction, and the way she played to the lights and the camera, like a fashion model, which was part of her biography. Before her ascent as a porn star, under a different mononym, the tattooed artist with the Mohawk had appeared in calendars, music videos; and adorning the hood of a car on the cover of a national automotive magazine. There was an affected tonality to her voice on-screen, giving her the compelling delivery of the presenter of an entertainment news show. Nicholas and Travis nodded to each other in approval after each take, each one equally surprised at her professionalism.

When all of the dialog in the firehouse was completed, Travis announced that they were on the wrong set, which, in the parlance of production, was not an astonishment to a disoriented crew, but a welcome direction that meant they were ready to move onto the next set-up. It was to be a night exterior, which called for at least an hour for lighting, as the day turned from dusk to darkness. Everyone knew that it would take time; nobody was rushed. Piece by piece, the crew began to move equipment to the parking lot where the filming was to take place; Jack positioned the camera; electricians set up lights on the rooftops and in hidden corners; the production assistants shuttled vehicles out of the way and prepared to wet down the pavement in which they made resourceful use of the actual firehoses that also served as props.

Mariana and Sebastian were assigned a break, and immediately took that as a cue to sneak off and smoke a bowl of marijuana. From a distance, peeking around a corner like a private detective on matrimonial surveillance, Nicholas kept them in his line of sight. When they returned to the green room, smiling fantastically, they stayed under Nicholas' watchful eye. There was always the possibility that either of them – more likely the capricious Mariana – might wander off and vanish in the vast landscape of the backlot. Instead, they nestled together on the couch, getting further acquainted on an intimate level in preparation for the upcoming sex scene, and, in their artistic enthusiasm, it was everything that the vigilant studio executive could do to prevent them from beginning the action right there on the cushions before any cameras were rolling.

The fire truck arrived twenty minutes ahead of schedule. It was shiny red with polished chrome, and, of course, practically the entire company had to come out and remark upon it, as if nobody had ever seen such a vehicle on the streets of California. It required some guidance and maneuvering to back it into place, and Howard had to make sure that it was parked where they would need it for the shot. Naturally, the production manager could not resist running the siren – as a test – which caused some consternation from one of the other companies who were recording sound and were forced to redo a take which was drowned out by the noise, and almost deafened the sound mixer who was wearing headphones.

With acute hearing, the spotted firedog went berserk at the high-pitched claxon, yapping, chasing its tail, and urinating against one of Tommy's light stands.

From one of the rival companies, a surly thirty-five-year old producer by the name of Menachem Amsalem marched into the parking lot to confront Travis directly.

He wore a navy blazer over a beige V-neck sweater, and charcoal jeans, and his beard was trimmed, barely more than a shadow. "When we shout rolling," he said dryly, "It means we are shooting. Maybe in your kind of movies, the dialog doesn't matter. But we are doing a serious drama."

His serious drama was a low-budget horror movie that involved buckets of blood, harpoons, and an evil fishmonger in a rubber mask.

Travis seemed to smile and glare at the same time. "I am sure your project is as important to you as mine is to me. Even though we're neither of us doing Shakespeare."

"I'm not saying it's *Gone By The Wind*," sniffed

Menachem, "But, for sure, we're spending more money here than you are."

From this moment, and with that assertion, Menachem made sure to quibble about even the slightest annoyance from his neighboring producer, as a way of asserting the pecking order. But the pecking order was bread and butter to Travis. Menachem would soon regret ever running across him.

* * *

On her second day of shooting, Mariana, who had been impeccable on her first day of shooting, fell off the face of the earth.

"It just goes to voicemail," Howard explained, when Travis came into the firehouse. The production manager had commandeered the spot as his office now that shooting on that set was complete, and he could get out of the musty broom closet where he had been stationed. "Billy Dallas can't get hold of her. She's not double-booked on anybody else's set. She's plummeted into the void."

"Let's get Nicholas in here," Travis instructed, not knowing how to solve this one.

It was already late in the day and they were planning night-work again, which would go well past midnight, so the excuse that Mariana was not a morning person did not hold up in the afternoon. Everyone had been scheduled for a late call, although somehow the note had not reached Nicholas who had been there since ten a.m. waiting hungrily for the caterer to arrive with breakfast.

The executive came through the swinging doors into the firehouse, with a Styrofoam cup of coffee in one hand and a toasted bagel, wrapped in a napkin, in the other. "Howard says we have a problem."

There was a desk with an office chair, and a row of plastic seats lined along one wall, but they all stayed on their feet.

Travis said to the production manager, "Tell the story."

"She left here with Sebastian last night after their scene," Howard recounted, pacing back and forth along an imaginary line to add a touch of drama to his narrative, "According to Sebastian, they go back to her house, hung out, and she was fine, but she falls asleep and Sebastian goes home. Billy sends him back over there this morning, and he knocks on the door, but no response. So, everybody is thinking, another dead porn star, and so he gets the building manager, and they open the door, and they find her bed had been slept in..." He paused for dramatic effect, "...But she wasn't home."

"So, we can assume that she's alive..." Nicholas concluded.

"Unless the body was moved," suggested Howard, who was a fan of television detective shows much like the programs formerly produced on the premises.

There was a genuine puzzle to the circumstances: Mariana's sex scene with Sebastian on top of the fire truck the previous night had, in the words of the observers, been so smoking hot that they considered using the extinguishers. She had not been paid for the scene yet, because she still had more work on the picture, but nobody in the industry expected to have sex on camera without compensation. The fact that she had not turned up placed her paycheck in jeopardy, hence the mystification.

Travis weighed his options. "My problem is that she's more than an hour late now, and she is already established in the movie. We are supposed to do the big boy-girl scene on the rooftop."

"All right," Nicholas said, finishing up his bagel, and wiping his fingers on the napkin,

"Is there anyone else on set who can do the scene? What about Ginger?"

"She's only doing girl-girl," Travis and Howard chimed in together, fresh from their recent experiences with Sunbeam Video.

"Traci?"

"She's coming in today for the dialog scene in the bar." Howard glanced at his clipboard, and checked his wristwatch. "She will be here at any minute..."

"But, she already did a sex scene with Colt." Travis shook his head in deference to artistic integrity. "It won't make sense to the story. She can't be having sex with the watch commander in the firehouse, and on the roof of the burning building at the same time."

"All right," said Nicholas, darting towards the firehouse exit as if – only audible to him – an alarm bell had sounded. "Give me twenty minutes. I've got an idea."

They watched him depart, like a puff of smoke, and Travis looked at Howard. "I hope he's not thinking what I think he's thinking."

If the production manager knew what they were all thinking, it showed on his face, because he slumped forward, with a hangdog look.

"He's the company man," Howard shrugged, catching his drift, "He's going to be the final word."

"Well, keep moving, as if we know what we're doing," Travis instructed, taking the helm of the rudderless vessel, "What's next?"

"The pyro guy."

"How is he?"

"He has albino skin and weird blue eyes that glow like they're on voltage when he talks about fire. He gives me the creeps. Can you go and explain to him how you want the explosions?"

Before Travis had the opportunity to follow Howard out of the office, Jack interrupted and said, "You'd better take a look at the set."

"The roof?" asked Travis.

"The bar," Jack informed him, "Your friend, Menachem, has painted it purple."

Travis followed Jack to the bar set, abandoning Howard who had assumed that Travis was right behind him on the way to meet with the jumpy pyrotechnician.

The walls and floor of the bar had been painted a rich magenta, glimmering under the costly illumination for Menachem's horror movie. The silver mirrors behind the bar reflected a galaxy of tiny bright dots across the walls. Vases of fresh flowers, sculptures, artwork, and plush furniture had been aesthetically placed by the art department. There was a full crew, including a Steadicam operator, a prosthetics artist, and a battery of electricians who were finalizing the smallest of lighting details while they waited for the performers to grace the resplendent set.

"Looks fantastic," Travis murmured, with a reaction that made Jack think of him as the lucky recipient of an unexpected inheritance.

Menachem approached, spoiling for confrontation. "We are still busy shooting on this set."

"We have it on our schedule for today," said Travis.

"You can have it tomorrow afternoon."

"We're off the lot tomorrow."

"You will have to wait," Menachem said snidely, "But you can have it as soon as we're done."

"And you have painted everything this gruesome color." Travis did his best to scowl.

Menachem saw right through the disingenuousness of his fellow producer. "We will make sure to paint it back to the original."

Before Travis could respond, Howard found him. "There you are." The production manager was pink from the neck to the brow as a result of going up and down the stairs. "I thought you were coming onto the roof to meet with the pyro guy. The fire department is here."

"Is that a joke?" asked Travis, referring to the theme of their movie.

"If Officer Fleet from the film unit is funny," Howard replied, making sure that this time Travis was with him on the way to the next set.

At the top of the metal stairway to the roof, like a sentinel silhouetted by the falling sun, Officer James Fleet of the Los Angeles Fire Department stood at attention in his uniform, with a glinting badge pinned on the chest of his spotless white shirt and a grimace on his dusky face.

"Come on, Howard, get the officer a hummer while he's waiting," the producer quipped, with a white-toothed grin, even though he had a hollow feeling in the pit of his stomach knowing that the fire department held the authority to shut down the centerpiece of his production.

Fleet gave a wry smile. "Hello, Mr. Lazar. Not sure how my wife would feel about that."

The pyrotechnician was hovering antsily among the vents and chimney stacks. He wore a red-and-black flannel shirt, and khaki pants with mysterious brown stains.

"This is Willard Fingerbrand," Howard introduced them.

"Don't shake hands with me," he cautioned nervously, "I have gunpowder residue. So if you're going through an airport, they'll arrest you."

Travis had no immediate plans for travel, but took advantage of the opportunity not to shake hands, which he avoided as much as possible during X-rated production, where the elbow bump was the conventional greeting.

Fleet said, "We've been through everything and your permit is in order. I am going to allow the explosions as long as there is no wind."

"What I understood from Howard," Willard said, dabbing the perspiration from his brow with the back of his sleeve, "your cameras will be on the roof, and you want the explosions to go off in the courtyard below..."

"So, we can see them from the roof..." Travis instructed, "Where the sex scene will be taking place..."

"That's not a problem," said the technical expert, not wishing to discuss the disconcerting technicalities of copulation, "But to see the blast from the roof, I will have to get some lift. That means a lot of charge."

For a moment, sensitive to the exactitudes of his budget, the frugal producer had an alarming pang when he misunderstood the word charge, and blurted, "I think we already agreed on the rate."

"That's fine," said the pyrotechnician, who was motivated not by remuneration, but by having a rationale to release ordinance, "I mean explosive charge. Now, I already have one bomb loaded in the courtyard...."

"There's a bomb in the courtyard?" Howard peered over the parapet.

"Yes," gulped Willard, "...and I would like to demonstrate what it's going to look like. If you're ready."

Since they were between waiting for the cast and waiting for a locale in which to shoot them, and finding themselves swept into the spirit of anticipation of releasing ordinance as was demonstrated by the rapture of their example, it was an opportune instance.

"Fire in the hole!" shouted the pyrotechnician and the fire officer in unison, to which full-throated proclamation, seized by the moment, Howard added his voice, and the cry rang around the backlot, as different members of different crews picked up the collective chorus.

When everyone had been appropriately alerted, to great excitement, a bomb exploded with a thunder in the courtyard, sending a tremor across the flat rooftop, and a spectacular red plume of fire and smoke into the air.

"That's perfect." Travis was impressed.

"Of course, it will look better at night," the pyrotechnician predicted, his blue eyes glowing, "And don't worry." He covered his mouth furtively and spoke to the producer through clenched teeth so that Fleet could not hear him. "When it comes to the actual filming, I will add more gunpowder to make it even bigger!"

Then Nicholas came onto the roof with his own bombshell. "I got us a girl."

* * *

Tiffany West emerged from her period of seclusion, after a persuasive telephone call from Nicholas who begged for her participation and reminded her that the President of AXE was growing frustrated at continuing to keep her on retainer with nothing to show for it. Her sorrow, which was exhibited by a preference for the lugubrious attire of bereavement, embracing vegetarianism, an inability to motivate herself off the couch, and the therapeutic balm of medicinal marijuana, had not subsided, but after Nicholas called, Tiffany realized that perhaps the best way to forget her woes was to throw herself into her work as a porn star, and get back to fornication.

She arrived at the location in her plum-red Mustang

convertible with Coochie (the dog) in the passenger seat. She was still dressed in her habitual widow's black, as if she had not changed her clothing since the funeral, like the macabre picture of a jilted bride in a perpetual wedding dress, and she wore dark sunglasses into the dressing room.

"Hello, Travis," she said in a husky voice, when she saw her least favorite producer, talking to his moronic production manager, in the make-up room, "You know, I'm only here because of Nicholas."

"We appreciate you coming," said Travis, quite sincerely, not only because the movie would be enhanced by a star of her magnitude, but also because, as a contract player for AXE, her participation would not add one penny to his expenses.

"Nicholas told you about the scene?" Howard checked.

"I'm not doing Sebastian Barge."

"No, it will be Storm," Howard assured her, "But it's going to be on the roof."

"I heard," she confirmed, with a roll of her eyes, "Why is it always the couch, the desk, or a fucking rockery? I think the last time I had sex in a bed was before I got into this business." She took off her sunglasses, and had an epiphany which prompted her to correct herself. "No, on my wedding night." Then, struck with grief, she broke into something between a sob and a gurgle, and put the sunglasses back on her sculpted nose, while everyone in the green room checked their cell phones or examined their fingertips.

Maria saved the moment. "Let's get you into the chair."

With an unspoken communication among them, Travis, Nicholas, and Howard left Tiffany in Maria's talented hands, and proceeded straight to the production office in the firehouse for an emergency production meeting, the firehouse providing a fitting setting given the urgent nature of the discussion.

"What does she think the scene is going to be?" Travis inquired, as soon as they had some privacy.

"I said a boy-girl," Nicholas confirmed, extracting a cheroot, "She asked who was in the movie. I told her who we had." He rolled the cheroot between his fingers, unsure if smoking was permitted in the firehouse.

"She said no Sebastian Barge, everything too large. So, I said no Sebastian."

"Did you tell her it was on the roof?"

"She knows," Howard stated, with a meaningless glance at his clipboard, "She's okay with the roof."

"We were very lucky to get her," Nicholas noted, in defense of his decision-making.

Travis was not sure. "Does she know that there are going to be explosions while she's getting hosed?"

"No. I didn't mention that." Nicholas considered his cheroot. "She didn't ask."

"What do we do?" posed Travis, "Just put her up there, and pretend we didn't know there was going to be bombing?"

"If we tell her, she might walk." Deciding against smoking, with all the talk of explosives, the executive put the cheroot back into his pocket. "Duncan was satisfied that she was coming back to work. And if she goes back to him, and puts in a complaint..."

"All right," Travis said, "I suppose I'd better talk to her."

"You'd better talk to her right now," said Maria, dramatically entering through the firehouse doors, in time to overhear the tail of the conversation.

"Why?" all three men asked at once.

The make-up artist reported, "The pyrotechnician just lit a fuse."

Travis instantly grasped the combustibility of Maria's bulletin, and, leaving Nicholas and Howard debating remedies in the firehouse, he made a beeline back to the make-up room, with her keeping step alongside him.

"She's been in the picture for thirty minutes," the producer steamed, "And already she's a bonfire."

"I don't know how much she knows – I kept my mouth shut like a pillbox – but *the* Tiffany sees the pyro guy, Willard is his name, and he's kind of creepy and he's kind of creeping about..."

Maria had to stride to keep up to his pace and keep filling him in on the situation

"So, you know, *the* Tiffany wants to know who's everybody on the set, and super sensitive about pervy types since that incident with the rock star who went to prison for being a sicko."

She paused outside the make-up room, so that she could finish.

"So, she confronts him, and he says he's the pyrotechnician."

Her account concluded, Maria crossed her arms, although her inclination was to cross her heart in anticipation of what the producer would do next. "That's all. I thought you should know."

"Travis Lazar!" Tiffany stood with her back to the make-up mirror, half in reflection, half-dressed, in fireman's boots, and leggings with her torso naked, and half her hair in curlers, while the other half fell down luxuriously. "Can you tell me why there is a pyrotechnician on the set, and what – if anything – it has to do with my scene?"

"Right," said the director, "We haven't discussed anything about the scene. Your character is a firefighter who has a love-hate relationship with your co-star, and, now, after he saves your life, you have sex, in the middle of a fire."

"In the middle of a fire?"

"You understand the symbolism. The fire is their passion."

"I understand that there is going to be a real fire not a symbolic fire. Because that's not a symbolic pervo-technician." She rested her hand on her hip, with her head cocked, adopting a pose. "Or are purple Martians living in my brain?"

"Well, more like blasts," admitted the producer, ignoring her sarcastic rhetoric.

"Explosions!" Tiffany pulled the remaining curlers out of her hair, tugging on them one by one with every next word she spoke. "You are the lowest form of humanity on the planet, and I mean that until hell freezes over."

Nicholas and Howard arrived at the make-up room, having missed most of the disputation, but in perfect time to hear the pithy ending, from which they were able to supplement their understanding of what had transpired.

"Tiffany," Travis tried to calm her, "This is the way the scene was planned long before you had anything to do with this movie."

"Oh, you don't have to worry about that. Because I am not going to have anything to do with this movie. I am walking. And don't think I won't tell Duncan about this." Tiffany pursed her lips, and narrowed her eyes at him. "After what I have been through – as a vegetarian – and this, my comeback picture – and standing in for Mariana *flaking* Trench – and you expect me to do a sex scene on a rooftop – which by the way, I didn't complain about because I am a professional – but with explosions. After I had to watch my husband's head explode in front of me. You are a creature from hell!"

As a result of an overzealous tug, the last of the curlers flew out of her hair, and right across the room to be nimbly caught by Traci, who had been sitting quietly on the couch ready for her own scene, and oblivious to all the commotion because she was listening to hip-hop on her headphones.

Nobody knew what to say, which was just as well, because

at this point, the prevailing consciousness was that it was more prudent that things should be left unsaid. In uneasy silence, Tiffany was out of her fireman's boots and back in widow's black. There was no stopping her. She scooped up her dog, and, glaring at the infernal producer, she was about to make her dramatic exit, which was upstaged when Jack and Tommy appeared in the doorway with breaking news.

"Menachem's crew has gone home for the night," the cinematographer disclosed, "So, if you want to get into the bar, now's the time."

"How long is it going to take us to light it?" asked Howard, expecting further delay, "You have half your truck on the roof."

"It's already lit." Tommy gave a twisted smile. "They left all their lights in place until tomorrow. I just have to flick a few switches."

Following the creed that the show must go on, and gratified to take advantage of his rival's absence, notwithstanding his extravagant lighting package, Travis agreed. "Let's get it out of the way quick."

In the fervor to comply with this new direction, everyone took off for the set, except Tiffany who smoldered towards her car with Coochie (the dog), and Traci, who deliberately lingered in the make-up room, so she could have a private word with Travis.

"So," Traci asked the director, "Has Howard talked to you about his project?"

* * *

The wind picked up as night fell. Script pages, call sheets, and production reports were caught up, and blew across the parking lot. The colored gels clasped to the metal barn doors on Tommy's lights fluttered at the edges. Additional sandbags and ropes were used to secure the light-stands. There was a sudden drop in temperature. To keep warm, crewmembers, working on the rooftop, had to go to their cars to fetch their jackets, and, in at least one instance, a shot of tequila.

Travis, Howard, Jack, Willard, and Officer James Fleet of the Los Angeles Fire Department stood at the parapet like sailors on the prow of a ship gauging an impending storm. With the exception of the intrepid producer, they all shared a forlorn look.

They had completed the dialog scene in the bar beneath them, and made sure to leave Menachem's equipment, exactly as they had found it; they were judicious enough to take photographs before anything was moved, so that it could be perfectly matched; nobody would know they had been there. All that was left was the final scene on the rooftop, but, even if the wind dropped, they still had nobody to play the female role. Worse, once Tiffany quit, Storm had taken it upon himself to logically assume that with no partner, and the unlikely and unwilling prospect of a solo male performance, the scene was cancelled. This was actually not an option under the limitations of their permit, which was very specific as to time, date, and details of the proposed pyrotechnics. But, not notified of the information and a little fatigued, the last male performer roared off on his Harley without notifying the production manager who left three sarcastic messages on his voicemail, requesting his direct return.

"It doesn't look good," Howard said pessimistically.

"Just keep preparing." Travis exuded confidence in the face of grim reality. "We've never shot an empty set."

"If the wind keeps up," Fleet exerted his authority, "I will not allow the shot."

"The wind!" Travis scoffed, "I can direct the wind."

Fleet sneered at the director as if he had claimed he could

fly, and the wind, as if in equal contempt, rattled the fronds of the palm trees across the street with a fresh jolt of turbulence.

From the rooftop, they could see into the parking lot, which was mostly empty, because, at that hour, they were the last crew on the premises. A cardboard box blew across the lot, scraping on the pavement. They kept their eyes peeled for Storm's motorcycle to come back, but there was no sign of him. Instead, an SUV approached.

"Now, who's that?" Travis wondered, always sensitive to the prospect of unexpected visitors, since an unfortunate surprise accession by the vice squad had left a bitter memory.

"It's Sebastian Barge's way-to-large SUV," said Howard.

"What's he doing here?" Travis asked, relieved that Tiffany had departed before she had the opportunity to jump to a rash conclusion as to the producer's veracity with respect to casting.

His sense of relief increased exponentially when they all recognized the passenger with the Mohawk who got out of the vehicle with Sebastian.

It was Mariana Trench.

Travis looked at Howard. "Okay. Back to Plan A."

* * *

"I don't want to hear it," Mariana said, raising one palm to ward off unwanted interrogations, as she sat down in the make-up chair. "I don't want to hear about it, and I certainly don't want to talk about it. You don't know what I had to go through to get here."

She started trembling, and Maria had to reassure her that nobody was going to attack her and that they were all sure that she must have had to endure absolute brimstone to fulfill her commitments, whereupon the matter on which the actress refused under all circumstances to digress unfolded none-theless.

It was shared, in confidence, first with the make-up artist, and then the tale soon traveled through the entire company, that Mariana, in the ideals of making a positive impression despite her reputation, had set an alarm for an early wake-up before falling asleep the night before. She had indeed risen at the designated hour, and set off for the location in good time, with steady traffic. Unfortunately, during her commute, she was pulled over for a license tag violation and arrested. In addi-tion to the expired tag, there was an old charge for driving under the influence, and a new charge for spitting at an officer. For the record, Mariana admitted to the first charge, and vehe-mently denied the second. Her vehicle was impounded. She spent the whole day in custody, and as soon as she was able, she called Sebastian to bail her out and bring her straight to the set so that she could satisfy her obligations to copulate.

When the story got to Travis, he gave Mariana a pearly-white smile and said, "I'm not mad at you. You're a trouper. You saved the picture."

She was ready for her scene, and, taking her by the hand, Travis led her up the industrial stairs to the roof, like he was escorting an angel into heaven.

Everything was ready.

There was a dolly track laid across the asphalt, balanced here and there on wooden wedges to ensure that it was level, which Tommy had verified with a bricklayer's bubble. The camera was parked on the dolly at one end. Jack peered through the viewfinder and swiveled on a seat on the dolly, which Tommy wheeled and nudged at the cameraman's instructions.

Under the lights, there was what appeared to be a concrete block but which was in reality a padded mattress on four apple boxes, held together by a bungee, upon which the action was to take place. Sebastian Barge was seated in the center, in a fireman's uniform, which was unbuttoned and unzipped, partly to accent his muscularity, but principally because the size of the uniform was not as large as Sebastian.

The couple had already partnered once in the movie, and it was unusual to reprise a scene, but given the on-screen chemistry between the stars, who would go on to enjoy a physical relationship off-screen, and the ardor of their lovemaking on top of the firetruck the night before, everyone agreed that a repeat performance would only add to the movie, a fortunate conclusion given that they had no other choices.

The angry wind had dropped, as the night grew later, and now there was the lightest breeze, rising and falling, but it was not cold.

Mariana giggled when she saw Sebastian, bursting at the seams.

"I'm sorry, Travis," he said, crestfallen, "I can't get nothing to fit."

"I think that was the biggest size we could get," the producer apologized.

"I got to have custom, too. Not just the girls."

"Sebastian Barge, everything large," teased Mariana, fondling his crotch, her familiarity a crucial preparation for the success of their imminent performance.

"So, this is what's going to happen," Travis announced to the company, "We only have one take on this, so we can't screw it up. As soon as the love scene starts, the dolly move starts. When I shout one, special effects will release the first bomb, two for the second, and I will shout three at the third mark..."

"That's the big one," Willard said proudly.

"Well, hold on, hold," Fleet interrupted, "I can't allow you to proceed if there is wind."

At the precise moment, the breeze completely subsided, and the night was as still as a bell on a shelf.

"What wind?" smiled Travis, the director's powers over the elements now proven.

Not a paper stirred.

Fleet shrugged. "Well, it's stopped now."

Travis shouted, "Right. Positions everybody!" There was a scramble for everyone to get into place, and the director muttered to the cinematographer, "Jack, let's get this quick before the wind picks up again."

They started rolling, and, on the call of action, the couple on the concrete block conjoined, and Tommy began trundling the camera dolly down the track, approaching the first mark which was signified by a piece of tape stuck to the rail.

True to plan, Travis yelled out the cue. "One!"

There was an explosion which rocked the rooftop, and sent fire and smoke and cinders into the night sky, bigger than anything which had been rehearsed, too big for the shot, and, as they were all profoundly aware, not the biggest yet to come. But, to repeat, the show must go on, was the creed. Nobody veered from the course.

Tommy kept the camera dolly moving down the track towards the second mark, and his head down in case of shrapnel. Without taking his eye from the viewfinder, with one hand, Jack released the tilt hold on the camera so that he could adapt the shot to catch the full explosion on the second effect. And nothing short of a nuclear mushroom would stop Mariana and Sebastian from soldiering on in continuous engagement.

"Two!" bellowed the director, through his cupped hands, as if he were directing a black-and-white comedy through an old-fashioned megaphone.

The second bomb was more powerful than the first, and everyone was rocked back on their feet, and, there was such a blast that the sound man ripped off his headphones and threw them onto the asphalt surface, as if they were instruments of torment. In the neighborhood, car alarms wailed, and dogs began barking; in the distance, there were sirens and helicopters.

But the camera kept charging down the track, and the pyrotechnician with his eyes beacon-bright kept his finger on the detonator. The backdrop of an enthusiastic fire was blazing in perfect symbolism with the director's artistic vision while the two fictional firefighters kept pumping.

The brave members of the crew braced themselves for doom.

When Travis shouted three, the bomb exploded so loudly that it was heard in Chinatown, if not China itself. The whole cast and crew could discern the crash of broken glass, wood, and plaster, which resounded from the courtyard, but Jack got the shot, tilting the lens into the blazing night sky to catch the rocket of fire that rose.

"And cut!" the director called, and then, there was a hush on the set, much like the funereal stillness in the make-up room after the wrath of Tiffany, and, as the complicit wind stirred up again, everyone steadied themselves, offered silent gratitude for being alive, and awaited further direction. Only Mariana and Sebastian, immersed in their roles, moved and moaned, oblivious to even the most cataclysmic of external distractions.

There was a crackle on a walkie-talkie. It was Howard's voice. "We need Travis to come down."

Leaving the rest of the scene - which did not involve further perilous effects – for Jack to supervise, Travis descended to the courtyard to be met by Nicholas and Howard.

The third bomb had been so impressive that it had destroyed Menachem's sets. The bar had been completely demolished. The beautiful pots and sculptures and vases were all bits and pieces of gypsum. There were shards of glass, rubble, and wreckage everywhere, under the rising smell of sulphur. Equipment was burned and twisted. All the lavish props and set dressing were obliterated.

"That pyromaniac Willard put too much gunpowder in the last bomb," Howard said, surveying the debris of splintered wood and dry wall.

"This is going to have to come out of the budget contingency," Nicholas advised, acknowledging that the studio would have to absorb the costs. "Duncan won't be happy."

"Neither will Menachem," Howard recognized. "But, he'll never give you any trouble again."

"Of course..." The producer was especially munificent when it was not his money. He flashed a gleaming smile and nodded. "We will have to pay for the damage."

CHAPTER SIX

THE PICTURE OF THE YEAR

Tiffany always enjoyed cruising down Sunset Boulevard with the roof down on her convertible, soaking in the sunshine with her faithful companion Coochie sticking her head out of the passenger side to catch the wind. The dog yapped and quivered with excitement, as the wind bristled her scruffy hair. Her little legs were so short that there was no way she could muster up sufficient spring in them to jump out of the car, so Tiffany was not worried, except that sometimes Coochie worked herself into such a flurry after an ambulance passed that she urinated on the seat.

In fact, Tiffany had once had a similar upset herself, after sneezing on a full bladder, which came from not doing her Kegels, so she was sympathetic to the incontinent animal. She sometimes left a magazine under the creature's paws to be safe. Tiffany always held a latte in her hand, or at least, a bottle of water, so that she could hydrate, and she always had the music playing loudly, so as to create a roving fanfare. She was invariably recognized by fans, and not just because she had a personalized license plate that read TFFNYX. She always considered how her fans would react. Even in mourning, she was dressed in the cutest pink leggings, with patterns and lettering, and a white top, which did not hide her acclaimed bust. Driving along the Sunset Strip was so exhilarating in the curves through West Hollywood, past the famous clubs and restaurants, with the hills rising above, and then, under the palm trees, where it rolls into Hollywood, but now she liked traveling down Sunset even more than ever. She drove it often and knew it well. In the late afternoon, heading toward the coast, it was a blind venture into the dazzling sun, hence the name. By day, the best direction was eastbound. She tried to find excuses to take the route, even during rush hour when traffic was bumper to bumper.

Sunset Boulevard was not the same as it used to be. It was a million times better.

The reason was simple. Just as you came around the bend with Beverly Hills behind you, looming above the boulevard, there was a colossal billboard where Tiffany was thirty feet tall, on the cover of the Best Picture of the Year, *Wake*. It sometimes choked her up because it made her think of poor Miles, but then she was comforted when she saw how stunning she looked on the poster, and besides, she was trying to move on now.

Selwyn Felwyn had paid handsomely for the promotion in such a prime spot, and right over where it said Best Picture of the Year was the logo of Paradise Media, Inc, and, underneath, only a little smaller, her name in twinkling letters, leading the cast of stars.

Thousands of people who drove down Sunset Boulevard could see her image.

It grew larger as she approached, and she drove by it as slowly as she could without getting rear-ended by an impatient delivery van, until her own enormous close-up towered above her. Of course, her cosmetically altered lips, nose and bosom had been airbrushed for the enlargement, but show business was not supposed to be reality. She looked beautiful, and she was as huge as a giant. It perked up her day, in antithesis to the cloudy mood that she had been ruminating in all morning.

Tiffany was on the way to the valley to the headquarters of AXE, because the story on the grapevine was that the Best Picture award was about to be revoked, a casualty in the ongoing rivalry between the moguls who led the studios. In defense of her late husband, not to mention safeguarding the lifespan of the sensational billboard, she planned to meet with Duncan and make her feelings known.

To put the studio boss on the defensive, and to enact her own vindication, she intended to protest in the most incendiary terms about the despicable way she was treated on the set of *Fireworks* by his demonic producer, Travis Lazar.

When she arrived at Duncan's office, she blinked twice through her sunglasses, as if she could not believe the report of her own eyes. Her arch-nemesis was already there. Travis Lazar, in black jeans and a black leather jacket, was seated in the horseshoe of leather chairs at the mogul's large desk with the leather blotter and the letter opener and the paperweights. A selection of desktop items would have served as sharp or blunt instruments for a spontaneous murder, for which no jury of peers would convict her, but she suppressed the inclination. The beleaguered executive, Nicholas Pasquale, hunched in one of the other leather chairs with one leather chair in the arc between them, as they finished up a meeting.

"So..." Duncan was saying, "You had a screw-up with special effects..."

"There is always some loss and damage." Nicholas tried to minimize the impact of the unforeseen destruction of

Menachem Amsalem's set. "That was the only problem on the shoot..."

Duncan was fortunately distracted by Tiffany's presence at the doorway –how could he not be flabbergasted given her striking combination? The president himself always dressed like he was ready for cocktails at the beach.

He waved an arm. "Come in, Tiffany."

Travis and Nicholas turned in their chairs to glance at her and then, it appeared, tried to communicate with each other by telepathy, but finding their mystical powers limited, to no avail.

She stormed forward, and stood behind the center chair, with Coochie twitching in her arms.

"Well, that was not the only problem," snapped the star, without exchanging pleasantries, and lowering her sunglasses to squint her eyes at the producer, "I think it was too much to expect me to do the scene with grenades erupting around me. After what I have been through. And as a vegetarian."

The mogul had already been well advised of the performer's travails on repeated occasions by the performer herself, and his sympathy for her circumstances was proven genuine beyond dispute by honoring his financial obligations, while she was inconvenienced. He turned to his right-hand man, swiveling in his executive chair. "As I understand it, Mariana did the scene in the end, right?"

"Right," confirmed Nicholas, "With Sebastian Barge. So that worked out."

The conversation was not going the way that Tiffany had envisioned, so she decided to press on to her next point. "The reason that I wanted to see you..." she said, slipping into the empty chair, and letting Coochie put her head down in her lap, "...it's to do with my late husband's award."

"That's not up to me." Duncan folded his arms on top of his

desk, and the lapdog growled at the motion, inadvertently providing an appropriate sound effect to the mogul's delivery. "That's up to the critics."

"They want to give it to one of the surviving directors," Nicholas filled in for anyone who was not up to speed. "It's probably between Alec or Travis."

At the evocation of his name, Tiffany offered the fiendish producer another fiery squint and a motion of her chin, which served to communicate her sentiments more than any utterance.

"Both directors belong to me." The president of AXE gloated as smugly as a spoiled child with two lollipops. "Either way, the award comes home to AXE. The hell with Paradise Media, Incorporated. I'll put up my own damn billboard."

The widow was swept with righteous indignation. "That's not right. Miles was the winner."

At this point, to her blank-faced astonishment, an unlikely alliance was hatched.

"I have to say..." Travis stood up. "For once, I agree with Tiffany."

Travis was not going to overthrow his friend's memory, especially because, in his expert opinion, Alec Zig was to be the beneficiary of the usurpation. The producer racked his brains to think of some way to influence the situation, but with the mogul as the engineer, there was no way to stop this locomotive in its tracks. Travis was always tense around Duncan, given the president's stormy temperament and their resplendent history. He felt relieved when the meeting was over and Tiffany needed a minute alone with the studio boss to explain why he was still paying her contractual stipend while she was not working. Nicholas walked Travis as far as the bullpen, but hurried back to join the interchange between the two hot personalities in the event that cooler heads would be needed to prevail, leaving the producer to find his own way out of the building.

Left to his own devices, he circled around the long way so that he would pass the open door to Evelyn's office, and although the influential lady was on a three-way telephone call, she covered the receiver with her palm to say, "Saw some of the footage, Travis. Magnificent."

The *Fireworks* production was complete, and the inevitable trip to the woodshed on Duncan's carpet had resulted in nothing more than a slap on the wrists, especially thanks to Tiffany's oral skills at sucking up all the air in the room.

Travis was ready to begin pre-production for his new project, the still untitled release for New York Pictures, which was the next one up on the whiteboard roster.

He took De Soto Avenue and made his way back to the production office at Sound Stage B, where Howard was sitting at his desk, staring at his clipboard, slurping through the plastic straw of a fast-food cup, which was empty of soda, and only contained ice.

The new production was to take place in a mansion and would be a melodrama about marital infidelity with everyone jumping in and out of different bedrooms. There would also be one scene at the swimming pool – as Howard said sardonically – for a change.

Howard checked in with the location service in Hollywood to see which of their regular go-to houses in the valley was available on their proposed dates. In addition to various sound stages, warehouses, backlots, bars, and ranches, there was a list of mansions with friendly owners who were well-paid by the production companies for the daily rental of their private homes in which outsiders were welcome to copulate.

Howard booked the crew – Travis had already put Jack on hold – and he called Billy to secure the cast. For the lead role, Howard had pushed Traci to Travis, whom Travis had pushed to Sylvia in New York who had agreed. This made life easier for everyone, but life in the movie business was still always complicated.

"Is there anything you want to tell me?" Travis asked his production manager.

"Like what?" Howard shrugged, looking at his clipboard, as if it were a matter pertaining to the shooting schedule.

The producer sat on the front edge of his own desk, like an interrogator, but mostly he was in amazement. "You're doing scenes now?"

He looked up from the empty soda and the clipboard. "How do you even know about it?"

"It's getting back to me. You're talking to girls, trying to recruit them for some new series. Traci told me, Jack told me, Tommy told me."

"They all ratted me out?" Howard was disappointed at the fidelity of his fellow man.

"Welcome to the human race," said the sympathetic producer, "What is the project?"

"It's called *The Love Life of a Loser*."

The producer's incredulity expanded. "Now, who is going to want to watch something like that?"

"I think there will be viewers. Guys who just want to see someone ordinary. Not some buff dude that looks gay." Howard realized that he was using his moron voice to explain. "I've shot a few scenes now. I paid everyone with my own money. I was going to tell you. I just wasn't ready."

"Well..." Travis began, with a white smile. "Perhaps, I can help..."

As Howard had anticipated, the wily predator was looking for a way to leap upon the bandwagon.

"What are you doing for distribution?" The predator sprung.

Travis had a plan for Howard's movie, namely to install himself as the executive producer, after the fact, and in his altruism, to assist the novice in securing distribution of his work. He already had a solid idea about where he would be able to lay it off. Here and there, Travis was owed a favor. He would call in a marker. Naturally, he would take a small percentage of any profits. Since Howard, in his genius, had already financed the project, Travis had nothing to lose. It was not that he expected any riches; but he could not allow something to occur on his watch and under his beak without deriving some tribute. Besides, as he had absorbed from the lessons of Motti Sunbeam, any profit was all profit.

Howard was hardly in a position to refuse, without distribution opportunities and without alternative employment options, and so, he put his hopes in the hands of providence and rashly gave Travis the go-ahead to act on his behalf. Travis left for a pre-arranged lunch with The Duchess to be followed by an unscheduled afternoon meeting in which *The Love Life of A Loser* would be on top of the agenda.

Travis met with The Duchess at the Thai restaurant on Ventura Boulevard. As usual, there were only a few other customers, so they were able to speak without concern of being overheard.

"It's been forever since we talked," she said, hardly touching her soup, "I don't know where to begin. What about you?"

Travis had no such hesitation about beginning to talk or to

eat. "I just came from Duncan." He put a spoonful of hot wonton soup into his mouth. "Trouble with the award."

"You know I'm on the board of the First Amendment Association. The publication is getting ready for press, so I have the inside scoop."

"Okay, so what's the bad news?" he asked, but he already knew the answer.

"You're not getting the Picture of the Year Award."

He fished for a wonton, a greater priority for the hungry producer since he was not disappointed by her announcement. "So, it's Alec Zig?"

"That's what the headline says." She stirred her spoon in the broth, took a sip, and rested the spoon in the bowl. "Don't feel so heartbroken, I didn't win either."

"I wouldn't accept it under these circumstances," Travis said, with a dismissive wave of his own utensil, "Miles won it. Tiffany is right."

"She's mounting a campaign, you know," said The Duchess, although this was not surprising given Tiffany's renown at using her mouth.

"The hell with Alec Zig."

The Duchess nodded. "I will use whatever leverage I can at the next meeting of the board, but I'm telling you now it's going to press."

The waitress came to clear away Travis' soup bowl, which had been swiftly emptied. She gave a little curtsey, as she removed the bowl, and The Duchess held up her hand to indicate that she was still busy. A second waitress appeared with two small silver trays containing broccoli and beef and chicken fried rice. She deposited the food in front of the ravenous producer, and the Thai waitresses backed away, disappearing into the kitchen through red fringe curtains.

A gong sounded somewhere in the restaurant, and like a

boxer emerging for the next round after the bell of the time-keeper, Travis began work on his second course. "What's the other news? How's the big acquisition?"

"That's what I wanted to tell you. They have gone back and forth on the figures, but the deal is on the brink of closing. By which I mean brinkmanship."

"What makes you so sure?"

She learned forward confidentially, even though there was nobody listening. "I know they have someone inside the studio working both sides like a double agent. But I don't even know if it's a man or a woman. I'm trying to find out. But I know exactly which studio they're targeting."

"I always thought it would be Selwyn," volunteered Travis, in the same discreet intonation, "My guess is Paradise Media."

"Wrong. It's AXE."

* * *

Tiffany could not help but wonder at what Travis Lazar was plotting. It was hard to believe that a producer of that caliber would take sides with a performer against the studio. As far as she was concerned, he was the kind of man whose handshake could be trusted as an opportunity to steal your fingers. She understood that he had been on brotherly terms with Miles, as a fellow director, coming up the ranks together, but the way that Tiffany figured it was that Travis was exploiting her legitimate grievance as leverage against Duncan. The producer always had an angle. Still, she knew how to use leverage too, and, even if he were an organism from hell, it was better to have him as an ally. You could never have too many.

She arrived at the headquarters of Global Models Management after Billy had returned from lunch and the place was full of people eager to see him. In the outer office, which was almost never used, two trashy ingenues, whom she had never seen before, were waiting to go inside for interviews. They gasped and giggled, jostling one another with their elbows when they spotted a star of such distinction, but she brushed right by them into the talent agent's main office.

There was a shag carpet and the walls were adorned with fake wood paneling, and glossy photographs. With the exception of Billy's large, glass-topped desk, the furniture – which could have told a tale if furniture could discourse – was not new, but still capable of years of service.

Traci, Storm, and Summer were settled on the long couch, waiting their turn to engage the agent, and taking advantage of the delay to catch up on the latest insights about absent friends; Blimp Pullman and a script took up the second couch; an Italian producer by the name of Luigi Pinocchio interviewed starlets in the back casting office which was used for auditions; a producer of wrestling movies cradled a thick catalogue of the current stable on the agent's roster; there were two other producers and a model photographer waiting to peruse the same catalog,

Billy fielded one telephone call after another from behind his desk, rocking back and forth in his executive chair, occasionally using the tip of his boot against the lower drawer to assist propulsion. There were two men with foreign accents and swarthy complexions sitting in the visitor's chairs in front of the desk, but they both relinquished their claims to the seats and Billy put down his telephone as soon as Tiffany strutted up to confront him.

"Are you going to do something about this?" Tiffany demanded without sitting down, and without any explanation of context.

Her three fellow performers on the long couch turned their attention to the exchange like audience members in the front row as the curtain rises on a variety act. All other conversation in the office dropped to a mutter, and Luigi Pinocchio twirled the ends of his waxy moustache. The two ingenues in the outer office slid in at the doorway to observe for their professional education.

"Now, I know what this is about," Billy admitted, stretching out an arm in some sort of effort to placate her or defend himself, "And y'all have a right to be agitated. But, honey, my hands are tied like hogs for a barbecue. This is between Duncan and Selwyn and the scholarly people at the publication who decide on the award." He rocked back in his chair. "I am just an agent. I am a burr on a fur. How am I involved?"

"You are involved exactly because you are an agent." Tiffany put one hand on the glass surface of his desk, and rattled her nails. "You represent me. You take a commission of my hard work having sex. I don't see you blowing anything more than your nose in your handkerchief. So, don't get all folksy with me."

"I will confer with the critics," Billy agreed, trying to refrain from metaphor, "I'm on the association. But they won't do anything for one lone cowpoke."

"Oh, don't worry, Tex," the actress said, mimicking his drawl, "We're not going to be alone. I already have Travis Lazar in my posse."

With that regional pronouncement, and a shake of her head, Tiffany made her exit, leaving her audience in the talent agency somewhat dumb-founded and much entertained.

Her next stop in her search to recruit allies was the modest headquarters of the number two studio in the industry, Paradise Media, Incorporated. The offices, and adjoining ware-house, were situated not far from the home of Global Models Management and near to the county courthouse in a nondescript industrial building in Van Nuys with two stories and a flat roof.

Equally modest, and unexpectedly small, much like its occupant, Selwyn's office was sparse, but also unexpectedly contained a prominent grandfather clock, which did not correspond with the rest of the office furniture, but kept perfect time and chimed on the hour. There was a refrigerator for Selwyn's private collection of Cokes. Summer or winter, the air conditioning was kept at a cool temperature.

When she stepped into the office, Selwyn stood up and came around the desk to greet her with a peck on her cheek, provoking a growl from the dog, who was tamed as soon as Selwyn stepped back to make sure that the door was shut for the sake of confidentiality.

The President of Paradise Media, Incorporated seethed with controlled anger. He displayed strong arms in a short-sleeved navy shirt, and all his veins and muscles bulged and reddened, as if fumes were about to pipe from his ears.

"Screw Duncan!" he hissed, "I wish there was something I could do about it."

"You're saying there is nothing to stop this?"

"Do you think I haven't tried?" He sat down in one of the guest chairs, and pulled the other one alongside it, motioning for Tiffany to take a seat beside him, which she did. "I talked to the lawyers. They laughed at me. It would cost too much to fight it. I talked directly with the publisher. I threatened to pull my advertising, but d'you know what he told me?" Selwyn shook his head gravely. "You won't believe what he told me." He squeezed his fists together. "The publisher said that Duncan already agreed to buy all my pages." The thought of his rapacious rival prompted him to add a disclaimer. "And that's in private, Tiffany, these doors are closed and I would deny it, but I am trusting you." He rubbed his fists on the arms

of his chair. "No, there's nothing I can do about it. But you..."
He considered the options, regaining his composure as a plan of
action appeared to him. "You should go on strike."

"I'm already not working because of the...you know...
tragedy." She hugged Coochie closer to her chest for solace.
"Duncan's not thrilled about that."

The grandfather clock in the corner chimed the hour,
signaling a natural ending to their appointment.

Selwyn put his hand on her leg in a paternal fashion, and
spoke in a whispery voice. "You know, the award doesn't really
matter so much in the grand scheme of things..."

"But you spent so much on the billboard, and it's so beautiful..." she said plaintively.

His voice was just as forlorn. "...I paid for a six-month lease
on it, and now I will receive a cease-and-desist to take down the
ad." He gave her thigh another pat, and so as not to become too
familiar and already one contact too far for comfort, he got to
his feet and navigated around to reach refuge on the safe side of
his desk. "It's not smart to get into a fight we're never going to
win. Duncan will have his day. "

* * *

Travis almost missed the on-ramp as he turned the Mercedes
from Sepulveda Boulevard onto the 405 North towards
Chatsworth because of how the wheels were gyrating in his
head.

First of all, he needed to find out as much as he could about
the shake-up at AXE. It was not that he doubted the veracity of
his loyal colleague, but this was the movie business, so no
matter what she believed, nobody knew anything for sure. But,
if what The Duchess said turned out to be true, then the repercussions could rattle the valley like a tremor. There was the

question of how the large corporation, if not to say the industry, would fare without the stewardship of Duncan. But, if what The Duchess said turned out to be true, then it would be The Duchess herself who would take the reins.

That could be a stroke of fortune.

The loyal producer resolved to do everything in his power to assist his loyal colleague to that responsibility. He would start by uncovering the imposter who was working the inside.

Secondly, he had not thought of a title for the new production for New York Pictures, and there was something bothering him about the project that he could not articulate. It was running too smoothly: Traci, as reliable as sunshine in California, was the star; he was in constant touch with Sylvia Bern in Manhattan who had given her solemn assurance that the wire would transfer from the deep pockets of New York Pictures to arrive in the account of Travis Lazar Productions on time; and he would make sure Howard booked more than one mansion so they would have back-up, if they lost the venue. This meant that the typical problems, which always occurred, would not occur. But Travis could not prepare himself for the unexpected problems, and that made him restless.

Thirdly, he could not figure out a way to make sure that the award stayed in Miles' name. The best he could come up with was to refuse to accept it, but that wasn't a solution as the prize was destined for Alec Zig, who would be thrilled to get his grubby hands around it under any conditions. The mission now was to try to foil Alec Zig, but Travis could not think of an angle. Sometimes, you just had to leave these things in the lap of the gods, which to the producer meant an opportunity would present itself.

The one item on the producer's list of things to do that he was certainly not concerned about was where to find a distribution deal for Howard's opus, *The Love Life of a Loser*.

Partly because of his prestige within the industry, and partly because of the slow afternoons on the torpid schedule of Majestic Movies, Travis did not require an appointment to meet with Beppo. In fact, unsure if the bell rang, the girl at the front, who interrupted her game of solitaire on the computer to slide open the receptionist's window, was surprised to find that there was a visitor.

She informed the acting president of the company, and Beppo welcomed Travis into his office, which he had chosen to keep in the dim light of shut blinds.

"Good to see you," he said, moving some files from a chair so that Travis could sit, "Did anyone see you arrive?"

"I parked across the street," Travis said, appreciating Beppo's preference for discretion being the better part of valor.

He cracked open a window blind, allowing a glint of sunlight. "What's up?"

"I might have something for you," said the producer, but he knew that since the influx of funds from Germany, Beppo was in no position to refuse him any request. He owed him a favor.

Beppo turned on the desk lamp for better illumination. "G'ahead."

"You know Howard, my production guy..." Travis began his pitch.

"Sure." Beppo was not expecting this conversation, but he was certain it was going to be informative, and the springs creaked under his chair as he settled in to listen to the presentation.

"He's made a picture. He produced it, and he's performing in it. It's called *The Love Life of A Loser*."

"He's performing in it?" Beppo frowned, patting himself down for a cigar, as the pitch took an unexpected twist, "Now, who is going to want to see something like that? Have you screened it?"

"Oh, no," admitted Travis, who only ever watched pornography with his finger on the fast-forward button, "I couldn't look at something like that."

"So, it's like what? A novelty?"

"It doesn't matter," Travis explained, with a wave of his hand, "He thinks there's a market. But if we sell a few pieces, we will all make money. All the expenses are already paid."

"I have distribution expenses too," argued Beppo, which was not an unexpected remark.

"Everyone knows those come out first..." agreed the producer, knowing that there was no way to stop Beppo from skimming, "...from whatever we recoup. As long as a few dollars come home. We will have to let Howard wet his beak."

"You never know," Beppo shrugged, "Something like that. It could go nowhere. But there's always the possibility that it could be a hit."

* * *

Howard was on hold for so long waiting for Billy Dallas to come to the telephone that he was tempted to leave the production office at Sound Stage B and get into his car and drive over there in person. This was motivated not only for a discussion of business matters, but also to participate in the inevitable frolic that was surely taking place around the talent agent's desk, given the length of the time that the production manager was held waiting. Foregoing his place in the line, he hung up without waiting any longer when an unscheduled visitor in pink leggings, white top, and sunglasses walked into the production office.

"Hello, *Howard*," Tiffany said, emphasizing his name as if its articulation left a bitter taste in her mouth. She swept her gaze around the office. "Is Travis Lazar around?"

"Went to lunch and a meeting," Howard replied, leaning back in his chair with his fingers clasped behind his pate, in an effort to appear more suave, "But he should be back at any moment, if you want to wait."

"I will wait for ten minutes, then I've got to go..." Tiffany perched on the edge of the opposite desk, clicking her tongue. "I have Coochie in the car."

His eyes glazed over looking at her. It was not that Tiffany's presence gave Howard an idea, but a notion, burning in the medulla region of his brain, focused upon Tiffany, like a parasite upon a host. Her unexpected arrival just as his mind was aflame seemed to him like a preordained opportunity.

"Since we're waiting, just the two of us..." Howard began unabashedly.

She lowered her sunglasses so that she could scrunch her eyes at him. "Don't even think about it."

"No, it's not what you think," Howard said, dismissing the notion of complimentary fellatio, which had apparently occurred to each of them, "It's about work. I wanted to talk to you about my line. I don't know if you know, but I'm doing scenes..."

"You are a disgusting, bug-eyed cockroach..." Tiffany began, but she stopped herself in mid-rant when Travis walked into the office.

"Hello, Tiffany," interrupted the producer, who did not seem taken aback by her surprise visit.

She adjusted her sunglasses on the bridge of her perfectly-hewn nose, and made a pronouncement. "I am here to thank you in person for your support in the meeting with Duncan."

"Yeah, well don't thank me yet." He knew that she was not there to thank him, but to make sure that he was still on board. "I have some news."

Tiffany put her hand over her heart. "I swear I won't say a word."

"They already decided the award is going to Alec Zig. The announcement is going to press."

"We have to do something," implored the star. "For Miles."

"I'm working on it," said Travis, although he held little stock on any leverage the Duchess might wield.

Tiffany was not persuaded of his conviction to the cause. "What does that mean?"

"I'm trying to sway the board. We need six votes. I have The Duchess."

"I have two. Billy Dallas is on our side. And Paradise. I talked to Selwyn."

It did not seem like news to Travis that Paradise would be an ally, given that Paradise would suffer the most misfortune in the event, but now Travis had to think about how Duncan would respond if the mogul thought Travis had aligned with his arch-rival. There was already conflict based on his hesitancy to accept the potential accolade, so he decided that he might as well keep going in the direction of the war. The cause, however, was lost. The Duchess would be able to attract one of her fellow board members, who was allegiant, but nobody else would want to risk a fight. Political capital would be spilled. There was no way to garner enough votes, and he was convinced that this was a battle he would not win.

They heard the drone of an airplane overhead, and they all instinctively bristled not because of impending bombardment, but because of the conditioning over the years they had all spent in production, when the hum of aircraft over recorded sound routinely caused the director to announce a cut.

"Oh, hell," Tiffany blurted, alarmed for another reason, "Coochie is going to pee like a storm drain."

Without observing parting ceremonies, she dashed for the door.

"It's going to Alec Zig?" Howard checked, after the star was out of earshot.

Travis nodded, "Tiffany is trying to build a groundswell, but I don't think that there's any way to stop it. Duncan has the board in his pocket. He's too strong." Then, taking his seat behind his desk, the producer said, with an upbeat tone, "But that's not the only news of the afternoon."

"You made a deal?"

"Congratulations, you have distribution on your picture."

Howard felt full of hope. "Who is the distributor?"

"Majestic Movies," Travis said, without further comment, which meant that Howard did not feel obliged to continue the conversation.

* * *

The call came from Nicholas a few days later, requesting an urgent meeting with Travis, who was able to appear in Duncan's office within two hours. Calling on the mogul's behalf, the Head of Production at AXE did not want to go into details over the telephone, but the producer surmised from his tone that it was a matter of importance, which – like so many vagaries on the currents along the grand river of the industry – might have a positive consequence on the fortunes of Travis Lazar.

Tiffany was also present at the meeting, a concluding juxta-position of what had begun with the same participants a few days before. Also providing a matching contrast, Tiffany was back in her widow's black, with long black gloves, a hat and her ubiquitous dark sunglasses, which played in rain or shine, although it was not certain whether she had relapsed into mourning the late demise of her husband, or was grieving for the fresh loss of the billboard on Sunset Boulevard.

The golf channel, which nobody was watching, flickered on the mute widescreen television. Duncan sat glowering behind his desk, his palms on his jowls, his lips pressed together, letting Nicholas do all the talking.

Nicholas explained that in an unfolding scandal, Alec Zig was arrested for "just looking around" his neighbor's apartment while she was at work. The aforementioned neighbor came home unexpectedly and discovered him there – fully clothed – in her living room. The place was as neat as she had left it, nothing was missing or disturbed, but she summoned the police, and Alec was arrested without much to say to anyone in his own defense. He had seen the young woman in the hallway on numerous occasions over the years. He felt "curious", he said, about how his neighbor lived, and swore that he had not touched her undergarments or anything like that, and just wanted to savor a slice of her life, for which appetite she filed charges for breaking and entering, criminal trespass, but, unfortunately, not for just being a creep.

Mrs. Hathaway was appalled when she discovered the conduct of the eccentric auteur, and consequently Duncan shared in the outrage, and refused to offer any support, particularly when the request was for a financial contribution towards legal counsel. In addition to which, effective immediately, the disgraced director would no longer be under contract to the studio.

There was no ethics violation clause in the contract, in fact, there was no contract at all other than the verbal understanding between Duncan and his contractual director. Part of that understanding, as far as the mogul was concerned, was the responsibility not to behave like a drooling pervert. The industry was traditionally lenient with respect to personal peccadilloes, but the deviant nature of this offence with an innocent civilian made it more egregious. Such a shockwave already electrified the grapevine and ground the presses to a halt, resulting in a dramatic change as to the proposed recipient of the re-awarded honor for Best Picture of the Year.

It was to be Travis Lazar.

The producer and the star left the building together in silence, and Tiffany stood face to face with him in the parking lot.

"I just want to say to you," she said, her eyes lowered, her voice trembling, "That I wish I could tell you what I am thinking about someone who is the lowest form of scum on this planet, but we are in Duncan's offices or premises or whatever – company – and I am a professional who will not jeopardize – never mind – I hate you."

Before he could reply, having said her piece, Tiffany turned on her heel and stomped towards her car, carrying Coochie in the cradle of her arms like a fluffy toy. She was so emotional that she snubbed Oscar Lowport who was coming back from lunch and who tried to engage her in a conversation.

He was more successful when he reached Travis. "What's she upset about now?"

"That I got the award," explained Travis, "But I didn't want it. And I'm going to refuse it."

"You can't do that." Oscar was dismayed. "It's not yours to refuse." He ran the back of his hand through his dark, oily curls. "Don't kid yourself, my friend, it belongs to Duncan. You've already had differences with him. All cleared up now. Happy ending. But he'll have your balls for breakfast if you tick him off again." He gave a chummy chuckle. "I mean, the man has his pride. Let him have his award. It means a lot to him."

Travis realized that the foreign sales agent had a point. "He's gone to a lot of trouble to get it."

"Be loyal to him, and you will always have a home at AXE." The broker gave him a sly look, and a confidential wink. "You know, there are going to be a lot of changes coming up in the near you-know-what, but no matter if it's hell or highwater, you will always have a home here."

As soon as Travis got back to the Mercedes, he called The Duchess. "I'm at AXE," he said, when she picked up, "I found out who the insider is."

CHAPTER SEVEN

THE LOVE LIFE OF A LOSER

A week later, Travis met The Duchess at the Thai restaurant on Ventura Boulevard. Most of the lunch patrons had already gone back to work on the muggy afternoon, so there was nobody to overhear their deliberations.

This was where things stood: Oscar Lowport, as Travis had surmised, was undoubtedly the busy go-between brokering the deal between AXE and a mysterious Internet conglomerate called Sinisex. Duncan was to receive a certain price for the sale, with an initial payment followed by six equal installments to be paid out over three years, upon which Mr. and Mrs. Hathaway were basing their plans for retirement. But in their investigation, and to their frustration, the two producers could not ascertain exactly what the price was.

Information was power. Producers needed numbers.

Travis heard one amount from Nicholas, but The Duchess was informed of a higher figure from her contact inside Sinisex. The producers agreed that the discrepancy in the totals reflected the involvement of the oily foreign sales broker, who was not only wetting his beak, but practically immersing his head to the shoulders.

Lowport International Licensing had engineered it all. The middleman had been shepherding the deal through for months, like it was shuttle diplomacy, going back and forth from one side to another, and swearing allegiance to them both. Oscar Lowport had presented the proposals, initiated innuendo, generated rumors, calculated figures, convinced the buyer and the seller that there was an interest from the other participant, and negotiated the terms. He had whispered in ears, greased palms, and shook hands. All his hard work appeared to have paid off.

Contracts had been prepared. Payment terms had been calculated. Lists of assets had been compiled. Due diligence was done. In accordance with their professional obligations, sharp-eyed lawyers and accountants on both sides had tried everything within their ability to blockade the deal. They were well-practiced in their sworn mission that business should not proceed. They went to work with overwhelming reams of paperwork containing definitions, parties of the first part and the second part, addenda, remedies, nullifications and complexities, but were finally obliged by the parties of the first and second part to shrug their shoulders, shake their heads, and give grudging assent. Having offered their most dire warnings to each party, though cautions were not considered, counsel could not be held responsible for whatever was to follow.

The repercussions of the sale of the monolithic studio would reverberate through Chatsworth like the Northridge quake all over again. The industry was about to lose its leadership. Without the prominent bearing of Duncan at the captaincy of pornography, there would be no moral authority to guide the vessel, and to offer an immaculate example. Alignments would shift, vacuums would be opened, disruptions would materialize, and at least one rival would be licking his lips. But, as always, as the insatiable global appetite insisted, movies would have to be made.

The Duchess had been forewarned to prepare herself to take the helm of AXE, following Duncan's departure. Her mission was to remake the industry flagship studio from a woman's viewpoint, so as to attract a new demographic of young female consumers who were Internet savvy and sexually inquisitive, and, in each case, inclined to exploration.

Her tenure at AXE could not begin soon enough for Travis, because his relationship with Duncan had soured again, as a result of Travis' reluctance to accept the award for which the President of AXE had worked so hard in his honor. Duncan was naturally piqued, Travis stayed out of range. The ceremony was scheduled to take place as a special programming note at the next convention in Las Vegas, so all-out war between them had not yet broken out; there was time. The studio boss was sure that, under strain, Travis would relent. The producer was already feeling it; there was nothing on the white production board except the lone production for New York Pictures, and now the long hot summer stretched before them.

On the East Coast, which was the prime market, with fine weather, consumers took to the sunny outdoors rather than staying home for indoor entertainment, so sales fell. In San Fernando, the valley floor would blister under the glare of the unforgiving sun. Nobody wanted to move in the lazy desert heat. Business slowed. It was a force of nature for the producer, an inevitable season on the calendar. And he did not need Duncan's iron pressure to make things worse. Once The Duchess took the helm at the studio, however, there would be many changes, among them the certain requirement for a new slate of big budget productions.

Fortunately, it was all poised to happen suddenly.

"Unless..." The Duchess pondered as they finished their meal.

"Unless what?" asked Travis, making sure that no food which was charged on the bill would be left on the plate.

"Unless we're all being *Lowportimized*."

The Love Life of a Loser, produced and directed by Howard Funx, starring Traci Gold and Howard Funx, was released by Majestic Movies at the end of spring in an effort to avoid the impending summer lull. Majestic Movies spared no expense in distributing the film according to where Beppo valued the movie, which is to say that as little as possible was advanced toward marketing.

The box cover design showed Howard with a sheepish grin ringed by naïve newcomers. The female principal, who was not available for the box cover shoot due to a question about her rate, appeared in an inset. There was also a foldout poster, sponsored by and depicting the producer-performer and the aforementioned bevy, that was included at no additional charge.

Beppo had low expectations for the movie.

The acting president of Majestic Movies stood in the warehouse, watching the warehouse manager pack the shipments. Occasionally, Beppo offered his assistance, reaching up to receive the odd selections handed down from the top shelf while the sole employee was on the rolling ladder. In addition to the new release, customers ordered cheap back titles. Not many had selected *The Love Life of a Loser*. There would be enough distributed to cover his costs, so Beppo would not be out of pocket, but only small change would come in from sales. Those that were disseminated were destined to languish on the shelves of adult bookstores, finding their place on racks behind more popular movies, and ending up in discount bins, or bundled in grab bags or special promotions.

In the end, everything moved.

There was no air-conditioning in the warehouse, but a fan the size of a propeller blew a futile zephyr of stale air, which only served to cool anyone who stood directly in front of it at close range.

The corrugated doors were rolled up half the way, so it was easy to see when the brown UPS truck arrived. The doors clattered up on the rollers. Beppo watched as the warehouse manager loaded up the shipments onto a dolly and wheeled them out to the truck. He made three or four trips, and then *The Love Life of a Loser* began its journey into the marketplace. It was always satisfying, even with a modest release, for Beppo to watch goods going out into the world.

He reached for a cigar in his pocket, rolled it between his fingertips and put it between his lips. He was about to light up, with his back to the whirring fan, when the girl from the front came into the warehouse from the other side. Her hair, which was tipped with purple streaks, was disheveled because of how she played with the strands when she got antsy, and her pale skin seemed even paler.

"Uh...Beppo...there's some people here to see you."

* * *

In spite of the low prospects held by the distributor, the producer of *The Love Life of a Loser* remained blissfully ignorant. In his mind, Howard was not only already counting the profits he would make, but he envisioned a library full of movies and the endless roster of roles he would have to cast as his partners. He foresaw personal appearances, and signings, and even a Howard Funx fan club of supporters. There would be posters, t-shirts, perhaps a newsletter. Admirers would recognize him on the street. Money would roll into his coffers. Nubile aspirants would seek him out for his prowess. He let his fantasies roam wild, but told himself that even in the worst case, he had everything to gain. He would be able to make his mark. He had witnessed Travis Lazar at work for long enough, he could do the same. He imagined himself as an influential producer who would one day recall the humble origins of his eminent career.

Howard stretched out in bed in his North Hollywood apartment, wearing nothing more than a pair of boxers and a pair of glasses, with the Cartoon Network on low. The window was open. Tomorrow was trash day, there was a faint smell of garbage, wafting up from the alleyway. Distant freight trains chugged through the valley. His neighbors were still awake, talking Spanish in loud voices. It was getting close to midnight, and as he often did around that hour, because that was when they both felt alone, he called Traci.

"So, our movie was released today..." Howard said, proudly sharing the credit with his leading lady.

"I can't believe I had sex with you," she commented, in a voice without bitterness but which conveyed her incredulity at her own recollection, "I still have bad dreams about it. Sometimes, on set, I think about you on purpose, if I don't want to come."

He smiled in his own fond reminiscence. "Now that I have my distributor, I can reach my audience. I'm going to turn the project into a series. I want to shoot part two immediately so I can get it right out."

"Yeah, who are you going to get as your star? It's not going to be me."

He could not stop thinking about his encounter in the production office. "I wanted to get Tiffany."

"Oh, you're disgusting."

"I tried to suggest it to her, but she looked like she was about to rip off my scrotum."

Traci tried to avoid the visual image. "Anyway, don't you think you'd better wait and see how the first one does before you run off and make a sequel?"

"If I could get Tiffany, I would shoot it tomorrow."

He was, of course, inspired by the limitless expansion by which both his personal prestige and his sales would soar were he to consummate the acclaimed star, but, for the fledgling artist, the dream of the consummation itself dwarfed any other motive.

"You know, Howard," Traci clarified, "We do this for money. If you pay her enough, she just might."

The innocent seed that careless remark planted in the fecund soil of his brain was about to grow into a treacherous thicket.

* * *

Tiffany was in the sourest mood, the black cloud of her disposition providing a stark contrast to the crisp California sunshine. She was seated in her Mustang, with the top up, parked in a valet parking lane on Sunset Boulevard, even though the restaurant serviced by the parking attendants was closed until lunch. To perk herself up, she had decided to forego her widow's wardrobe, and was back to vivid tops and clingy leggings. She wore her dark sunglasses and peered across the street like she was a hard-boiled detective on stakeout in one of those television shows they filmed on the Fireworks lot. But she was not stalking a suspect. Tiffany was staring at the Paradise Media, Inc billboard.

She had a good view of it from where she was stationed on the opposite side, and the traffic in the late morning was light in each direction. What she saw left her slack-jawed in disbelief.

There were workers on the catwalk attached to the structure who were in the process of removing the poster for the Picture of the Year, in accordance with the receipt of a letter on embossed stationery from legal counsel, demanding its timely extirpation. They worked methodically, in no rush to complete the task, which was curiously gratifying. Panel by panel, they peeled away the strips. Her head was decapitated, and her sensual supine body ended at the neck. From where Tiffany was sitting, it looked like she was nothing but boobs, defacement made more insolent by the antics of one of the laborers.

Piece by piece, as she watched in horror, they pulled away what was soon a jigsaw of colored blocks from which no definition could be discerned. The pithy text was just random letters. The logo was a shapeless fragment. The blank canvas below poked holes in the picture, and gradually, more and more white areas emerged.

Cars went by in the morning traffic, oblivious to the insufferable injury to her dignity. From beneath her sunglasses, tears rolled down her cheeks, and she wiped her face with the back of her hand. She was filled with the same emptiness that engulfed her at the funeral, and she swore to go back to her black attire to mourn this latest loss. She did not know how much tragedy she could stand.

Her image was gone. Everything was stripped from the billboard. All that was left was a huge white rectangle that made her feel that she had turned invisible. She could not believe that this was where the glamorous shot of her had loomed, and now there was nothing.

When Howard called, she was not inclined to listen to the ramblings of someone whom she considered to be the village idiot of the industry.

"I know we discussed this the other day," he babbled, "but I am not sure if you knew that I was serious."

"Discussed what?" she snapped, "I know you are seriously disturbed, that's all." She stared in numb disbelief at her former billboard across the street, as if, by the force of will, her presence in the vicinity would somehow cause her image to reappear on the blank surface, like celluloid projected onto a cinema screen.

"What I wanted to explain is that I would pay your full rate, and the scene would only take an hour, at the most...."

Some fans drove by, honking when they recognized the famous porn star parked in her convertible outside the Sunset Boulevard restaurant, where the valet parking attendant was setting up a yellow umbrella and a sign.

"What scene?" Tiffany demanded, not remembering any conversation with Howard about anything, "I can't do scenes, you hollow, come-dumb pervert, because I am too grief-stricken for sex." She started up her car, and got ready to pull out so she didn't have to deal with some valet parking attendant swelled with the authority of his office, which would result in a ticket. "And besides, I can only have sex for AXE." She was under the impression that Howard was trying to book her for a scene in the new project for New York Pictures. "Duncan would drop a mud streak in his golf pants."

"Oh, I forgot about that. I thought you could do something on the side."

"What scene?" she asked again.

"For me," he explained meekly, a little thrown off his surety by now, but too far gone along his path to make any retreat, "I told you, I have my own line that I appear in..."

"Okay, listen to me, you worm-coiled, stool-brained freak," Tiffany could not be contained, "Did Travis Lazar set you up for this bullshit?"

Howard did not want to get Travis involved. "Oh no, this is all my own bullshit."

"I am going to report this call to Duncan and to Billy. You are a repulsive loser, and you can tell Travis I mean it until hell freezes over!"

* * *

On the other side of the hills, in direct antithesis to Tiffany's disposition, The Duchess was filled with the joys of life.

There was a skip in her step. Her avant-garde wardrobe had been replaced by a pinstripe skirt and jacket over a cream blouse with uncharacteristic ruffles, her jangling earrings had been shelved in favor of studs, her artsy pendant had been usurped by a sedate string of pearls. She carried a briefcase wherever she went. Her new look was corporate.

In anticipation of her upcoming engagement as the new President of the new Sinisex Studios, formerly AXE, the lady producer went shopping for a new SUV, befitting of her impending distinction. Her primary concerns with the new vehicle were the color, which was to be silver, and the assurance that she could retain her old license plate, which read, SHTGRLS, an acronym that was much played upon by inventive members of her production crew. The petite brunette hated haggling with car salesmen, so it was natural that she was accompanied by Travis, for whom car salesmen were fish in a barrel generally left in enough tears to fill a barrel after enduring his negotiating proficiency.

Even though it was a dry day with endless blue skies, there was a sultry wind, which rustled the promotional pennants strung above them. The two collegial producers – who were spending an uncommon amount of time together as the impending deal grew nearer – ambled along the line of vehicles at the dealership on Van Nuys Boulevard. They were so preoccupied with business that they paid little attention to what they had come to purchase.

"Let me ask you a question about the deal," Travis wondered, clearly not referring to anything automotive, "Duncan is selling all rights to his entire library of films?"

"Yes. The building, the racks, the replication division, and all rights to the line. Everything he owns."

Travis frowned. "He doesn't own everything in his library."

"He thinks he does."

"Duncan has movies which I made for him, but in some of those deals, I retained certain rights. On behalf of my guys in Germany. I know he made deals like that with other producers, because that's exactly the kind of thing that Lowport Licensing does for him." Travis stopped walking and he said to her slowly, as if he were also telling something to himself, "Oscar must be aware of this. Duncan can't sell what he doesn't own. You'd better warn Sinisex."

A car salesman with a youthful smirk and slicked straw-colored hair swung open the double glass doors of the display room, where he had been lurking on the lookout for potential customers.

"If I breathe a word to them," said The Duchess, "It could blow up the whole deal."

"It's a poison pill," Travis concluded, giving the car salesman a white smile. "Somebody is going to get less than they bargained for."

* * *

The telephone just rang and rang at the worldwide headquarters of Majestic Movies with no response. It was the only sound in the front office. There was no shuffling of papers, no bell at the counter to announce visitors, no scrape of the sliding glass panel. There was no clacking of the computer keyboard as the long fingernails of the receptionist prepared invoices, or sent emails, or updated her status on the Internet. The receptionist was not at work, and the monitor was dark. The ringing of the telephone echoed in the empty warehouse, where the warehouse manager was absent. The coffee pot was cold. The fan stood motionless in the stale air. The pens and packing tape and freight documents were undisturbed. The raunchy centerfolds taped to the wall remained unseen. No shipments were ready for the UPS trucks. And in Beppo's dim office, where the blinds allowed a sliver of sunlight, the telephone rang among the piles of dusty papers on his desk, but nobody came to answer it.

Travis was baffled. It was not like Beppo to ignore the rare prospect of business on the other end of the line. He tried Beppo's cell phone, and, like the telephone on his cluttered desk in Chatsworth, it just rang and rang.

If Travis was worried, Howard went into a panic. He was so eager to hear the initial sales reports on his movie that the mysterious absence of Beppo created a swirl of alarming questions. What if his movie had turned out to be a blockbuster, and Beppo had run off with the earnings? What if the release was a disaster, and Beppo was hiding his head in shame? Where was Beppo?

Travis did not share his own insights with Howard, but the options – none of which had anything to do with Howard's movie – seemed obvious. He considered their rendezvous at

The Chatsworth Diner, and the heads-up which Beppo had been considerate enough to provide. He would reach out when he was ready. Beppo was laying low because he wanted to lay low, which meant that it was better not to look for him. Either that, or the jig was up, in which case, it was really better not to look for him.

* * *

The first day of shooting on *Cheats*, the new production for New York Pictures, took place at a mansion in the flat lowlands of the west valley, on a day in which the seasons seemed to offer a preview of the sweltering attractions lined up for the months which lay ahead.

There was a wall surrounding the property, which guaranteed privacy, and a driveway with a metal gate between two brick gate posts upon which adroit lions balanced on stone balls. The house itself had two stories, in a mustard shade with white trim, with a sparse, modern style to its architecture and furnishings. The main attraction was the swimming pool at the back, which was shaped like a hidden lagoon, an effect aided by foliage and palm trees, and a dark, green underwater tile. In all likelihood, water was probably not the only fluid in the pool. They had all shot here before, and there had been coitus on every dry or wet spot on the property.

Traci, true to form, arrived fifteen minutes before anyone else, but the experienced trouper knew better than to enter the premises, and consequently initiate the ticking of the clock by the count of which the production company was obliged to pay the rental of the location. She waited in her car, checking her messages. It was the habit of the producer to arrive twenty minutes later than the call time by virtue of his stature as producer, so consequently the rest of the crew had developed the habit of arriving fifteen minutes past the call time so as to be present when Travis appeared. But, after waking up early to comfort his youngest child, who had been troubled by a restless night after late ice-cream, the producer arrived on time, and was astonished to find that nobody was there besides the punctual actress.

The crew was equally astonished fifteen minutes later, when they all arrived to find their boss pacing up and down between the leonine gateposts, itching to begin the day but also cognizant of beginning the hourly meter on the location before the latecomers arrived. They hurriedly got to work.

Maria unloaded her brushes, curlers, sponges, Q-tips, powders, glosses, vials of makeup, and a hair dryer, and laid everything out on the dresser of the small bedroom that they always used for the talent, and got Traci into the chair. Howard set up his production office in the formal dining room, which had a grand, polished table upon which he laid out a stack of model releases, call sheets, schedules and scripts, and a portable Xerox machine. The production assistants commandeered the kitchen, unpacking trays of soda, fruit plates, donuts, bagels, cream cheese, confectionery, paper plates, plastic utensils, Styrofoam cups, trash bags, and a coffee machine. Jack and Tommy carted in the camera and lighting equipment, cables, monitors, battery packs, and microphones, and began setting up at the pool, which was scheduled as the setting for the first scene. It was standard procedure to shoot an outdoor scene first so that they would not run into trouble with the diminishing light or inclement weather.

This turned out to be a lucky accident of scheduling because when Tommy went to plug in his lamps, he found that there was no electrical power, a discovery which was simultaneously made by the production manager attempting to make copies of the script and the production assistant attempting to make coffee.

"Uh, boss..." Tommy reported to Travis, who was at the pool trying to figure out the most aesthetic placement of the pool chair upon which the first sex scene was to take place, "We've got a little challenge. There's no power."

Travis was not surprised. There was always a crisis on the first morning of the shoot, more often than not in connection with a performer who had confirmed the night before and cancelled in the morning, but sometimes it was a technical issue. "Did you trip something?"

"I haven't even plugged in yet...slow start...my own fault, no excuse...but not me. Dead as roadkill."

"Howard!" bellowed the producer, but the production manager was already halfway across the lawn.

"I can't get the copier to work," Howard complained, shooting a glare at the chief lighting technician, "I suppose our crackerjack electrical department blew a breaker."

"It's not me," Tommy mumbled, "I got nothing either. The circuits are overloaded. Every air conditioner is blasting coolant from here to Mexico."

The unforeseeable had revealed itself.

Travis took the helm. "Call the City of Los Angeles Department of Water and Power, and find out if there is an outage in the neighborhood. And find out how long it will take them to fix it. Order a small generator, and find out how long it will take to get here..."

Howard made notes on his clipboard. "And the cancellation fee." He knew his producer well enough to anticipate the confrontation that might occur if it turned out that the rental was not needed. "If the lights come back on..."

"Move quickly on that jenny," Travis instructed, "because

every other crew shooting in the valley will be dealing with the same thing."

Jack walked up, now also familiar with the problem. "We can get started outside. That's sunlight. But what do you want to do about the bedroom scene that's coming up after the pool?"

"Open all the curtains, and let's see how it looks with just the existing light."

"It's supposed to be a night scene," Howard reminded them.

"We can do night on the lens," the cinematographer suggested, "If I stay off the windows."

Howard said, "I'll have a generator here before you get to the bedroom. You have to do the pool first. You might be able to shift some of the dialog outside too."

"Oh, don't worry." Travis forged ahead. "Nothing is going to stop me from shooting."

* * *

At Paradise Media, Inc in Van Nuys, the lights had also gone out, and Selwyn sat alone in his dim office where he formulated a plan.

It was tranquil in the still shadows, without any interruptions, and there was a unique silence in which he could gather his thoughts. On his desk, beneath his reading glasses, lay the lawyer's letter on embossed stationery, demanding the removal of the Picture of the Year advertisement. He recognized that he had lost this round to his arch-rival, a suspicion supported by the fact that Duncan was crowing all over the valley. But there would be another round. The president of Paradise was determined to triumph over him the next time.

Now that Alec Zig had withdrawn from the community, Selwyn guessed that *Fireworks* would be the favored contender for the next bounty of awards in Las Vegas. He had to block it. He had to make sure that he had a winning picture to compete. It really was too bad that Miles was dead, and consequently not available to direct it.

He considered his second choice – Blimp Pullman.

The rotund director was coming to the end of his contractual agreement with Paradise, and Selwyn was not planning to renew it. He had nothing against Blimp, but he had a plentiful stockpile of the director's work and he wanted to bring in fresh blood to skew to a new generation of consumers. Blimp was not the virtuoso that Miles had been, but he would be capable, especially if Selwyn nudged up the budget by a few notches.

Since he still held the lease on the billboard, he thought that he might solve another problem and rub some salt in his rival's tender spots. The blank billboard was useless, advertising nothing. He had originally considered just putting up an image of the company logo, but now he decided to use it to begin the promotion for the upcoming new blockbuster, which did not yet have a name.

With the outage, the air-conditioning was not working, and the office was warm, but it was not uncomfortable. He realized at that moment that he did not really like the cold air, as if there were something artificial about it. Then he remembered that the refrigerator where he kept his personal collection of Cokes had gone out too, and that the ice would melt.

He needed a name for the picture that would build up expectations, and suspense.

The name would have to be something that would needle Duncan even further. Selwyn knew it was bad enough for his nemesis that he had snagged the choice spot on Sunset Boulevard for his promotional display. He wanted to pummel it in the mogul's pompous red face. Selwyn sat in the dimness, forgetting now that there was no electricity. The gloom was conducive to meditation. He received an inspiration. The movie he was up against was *Fireworks*; Selwyn decided at that moment to assign Blimp Pullman to direct *Ice Queen*.

He had no other ideas about it, other than it would be the perfect vehicle to launch his new contract player, Mariana Trench.

* * *

When The Duchess drove up in her brand-new silver SUV, adorned with her former vanity license plate, the sex scene at the pool between Traci and the ever-reliable Colt was just concluding. They had tried to stage the scene on the diving board, for the sake of variety, but Colt's forceful thrusting risked driving both the performers off the edge and dunking them into the water, like pirates walking the plank, so they ended up back on the chaise-longue. They had already shot the softcore version of the climax, which consisted of a reaction shot in which Colt grimaced and grunted to simulate orgasm, and were now ready for the real thing. The lady producer – like Travis Lazar – did not need anyone's permission to walk onto an adult set in the valley, and she knew the location just as well as anyone else in the industry. She had made three movies there herself for New York Pictures. With a frown at Howard, who motioned to her with a rotation of his wrist that cinematography was in progress and then transformed his gesture into a authentic mime of self-pleasuring, she rolled her eyes and waited on the patio beneath an awning while Colt began the process of stimulating himself to reach the finale.

It took the seasoned performer a palm full of spit and a few well-practiced strokes, with his eyelids shut, before he gulped, "Ready," and Jack started up the camera again, and moved in closer for the shot.

Exactly on cue, Traci writhed and panted, even though by now there was no actual physical contact between the performers, and Colt reached the splashy culmination, for which, as they all joked, he received the big bucks. Male performers typically earned less than the female stars, so the wit was much appreciated.

With a black bolt of cloth covering his head and the monitor like a hangman's hood to shroud the brightness of the sun, Travis was concentrating on the action, and so, he did not notice The Duchess until it was all over.

"Wrong set," he announced, emerging from beneath the canopy.

The production assistant rushed in with paper towels for the performers to wipe themselves down.

They all began the cumbersome journey from the pool to the upstairs bedroom, which was still not powered by electricity or enhanced by cinematic illumination. As the crew moved in their deliberate pace, Travis took the opportunity to engage his colleague. Her presence indicated there was a matter of urgency to discuss.

"What's up?" he asked, stepping into the shade of the awning where The Duchess was standing.

She did not waste time with small talk. Good news could never wait, but it was better to spit out the bad news quickly too, and this was bad. "They pass. Sinisex. It's off."

"I thought it was a done deal." He was shocked. "They all agreed on the terms."

She shook her head, too dejected to spell out the details. "Fell apart at the last minute. It's over."

"Oscar Lowport must have been knocked over with a feather," commented Travis, although he could have been floored with the same plumage himself.

The producer pondered the sudden realignment of the pornographic planets.

First of all, it meant that, like it or not, Duncan remained in control of the major studio. Travis considered how his own relationship with Duncan would be impacted, which put him under renewed pressure to accept the re-awarded honor for Best Picture against his highest intentions. His hope rested on the rock of sympathy he would find at AXE once The Duchess was installed, but now the mogul was still in his place. He would be in a foul mood too, Travis realized, not only in the face of such a setback in business, but also from suffering a disappointment for Mrs. Hathaway's retiring years.

It was so frustrating to be so close, and to have it slither away.

He had to consider the interests of The Duchess too, newly extended in the prospect of blossoming expectations. She looked forlorn in her pearls and ruffles with her briefcase. He had not seen her so broken-hearted before. He did not count her out, which was to say, the deal was still alive, though it was dead for now.

They had to accept that it was dead for now.

Then Tommy interrupted his calculations to remind him that not only was he dead, but he was also blind.

The electrician said, "Uh...boss...sorry to...not my place... but we need some direction..."

"What's wrong?" asked The Duchess, who had noted that all the traffic lights were out on the way to the location, "No power?"

Howard walked up with his clipboard in his hands.

"I ordered a jenny," replied Travis, "But that's in Howard's capable hands."

"It will be here in twenty minutes," Howard boasted, smug at his own exceptional competence, "But the city says the power will be on in thirty. The jenny is five hundred dollars when it gets here, or fifty dollars if I cancel before it arrives." Howard relished the look on his boss's face, and asked pointedly, "What would you like to do, sir?"

It did not take a second for the seasoned producer to come to a decision. "Cancel the jenny. And call lunch."

* * *

The next and final day of shooting for New York Pictures took place back home on Sound Stage B, where they were planning to use the bathroom with the breakaway wall to double as the bathroom in the mansion, which would make it simpler to film the sex scene but would require a strained suspension of disbelief on the part of the viewers. Fortunately, their audience was forgiving.

Everyone on the crew noted that it was also worth reminding the new girl who was to play the part of the maid not to use the toilet in the bathroom set on the stage, because it was fake and not attached to any plumbing, the omission of such a reminder having caused an unfortunate and embarrassing spatter on a previous production. The announcement of a clean-up on aisle two was the typical industry jargon used to apprise the crew of such unfortunate mishaps.

The door of the production office on Sound Stage B usually stood open because there was so much traffic coming and going through the busy hub of Travis Lazar Productions. There were performers, prospective performers, agents, crew, press, vendors, invited guests, and the odd extra, all with pressing queries. On occasion, the door was closed whereby it was well-understood that the occupants were not to be disturbed, there was the possibility that Travis was conducting a private meeting, or, less likely, yet more unpleasant, that Howard might be receiving oral favors.

In point of fact, on some occasions, it was shut just because they needed a moment of respite in the barrage of management duties.

They could catch their breath.

They did not expect the door to burst open followed by the entry of two men, a square-jawed, square-cut, square-shouldered stranger, dressed in a dark suit with wide lapels and a narrow tie, and another, who was known to Travis as Officer Perez of the LAPD Vice Squad.

"We have a permit," Travis said, getting to his feet behind his desk.

"We're not here about that," said Perez.

"I'm Special Agent Frank Hassenger," announced the other, in a deep, formal tone, "FBI. We would like to talk to you."

"About what?" Travis asked.

"About your association with felons," said the Special Agent.

Perez said in a low voice, "Beppo the Bear."

Travis went pale. "It all has to go through counsel."

"He knows his rights," Howard commented.

"Shut the hell up, Howard," Travis mouthed to him across the room.

"Make it easy for everybody," said Perez, "You're not being charged. Nobody wants you."

"That's good," the producer said, "Because I haven't done anything." He complied with permits and insurance, paid fees to the city of Los Angeles and filed his taxes, in addition to providing written documentation which certified that every performer he employed was above the age of consent and free of transmittable diseases.

Travis was not at all consoled by Perez' assurance that nobody wanted him as a suspect, because that just meant that they wanted him as a witness to testify against Beppo, thus relocating the adult producer's metaphysical geography precisely midpoint between a rock and a hard place.

CHAPTER EIGHT

FINKEL VERSUS LAZARUS

When Ginger called, Travis could tell that she had been crying.

It was a clear, mild day promising the temperature would soar in unison with the sun as it climbed to noon in the perfect blue sky. The producer had just kissed his wife goodbye, hugged the boys, and was on his way to the post production facility to consult with the editor of *Cheats*, which had successfully wrapped production. Travis took the call in the Mercedes, watching his wife at the white picket gate recede in his rearview mirror.

"I don't want to make trouble for anyone," Ginger began, inhaling a breath between each word to steady her emotions, "But I am upset." Here she took more than one breath, girding herself up to get through the rest of her story. "Some of it was the pervy way he spoke to me, but I am not even doing boy-girl anyway, so I didn't want to do the scene, but he was so insistent about it..."

Travis tried to calm her down so that he could better understand. "You're talking about...?"

"Howard," she burst, with a sob, "He called me to do a scene in his movie. And it's supposed to be with him? *Gross.* I tried to tell him no, but he kept pushing. I don't have to do the scene, do I?"

Exactly at that moment, the call-waiting feature interrupted, and Travis had to place Ginger on hold, and in suspense, so that he could click over to Billy Dallas.

"We have a little dust-up," Billy drawled, "And it's to do with your favorite movie star, who stormed in full of piss and gunpowder..."

"Go on..." said the producer, not wanting to get ahead of himself before he knew any facts.

"According to Ms. Tiffany – and I understand that she is mightily opinionated, and lord knows, as stubborn as a blonde mule with red lipstick – your production manager tried to book her for a scene behind my back." The agent took a breath here too, much like Ginger, so that the producer could absorb his words. "Now, y'all have always been a straight shooter, so that's not what this is about, and I reckon it's just your boy running maverick off the range. I don't know the particulars, but y'all have enough problems with Duncan – I'm on the board and the big fellow is not shy with his perspective – but if he finds out you're going around him like a rustler to poach his branded star and the word was for New York Pictures – y'all won't be safe in the valley."

"Billy, I'm telling you, this is the first I've heard of this, but I'll get to the bottom." He switched back to Ginger, who was much relieved to hear his pronouncement. "No, you are not doing Howard's movie. There isn't going to be one."

He cut short his telephone calls and his meeting with the editor, so that he could get from Van Nuys to Chatsworth before the traffic built up on the 405 freeway, and face off with the apostate at Sound Stage B.

As if he did not have enough on his mind after the visit from the FBI, and the collapse of the Sinisex acquisition, he now had to deal with trouble under his own roof.

The revelation was not just a surprise, it was perilous. A swift response was imperative. Travis entertained no illusions with respect to Tiffany delivering her indignant report to Duncan in the most expressive terms, but, as things stood, AXE was a lost cause anyway. He was off the roster. There was nothing more to lose with Duncan. Even with the inevitable blast of outrage from the studio boss, that was not quite where the danger lay. It was only the fuse to the dynamite. The problem could be Sylvia Bern at New York Pictures. If Duncan, in his impulse, picked up the telephone to attack Sylvia on the assumption that New York Pictures had made a play for his contract player, Travis could lose his bread-and-butter account. Thanks to the quick heads-up from Billy, his information was hot; like tongues of flame crackling along a wire to a powder keg, it would take a few days for the news to travel up the ranks.

For once, he was actually innocent of any wrongdoing, but, more often than not, Travis had eluded culpability when he was guilty as scarlet, so he supposed the universe imposed equilibrium. He did not know which was worse – to be accused with an unclear conscience or to be suspected when innocent. Everyone assumed the worst, there was no way to prove that he was clean. This situation required a leak that would rise up the executive ladder like fluid from an erection. The move to make was to reach out to Nicholas in advance so he could blunt any reaction from the mogul.

That was only the first part of the problem.

Performers were complaining. Ginger was upset, Tiffany was enraged. Howard's mission was perceived by everyone, except the perpetrator himself, to be propelled not by the admirable pursuits of art or glory, but by his grubby libido. That base motivation created a tarnish that, by association, would ultimately rub off and taint the luster of Travis Lazar Productions.

It was not just that Howard was blundering around, knocking over the scenery. This was a one-man mutiny. He had undermined the producer. That was inexcusable in Hollywood. The entire system would crack and collapse if it were acceptable for crewmembers to subvert the hand that fed everyone. Travis could not allow himself to be disrespected.

He charged into the production office, where he discovered the offender on the telephone waiting for someone at Majestic Movies to pick up. Nobody did. The production manager hung up, blithely oblivious to his own prevailing fortunes.

"Beppo the Bear must have gone south for the summer," Howard complained, rocking behind his desk in his office chair, "Or he's in some cave counting his nuts. But, wherever he is, he's not answering his phone."

"Still no word?" said Travis, playing it cool, though he was cautious about having any engagement with Beppo while the acting President of Majestic Movies was under investigation, a fact which Beppo himself surely appreciated. "Stop calling."

"But my movie..."

"And on that subject..." Travis did not waste any more time, "Is there anything you want to tell me?"

"About what?" Howard demanded, thinking of many options that he preferred to withhold.

"About Ginger. About Tiffany. About – I don't know – who *else?*"

"So?"

"So, you don't have a relationship with them other than the fact that I tell you to book them. For which I pay a fee to the performer and to the agent and to you. Now, as a result of you taking matters into your own hands, I have problems with Billy and with Duncan..."

Howard gave a reckless response. "You're just mad because I was going to bone Ginger."

"We're done here, Howard," Travis said without displaying any emotion, and thereby communicating his meaning in crystal clear terms.

Howard understood. "So, that's it?"

"That's it."

* * *

The termination of the employment of the production manager of Travis Lazar Productions did not send a seismic spasm through the industry, but nonetheless traveled along the grapevine fueled by the delight of simple minds for idle gossip. Scandals streaked along at a more lightning pace than any other rumor, gaining in speed by the severity of the misfortune suffered by whoever was the butt. Everybody talked. Howard was sure that people who had cozied up to him the week before were cracking jokes behind his back, which was indeed a fact repeated many times.

He did not leave his apartment for three days, spending most of his time curled up in bed wearing nothing but his boxers and contemplating his prominent poster and his unemployment.

He got up at odd hours to eat a bowl of cereal, or cold pizza, and putter around from the bedroom to the living room, kicking the wall when the Spanish-language broadcast on the television next door was too loud. He just wanted silence. He had turned off his own TV because, after flipping from channel to channel, he was so distracted that he could not even concentrate on the cartoons. There was nothing in the refrigerator besides thickening milk and rotten fruit. The apartment unit was stuffy. He did not want to open the windows because of the smell rising from the garbage in the baking alleyway.

Overworked, the air conditioning emitted a supernatural groan at the stroke of noon and stopped functioning, and when he lay supinely on his bed without moving, sapped of motivation, like someone in a trance, the blankets soaked with perspiration. He could not believe that his X-rated career, so freshly launched and with such optimism, was so precipitously crushed.

Traci and Maria both called to find out if it were true, and Tommy left a rambling message about going out for spaghetti and meatballs, but he did not want to talk to anyone. He felt a stinging sense of shame in his dismissal, and the loss of his significance as the right hand man of the influential producer. He did not have any prospects for income, outside of Travis Lazar Productions. He could not believe the cavalier way he had been treated after so many years of service. He had felt secure in his post, essential, and a trusted keeper of secrets. He would have to start again at the bitter bottom, cleaning up soggy towels and standing by with a bottle of lubrication. He lay on the bed in his stale apartment and ruminated. As his sense of resentment grew, like an imp squatting in a cavern, Howard plotted his revenge.

* * *

Under the circumstances, it was not deemed prudent for Travis to meet Nicholas at the headquarters of AXE, where, once again, he found himself unwelcome in the building. Instead, the most apt place to rendezvous was The Chatsworth Diner, which, even with its colorless décor and drab atmosphere, was more hospitable.

They sat in the same booth along the window where Travis had met Beppo months earlier on the happier occasion of a wire transfer of funds. Travis was punctual, Nicholas dashed in five minutes late. They ordered the meatloaf special from the well-preserved waitress, keeping their culinary expectations low, and each remarking that the establishment was convenient for geographic reasons rather than the high standards of the cuisine.

Travis explained to Nicholas the circumstances behind Howard's dismissal, and was relieved to find that the news had not yet reached the fleshy ears of the studio boss. The brilliant executive agreed that the producer had made the right decision to reveal the information before the bulletin broke. It was not wise to blindside anyone, in particular someone whom they both knew would not take kindly, unless there was a tactical reason for the element of surprise, which in this case, there was not. In strategic terms, another word for surprise was ambush. There was no sense in waving a red flag at a storming bull without reason.

The winner was always the first one to tell the story. Nicholas agreed to broach the matter with Duncan before Tiffany could deliver her version of the events. She had been calling. She wanted a meeting with the studio boss. The mood at AXE was bleak, following the collapse of the Sinisex buyout, which Nicholas touched on obliquely, not knowing in what heartfelt proportions the producer shared the general disappointment. Duncan, who had been looking forward to a retirement of gin and golfing, did not have the appetite to address any further demands from his contract player, which was what he assumed was on the agenda. She had successfully managed to extend her bereavement month by month so lengthily that she had not performed in any movies all year, although he was still following the financial obligations of their agreement.

Sales were slow in the summer, and AXE suffered, just like all the other studios. Duncan still had to cover his costly overhead. Money came in slowly. Projects were languishing. Production was at a standstill.

With both Alec Zig and Travis Lazar out of favor, the studio had no marquee directors to fill their slate. Miles Flannigan was still dead. Blimp Pullman was coming to the end of his tenure at Paradise. There had been talk of bringing him into AXE, but, even without a slur on his creative prowess, nobody could see any panache in using Selwyn's hand-me-down shooter, notwithstanding pervasive personal distaste for the expansive director who had a reputation for helpfully prodding the orifices of female performers.

In addition, and importantly, Selwyn's rich stockpile of Blimp's movies would dilute the prominence of a single big new release from the rival studio. Travis made the point that he did not like to speak ill of a fellow director, but, of course, agreed with this summation, thereby negating his own caveat.

They ended their lunch, leaving much of it on the plates, and Travis made sure to pay the bill, since he was the one who had requested the meeting.

As they were walking out, Nicholas said, "You know you are better off without Howard."

"I should have fired him a long time ago," Travis shrugged, "But I'm loyal." He stopped, causing Nicholas to stop, and looked him in the eye. "So are you."

"I'll explain the situation to Duncan as soon as I can get a meeting," Nicholas assured him.

So far, the defensive plan was working. But Travis knew he had to watch his flank.

* * *

In pursuit of further such protective armor, Travis made his way along Nordhoff Avenue heading to Sound Stage B that was rented out to The Duchess since it was her month on the checkerboard for New York Pictures. He found the parking lot jammed, because of a grand production that was taking place on Sound Stage A.

It was Paradise Media's blockbuster banker, *Ice Queen*, which Blimp Pullman was directing to contend against AXE's *Fireworks*, directed by Travis Lazar. Being that Selwyn was determined to beat Duncan for the second year in a row at Best Picture, he was happy to spend lavishly on the extravaganza, and being that it was Blimp's swan song at Paradise Media, and thus the last crack at Selwyn's checkbook, he was happy to ramp up the budget.

On the large sound stage, set designers and carpenters had constructed an arctic village with Styrofoam igloos and snow machines, and there was an interior hut set, with a fire gag, where Mariana was to perform her scene with Sebastian Barge as a cave-maiden and a warrior, respectively. It was a direct challenge to the rooftop inferno in *Fireworks*, thus the use of pyrotechnical effects, which was becoming a signature pattern for the intrepid performers.

In anticipation of the live flames, Officer Fleet was lingering in the parking lot, taking advantage of the production delay to scrutinize the gridlock for any potential offenders who might be blocking a fire lane. Travis, who had a reserved spot, was compliant with the law, and saluted the fireman who returned a crisp salute.

Travis walked onto Sound Stage B, where The Duchess was setting up a shot for a bedroom scene starring Summer and Storm, as a husband and wife in *Underscore*, her romantic melodrama for New York Pictures. They played the parts of classical musicians in a rocky marriage. Since they were actually husband and wife in real life, the casting did not require much of stretch in the characterizations of the roles, and more to the point, nobody anticipated any uncertainty as to the comfort levels of the performers in the sexual depictions. Neither of them being a virtuoso outside their chosen artistic field, the dramatic scenes in which they were obliged to play string instruments would be simulated – simulation being a practice in which they were both well-versed.

The set consisted of three ten-foot high flats, including a decorative archway to a vestibule, which created some depth, and a bay window covered in tracing paper to read as opaque glass on camera. Having supported more fornication than there were fish in the Pacific, the bed stood between two pedestals that, like the hapless bed itself, had seen their fair share of complicity. There was a sullied bedspread that likewise memorialized many engagements. At the foot of the bed, Jack was positioning the tripod.

Summer, in a negligee, and Storm, in sheer boxers, were positioning themselves across the bedcovers. As Jack focused the lens, the performers, by way of warming up, focused their attention on one another's genitals.

The Duchess – without the suit and pearl ensemble now – was sitting in a director's chair in front of a bank of monitors, scrutinizing the shot.

She dropped from the high chair, and stepped away from the monitors when she saw Travis. "What's up?"

"You hear anything from New York?"

"Not a word. It's very far from the valley."

"This thing with Howard..." he began, without belittling her by explaining the details which she was sure to have acquired from her many sources on the grapevine, "I don't want Sylvia to get the wrong end of the stick."

"What do you mean?"

"That I somehow created a problem between her and Duncan..."

"Nah," the Duchess waved her hand, "You're just being paranoid. They don't think the way you do..."

"But you'll check...?" Travis requested, even though it did not have to be said.

"Yes, I'll have a word with Sylvia," she agreed, with an exaggerated sigh demonstrating that she thought he was being over-cautious.

Jack left his post at the foot of the bed, making sure to pay his respects. He nodded a courteous hello at Travis, sensitive to the fact that tenured crewmembers had lately proved to be dispensable, before he informed the lady director that they were ready.

Travis had no interest in witnessing pornography being filmed, an apt metaphor being the unpleasantness of watching sausage being made. "I'll let you get back to it. I have to drop in and say hello to Blimp next door..."

"I would be careful," Jack advised. "Could get ugly."

"Oh?" said Travis, and The Duchess frowned.

"He's there," Jack informed them.

"Who?" they both demanded.

"Howard." The cameraman received his chatter from a different grapevine to the producers. "He got a day job on Blimp's overblown crew as a production assistant."

"He's fallen down the ranks..." mused The Duchess, who had always considered Howard to be underqualified for any position that did not involve hamburgers and a griddle.

"Now, I really do have to talk to Blimp," said Travis, heading for the exit.

"I want to see his sets," The Duchess said, leaving her own set in the cinematographer's capable hands. "Go ahead, Jack, get them started."

Jack tried to corral the performers, who on hearing the action was about to begin, developed a sudden need for last-minute adjustments and bathroom breaks, which was not motivated by any suspicious reasons, but was just another natural delay in the uphill struggle to complete the day's work.

The two producers walked over to the large Sound Stage, which was bustling with crew members who were all strange faces with the exception of Maria. She was working as a makeup assistant for the day to help with the ensemble of inhabitants in the Styrofoam ice village.

"Aren't you guys on the wrong set?" she asked, when she spotted them.

"I just want to say hello to Blimp," Travis told her.

Maria led them down the hallway, passing Willard Fingerbrand, who was playing with a matchbox. As soon as the special effects technician spotted the producer, he turned his back and pretended to be busy, an instinct arising from his discomfort over the prior unfortunate incident of excessive ordinance usage.

Maria brought them to the arctic village where the corpulent director was paying attention to the smallest wintry details, by personally dabbing the nipples of the extras with an ice cube to make them pointy for the sake of realism. They all wore faux fur coats, fur boots, and nothing else. There were snow machines, fog machines, and crates of dry ice on a white set under cyan light.

He seemed honored to see the other producers. "Hello, hello," he welcomed them, "To what do I owe the pleasure of this rendezvous?"

"In case you drop dead of a heart attack," Travis said, trying to be congenial, "I just want you to know that we are here to carry on the show."

"It's good to know," Blimp responded, popping the melting

ice cube into his mouth, and wiping his moist fingers on his director's smock, "Investors always ask me about that when they give me the money."

"Now, seriously, I have some information for you," offered Travis.

"I'll be looking at the igloo," murmured The Duchess, discreetly allowing the other two directors a private consultation, although she had no doubt that Travis was plotting to impede his competitor from approaching his client, AXE.

Travis said in a confidential voice, "I'm hearing that your time is up with Paradise."

"There's no hard feelings. Selwyn just wants some new blood. We overshot. I had to take over from Miles. We're backed up for months. He has so many of my movies in his vault he has to release them in phases or he'll swamp the market."

"I'll keep my ears open to find you a home," said the altruistic producer, who wanted his competitor to be housed as far away from his clientele as possible. "But, for the moment, if I were you..." He glanced around furtively to emphasize the secrecy of what he was about to divulge, "Stay away from AXE. You probably heard about the Internet deal that fell through..."

"Yeah," Blimp considered, "Oscar Lowport mentioned that..."

"Well, they're broke. Their checks are bouncing like ping-pong balls in Pattaya."

"Duncan, broke? That's hard to believe."

"When was the last time they shot anything?"

"You're right," contemplated Blimp, "Well, thanks for the heads-up. I owe you one. What can I do for you?"

"Blimp," Travis put his arm on his shoulder like an old friend, "I don't want to tell you who to hire or fire, but the guy was my production manager for years. You're asking for calamity. He's all over the girls."

Blimp, who was all over the girls himself, did not appreciate such behavior from a subordinate. "I just need a big crew for this project. I won't keep Howard."

At that moment, and at the mention of his name, they heard his voice, and an astonishing string of colorful rhetoric. "You can go and drown yourself in a bucket of piss, and the same goes for Travis Lazar, the slimiest producer who ever crawled out of the sewer."

The Duchess, to whom the invective had been addressed, was stupefied. "If you want to speak to me like that, it just proves that you are a brainless moron who has jacked himself into dementia. But I won't allow you to speak like that about Travis Lazar, who carried your dumb ass for years."

"I will speak how I like," Howard unloaded eons of pent-up emotions, "I don't work for him anymore, and for all those years, I have been dying to tell you my opinion. Ha!"

Travis hurried over to restrain his bantamweight lady champion, who was ready to come out swinging. "Let it go, it's beneath you."

"You'll be the one twisting in the wind," taunted Howard, and then, unable to suppress himself, revealed his ace in the hole, "The lawsuit has already been filed."

* * *

The law was on the producer's mind as he cruised down Sunset Boulevard the next day, heading into the afternoon sun.

Travis had spent the morning with his attorney on sundry matters. He did not agree with the lawyer's advice, but he was obliged to follow it, especially at the rate he paid to receive it.

He did not know if he should take Howard seriously, but he

guessed that his former employee probably had some spiteful angle. Travis was not rattled in the least; in a battle of wits with Howard, it was not an equal match. He had weightier matters to tackle.

As he came around the curve towards West Hollywood, he passed the billboard that once portrayed Tiffany West on the cover of *Wake*, and was now replaced with the image of Mariana Trench in *Ice Queen*, which had yet to complete principal photography.

He turned left into Sunset Plaza, where there was a row of upscale restaurants with a terrace view of the traffic, and a rear parking lot which offered a spectacular view of the city, all the way from the distant ocean to downtown on a clear day.

He made his way through a back entrance of one of the restaurants, which was as far from the Chatsworth Diner within the perimeter of Los Angeles County as could be asked, both in terms of urban geography and social context – and menu fare. It was not the type of place where prying eyes might be watching. The establishment was practically deserted between the peak hours of lunch and dinner. Given that this was his second clandestine rendezvous in a restaurant within a week, much might be inferred as to the producer's moral character. Luckily for Travis, his character was not likely to be called into question.

Sitting alone at one of the tables in the rear was Beppo the Bear.

He looked a little haggard. The creases on his button-up shirt suggested that he had worn it for consecutive days. He had lost weight, which showed in his face, under the bristles of faint white stubble. Never too particular about his appearance, he had stopped shaving daily since he was no longer going into the office in the mornings, and there was no reason to be presentable. He was tanned though, as if he had been spending time outdoors, in the uncertainty of how much longer he might enjoy that privilege. He was staring into a cup of espresso and smiled when he noticed Travis.

They exchanged a few pleasantries – Travis said how well he looked, Beppo asked after the family. He told him about the situation with Howard, keeping him apprised, because he did not want him to hear rumors elsewhere, and because he never knew when he might need Beppo's abutment. For now, Beppo gave him his best guidance when it came to legal entanglements, which was, no matter what, say nothing. Travis agreed with this advice, noting that if one didn't say anything, one could not make any mistakes.

The slinky waitress, for whom Beppo was a regular patron, brought Travis an espresso for which there was no charge, an encouraging omen to the producer.

"So, what are we going to do?" he asked.

"You got to testify," Beppo said grimly, "I get it."

Travis dropped a sugar cube into the cup and stirred it around. "There's nothing on me about anything, but they want to rope me in with you."

"You never did nothing," Beppo snorted, "It's ridiculous. It all goes back to who I am long before any parole violations on crimes I already served time for. Banned from being in the industry. We are all just trying to scrape through life."

"I've got an idea," said the producer.

* * *

Travis understood that strength came from allies *and* adversaries. You could not have the one without the other. Your friends had enemies, rivals, competitors, and challengers; they became yours with every allegiance.

Up and down the ladder, Travis was loyal to his friends; he

expected they would be loyal in return. No latitude could be given to treachery. Like cheating spouses sweating between hot sheets, jealousy and greed easily spawned betrayal.

Just after seven one morning, shortly after rising, Travis went to answer a knock at the front door of his home in the suburbs of the valley. The eminent producer was still wearing pajama pants and a white robe, which had once appeared in a movie before suspiciously traveling from the wardrobe department into the producer's closet. He felt a little self-conscious, opening the door, in the free support of not wearing underwear for sleeping.

As he opened the door, he performed an involuntary Kegel exercise, with a therapeutic efficacy that would have made Tiffany proud. He was not surprised, but not delighted, to see a U.S. Marshal in a freshly laundered uniform on the threshold. Nobody else would come knocking at such an hour. He was relieved that his wife was monitoring the boys over cornflakes at the breakfast table.

The sun was bright on his front lawn. Birds chirped in the trees. Across the grass of the frontage, through the picket fence, there was another marshal in an official car parked outside his house.

"Mr. Travis Lazarus?" inquired the marshal on the doorstep.

"That's me," acknowledged Mr. Travis Lazarus.

The marshal handed him an envelope. "You've been served."

Nobody could hear anything else after that because a neighbor started a lawn mower.

The marshal turned smartly and strode off. Travis did not shut the front door. Without going back to the breakfast table, he opened the envelope to learn that Mr. Travis Lazarus (defendant) was being summonsed to Van Nuys Small Claims Court in a claim against him by Mr. Howard Finkel (plaintiff).

The enemy always delivered the weapons of his own destruction, thought Travis, as he watched the marshals drive away down the leafy street.

* * *

On the way to her meeting with Duncan, Tiffany suffered the second worst morning of her life.

It all began for her when she was out of coffee, – and she had to have it first thing or she was not herself. So she stopped to pick up a latte from the drive-through Starbucks, which she almost choked on when she came around the bend on Sunset when she saw the giant billboard, where her face once gazed haughtily over the celebrated boulevard, gazing back at her with the limpid eyes of the Ice Queen, Mariana Trench.

She gulped on the hot latte, spluttered, screamed, and pulled over to the side. Her fingers trembled. Her famous chest heaved. She gasped for breath. Mesmerized by the billboard of *Ice Queen*, she stared at it with a numb feeling going through her like a shot of arsenic. She could not believe that just when she thought she had sustained her share of tragedy, there was more.

She knew that all around the world, she had a million fans. She did not need an obnoxious billboard on Sunset Boulevard to prove her stardom, but she thought how ironic it was that all those admirers who let her image burn into their brains and thoughts and fantasies –who wanted her, who dreamed of her – did not know how much a star could suffer. Little did they imagine what she was compelled to endure. It was not all flash and glamour; there was pain. It all accumulated. It compounded. She felt worse now than she did at her husband's funeral.

It was fitting that she had returned to her widow's black, she thought, as she took a deep breath, adjusted her sunglasses, pressed her fingertips together and regained her composure, simmering all the way to Duncan's office.

* * *

The studio boss was in his usual Hawaiian shirt, but he was in shorts with his kneecaps showing. There was a white tam o'shanter cap on his head that made his face look even ruddier as he was swinging a golf putter.

The widow and the mogul cast a striking tableau in their contrasting garb.

"Hello Tiffany," he said, "This can't take long because I am playing golf." He took a few practice strokes to illustrate the point in case the clue of his attire had been lost on her.

Not invited to sit, she remained on her feet and rested her hands on her hips. "Then, all I have to say is that you got circumcised..."

"Come again?"

"Gone around...somebody tried to get me to break my contract..."

He rested the putter over his shoulder. "Do you mean circumvented?"

"Yes. I said that. By Travis Lazar."

"Yeah, I know all about that." Duncan lined up another imaginary shot. He had been well-prepared by his right-hand man. He was not going to take the bait, and get drawn into a conflict prodded on by the performer.

Tiffany was baffled by his reaction. "Are you going to do something about it?"

"Nothing to do," Duncan shrugged. He glanced up from the chimerical green. "Was that about it?"

Tiffany was at a loss for words. She had been thwarted again.

"My dog is in the car," she blurted, turned on her heel, and walked out of the office.

Whereupon Duncan, who had been quite indolent in her presence, suddenly sprang to life, twirled his putter and circumvented his desk.

He picked up his telephone. "Tell Nicholas to come in here."

At his rapid pace, Nicholas reported as summoned to find Duncan chuckling like a schoolboy and rolling the putter between his palms. "You should have seen her face. Didn't have the balls to ask me for a thing. But the real loser here is your friend Travis Lazar." He put the putter across his desk so that he could raise his gold-rimmed spectacles to wipe his eyes. "He looks like a damn fool for not keeping his people in line."

* * *

The morning of the trial began auspiciously for the defendant.

The Mercedes was scarcely out of the driveway, when the call came in from The Duchess.

"You're off the hook with New York," she reported. "I talked to Sylvia Bern, and, in the conversation, dropped your name. She said yes, you're already on the schedule. After the summer hiatus."

"I'm up?"

"Yes, you'd better come up with a production manager," advised The Duchess, "I told you they don't think like you do."

He veered into the lane of cars waiting to merge onto the on-ramp of the 101 Freeway towards the central valley. The early morning traffic was so thick that he wondered if everyone had a court date.

"This is how I think," he said. "I think you should tell Sinisex about the poison pill. It might bring them back to the table."

"I suppose it's the ethical thing to do," she agreed, her conscience roused now that there was nothing to lose.

The call waiting beeped and he had to put The Duchess on hold because it was Nicholas.

"I just want to let you know that Tiffany played her card," Nicholas said, "Don't worry, I was ahead of her."

"How did Duncan take it?" Travis asked, finding his way into the fast lane, which was moving at moderate speed.

"He hasn't stopped laughing since yesterday."

"Tiffany can still be trouble."

"She always is," Nicholas agreed, before they said their goodbyes.

Travis clicked back to the Duchess.

"I'm off the hook with Duncan too," he told her, approaching the exit for Van Nuys Boulevard, "Sort of. Nobody's rocking the boat. Stand-off. Until Vegas."

"It's a good start to your day. Now, all you have to do is squash that cockroach who is suing you..."

The Van Nuys courthouse emerged in the distance.

"Beppo says the best thing is to say nothing."

"I would do exactly what Beppo advises," she said somberly.

* * *

The Van Nuys Municipal courthouse in the heart of the valley stood like a tower among the opposing magisterial towers of the Los Angeles County Court and the United States Federal

Court on a flat, grassy plaza to the east of Van Nuys Boulevard. The plaza was also home to a police station, a library, a refreshment stand specializing in Mexican beverages, and surrounded by various bureaucratic offices which issued everything from work permits for minors to marriage licenses for those of sufficient age. Because they were so close to the court, and consequently the jail, there were bail bondsmen up and down Van Nuys Boulevard, advertising their 24 hour availability in bold neon signs, usually in more than one language, including Spanish, Russian and Armenian, so as to appeal without discrimination to a broad cross-section of detainees. It was always muggy there in the summer, as confused motorists searched for parking in the small streets with similar names around the government buildings.

Travis paid the extravagant fee to park in the underground garage and mounted a short staircase, which deposited him right in the middle of the plaza under a sharp sunshine. Dressed in his gala-event suit and his burgundy tie, the producer carried a small folder, which contained his summons to court and the prospective evidence of his probity. In polished shoes, he walked along the pathways to the Municipal courthouse, but he could not help considering the Federal Courthouse, which loomed not only over the plaza, but also the producer's future.

Beppo would stand trial in a few short weeks, and Travis was uneasily reminded that he was bound to present himself on the witness stand on behalf of the prosecution.

But, first things first, the producer, confronting one trial at a time, went through the metal detector into the Municipal Courthouse. The floors smelled of polish, and there was a certain mustiness to the old building. He took an elevator to the third floor, joining a sorry-looking group that was addressing a variance of concerns, mostly to do with vehicular matters or the challenges of dwelling in the vicinity of offensive neighbors. Given the bottled-up fury that was prevalent, Travis considered how fortunate it was to live in a society under the rule of law where disputes could be settled in a civilized manner.

On the third floor, there was a long hallway, that if it were split in two across the width, would have offered equal reflections of the opposite half – namely a row of windows looking out over the plaza along one side, and, on the other, heavy doors, a notice-board, two hard long wooden benches, and a bailiff.

By deliberate calculation, Travis was early. Predators lay in wait. He wanted the advantage and did not want to put himself under pressure by getting to court late. This was not his first visit to the court – he had dropped in a week before as an observer, so that he could get a look at the judge. He was familiar with the proceedings. There was no way that the producer was going to lose the case. Travis never did.

There were a few people sitting on the benches, a few more standing at the window, and a handful farther down the hallway at the other court, again as if it were in matching relief. Conversation was muted. Everyone shared the same forlorn anticipation. Even Travis, confident in his advocatory skills, was so tense that he had no appetite for the breakfast which his wife had prepared for him.

In a khaki uniform, the bailiff was a dour, scrawny figure with long, pale fingers and waterless eyes not focused on any of the attendees – much the same motley group as on every preceding day – but rather on a large clock with large letters ticking audibly above the courthouse doors.

On the notice board beside the doors, there was a printed sheet indicating the list of cases to be brought before the court, and there it was, Finkel Versus Lazarus, slated for the third trial.

Lazarus had no doubt that Finkel would show up for the event, but he was nowhere to be seen yet.

Some other unfortunate parties who had business before the court began to arrive, and, even though Travis kept his eyes on the elevator, he did not see his adversary. He surveyed the plaza from his high aerie at the windows. He could see the faded umbrella over the refreshment stand, busy lawyers and uniformed officials along the pathways, and the blue skies extending over the hazy valley. There was no sign of the production manager, but Travis did not believe that he would default. He was probably stuck in traffic. Wherever he was, Travis was satisfied that Howard was under stress.

The bailiff, who had been dutifully watching the clock, abruptly became energized, and flung open the heavy double doors. He made his proclamation in a loud and slow voice, but he had long ago surrendered any bombast in his delivery, as he advised everyone to stand in single file along the wall, and answer to their names before entering the court. It was hard enough just getting citizens organized; everyone was special, nobody wanted to listen to simple instructions. Confusion was the result.

The bailiff had to repeat a shortened version of the drill. People began to shuffle into place. Down the hallway, the same ceremony was being executed by an equally exasperated official.

Travis did not see Howard get out of the elevator, but he spotted him all at once among the rest of the litigants milling about as they tried to fathom the concept of a line. His pink face was freshly shaved for the occasion, and he wore a jacket with no tie, a starched gray shirt, and carried a new leatherette briefcase.

Travis said, "Hello, Howard."

"So, you showed up...?" responded his nemesis, whose hopes of an easy victory were thus demolished.

"You summonsed me," explained Travis, wondering how much the plaintiff understood of the judicial system. "What do you have in your fancy briefcase?"

"I'm not showing you my evidence," scoffed Howard, who was clearly not well-versed in the legal principle of discovery, and swung the briefcase away as if he feared that Travis might lunge for it.

Then the bailiff called their names, and they were obliged to end their exchange for the moment. They followed the bailiff's directions to enter the courtroom and take their seats in the hard wooden pews. Travis made a point of filling in the row to sit right beside Howard, partly to unnerve him, and also because it seemed ridiculous to him to sit apart after they had spent a decade sharing a production office.

Everybody rose when the judge entered.

Judge Bernice Grundle was a wizened, gray-haired woman, with surprisingly short patience given her occupation as a minister of justice on the bench. She peered at the world through spectacles, hunching her shoulders and screwing up her face, as if this would aid her sensory perception. She hissed her rulings in a raspy voice.

The first order that she gave was for all plaintiffs and defendants to leave the courtroom so they could present one another with their evidence and make one final attempt to resolve matters between them, thereby absolving the court of such a burden.

They went back into the hallway, and sat on the hard wooden benches.

"Now, come on," said Travis, "If I owed you any money, I would pay you. No matter what you want to say about me, everyone always got paid. So, I'm not trying to rip you off. But I never collected anything from Beppo. Whatever profits there were went to cover his costs. Majestic Movies have their own problems at the moment. You know that."

"I don't care," challenged Howard, snapping open his briefcase, "According to the trade magazines, my movie was number three on the charts." He produced a page torn from the magazine to verify his claim. "What do you have?"

"That's not exactly scientific," noted Travis, opening his folder to show nothing more than the cover of the movie, the front depicting Howard surrounded by the bevy of skimpily-dressed starlets, and the back showing Howard and the starlets without even the aforementioned modest covering to conceal the throes of hardcore action.

"What are you going to do with that?"

"Open it all up to the judge," said Travis, always aiming for the high moral ground.

"Well, we'll find out what the judge says," retorted Howard, who was determined to have his day in court, "You know, if you lose, it's going to destroy your credit. Ha!"

When they were called back into the courtroom for the scheduled third trial, the judge asked, "Well, were you able to mediate a compromise?"

"Your honor," Travis said, "I have tried, but to no avail. The imbecile is determined to have a trial."

"Very well," allowed the judge, to whom anyone wasting time in small claims court was imbecilic by definition, "Approach."

Travis went through a low swinging gate that fenced off the public gallery and took his place at a small table with a sign that read DEFENDANT in large block letters. In front of the entire court, Travis reached into his folder and laid out the cover of *The Love Life of a Loser*, making sure that the hardcore action in which Howard was the star, was face up to the judge.

There were some titters from the pews, and the rest of the litigants pricked up their attention in anticipation of what was surely going to be an entertaining case.

Howard lingered in the gallery, not quite sure what to do, since he had not taken advantage of the complimentary legal education that Travis had acquired the week before when he had attended court as a spectator.

The bailiff grunted out a prompt to Howard, who lurched forwards in the realization that his long-awaited vindication was at hand, and somehow collided with the swinging gate before he and his briefcase reached the table with the sign reading PLAINTIFF.

The judge turned to him inquiringly.

"My name is Howard Finkel," he stated for the record, "I have been working for Travis Lazar for more than ten years..."

"Who is that?" interrupted the judge.

As he had been well-advised by a veteran of the defendant's box, Travis did not say a word, allowing Howard to do all the talking.

"That's him," pointed Howard, "The one I'm suing."

"I have Travis Lazarus." Judge Grundle reviewed her notes, scribbling in the margins with hard strokes. "Is that who you mean?"

"Yes, Lazarus. His screen name is Lazar. He's a producer. His company is Travis Lazar Productions. He does sex movies. Well, why should he make all the money when I could do just the same? So, I have these movies that I made, and his company was supposed to help me with the distribution and I haven't seen a penny..."

She pointed a pen at him. "What do you mean that you made? Are you a cameraman?"

"No," Howard gulped, his voice rising an octave, "I'm a performer."

At this disclosure, there was a reaction of amazement from the gallery, and much contemplation of Howard up and down, with accompanying murmurs and headshakes. The judge looked up fiercely and struck her gavel to silence the response.

Travis, true to his plan, said absolutely nothing, but squared up the position of the box cover on the table, inadvertently drawing attention to the sordid images.

The judge glared at the box covers and at both parties before her, but, not reading the room well, Howard jabbered on undeterred.

"I have worked for him for ten years and seen all his tricks first hand. He is known in the industry as a total slimeball, not to be trusted as far as you can throw a dime..."

"Well, do you have some written contract with respect to your agreement?" inquired the judge.

"No."

"Why not?"

"I took his word," he responded sheepishly, undermining his own previous characterization of the producer.

The judge clearly had no interest in hearing another utterance. "You are suing him personally, but you claim you made an oral agreement with his corporation."

Triggered by the word oral, the rapt audience in the gallery perceived a double entendre and broke into laughter, which was not well received by Judge Grundle, who banged her gavel again. She had no further patience for this case or the characters before her.

"The paperwork is a mess," snarled the judge. "You have the right to refile, but for now, you can both get out of my courtroom and take those filthy pictures with you."

"Thank you, your honor," was all that Travis spoke through the trial.

He did not lose a moment. He swept the offending covers

off the table and into his folder and marched out of the court-house in triumph. How appropriate, he considered, that Howard, whose primary function as the production manager of Travis Lazar Productions was the rigorous preparation of paperwork, had bungled the paperwork for the court, thereby succeeding in proving his own utter incompetence beyond any reasonable doubt.

One trial done, one to go.

CHAPTER NINE

THE UNITED STATES VERSUS BEPPO BARI

There was no beach in the valley. The inhabitants of the San Fernando Valley were so geographically removed from the ocean that it was sometimes hard to imagine that the Pacific lay a mere twenty miles away, across the town, just as those sun-bleached citizens who lived along the shore and breathed the fresh salt of the sea-air were surely oblivious to the fact that there was a vast inhabited dale between the far-off mountains. Along the California beach-front, shapely young women tanned in the sun, rode their bicycles or skateboards along the boardwalk, and strutted around in swimsuit tops and short pants. There was no beach, but there was no shortage of girls in the valley.

Tiffany did not ever want to be just another anybody. She figured the shelf life of a hot newcomer in the business was six-to-eighteen months, so she was well past her sell-by date, but she was iconic. Legends had no date of expiry. She had a body of work. She still commanded a presence. She had a fan base. She had her reputation. But what she did not have any more was a contract.

The axe had fallen on the AXE contract star. Tragedy kept dropping on her like rain on mud. Duncan had not renewed, the rumor being, as it was explained to her – first by Nicholas and then by Oscar Lowport – that the mogul was still hoping to sell the company, so while it was all in a cloud of limbo, he could not really enter into any long-term limitations.

That all made sense to Tiffany, and it put her somewhat at ease that it was not a matter of her popularity, but she could not help wondering if she might have been *Lowportimized*. Still, she was flattered at the idea that the executives were sensitive to her stature.

Now, she had to start earning some money, preferably without the inconvenience of having some dude squirming around inside her.

She drove her convertible along the Pacific Coast Highway on the way back from a photo shoot at a mansion in Malibu. She was picking up modeling work doing layouts now that the spigot of Duncan's funds had stopped, and she was independent. As the saying went, the only thing that lasted forever was herpes, especially in the sex movie business, so notwithstanding the money, she could care less that the contract player chapter of her life was over. Been there, done that. The wheel of fortune turned. She did not have to feel anchored to one studio any longer, and she was free to spread her wings.

She would survive.

Her next appointment was with Billy Dallas to see if her check was ready, but, even though her destination was the valley, she took the long way down the coastline looping around to the 405 Freeway north rather than follow the shortcut through the forbidding curves of Topanga Canyon. She wanted to brighten her mood. She loved driving with the top down along the oceanside, with the spray on the air, and the sun in her face and the wind blowing her blonde hair. She had the music at high volume. The sky was blue and cloud-less. In the distance, the Ferris Wheel turned on the cotton candy boardwalk where the Santa Monica pier jutted into the sea. She was still wearing her flashy wardrobe and make-up from the shoot. Contract or independent, she felt just like a star.

But that was before she got to her agent's office.

"You've been served," Billy said when she came in, through the gathering of the usual hangers-on awaiting her arrival with the suppressed expectation of guests at a surprise party – her theatrical costume enhancing that effect.

Tiffany gave a disdainful look around the room.

Traci sat on the long couch commiserating with Sebastian Barge, who was suffering through a recent break-up. In keeping with his signature theme of largesse, it was generally noted that the male lead was taking it hard. Luigi Pinnochio – who was so particular about his casting that the Italian maestro never seemed to go into production – was in the rear office, inter-viewing nubiles. Low-level crew members milled around, hoping for the arrival of a producer in need of the skills they might offer.

All eyes focused on the former exclusive star.

On the desk blotter was an envelope upon which was pasted a lime-green sticky note with her name.

Tiffany did not sit. "Is that my check?"

Billy shook his head, chewing a toothpick at the corner of his mouth, since it was after lunch. He stretched out his long arm in a checked sleeve, buttoned at the wrist, and handed her the envelope, with an official seal, which was clearly not the instrument she had been expecting.

"A marshal dropped it off for me to hand to y'all," said the Texan, sounding every bit like a brothel-keeper in a Western.

She pushed her ever-present sunglasses onto her forehead

in disbelief to better verify that the document was not a check but a subpoena. "They can't do that."

"They can." He maneuvered the toothpick from one side of his mouth to the other. "Like you said, I represent y'all. They know that y'all frequent this place of business."

At these words, she glanced around the establishment, her eyes lighting on a fresh poster of Mariana Trench in *Ice Queen* adorning the faux-wood-paneled walls, which prompted her to think of the usurped billboard. She shut her eyes in the hopes that it would vanish, but when she opened her eyes again the laws of physics had not been suspended, and it was still in front of her.

"This is just another joke from the universe," Tiffany moaned, "What the hell have I done to get a subpoena?"

"You're a witness against Beppo the Bear," the agent informed her. "They say he financed a movie – *Hard Time* – and y'all were in it."

The crescendo the denizens of the office had anticipated was poised to erupt.

"I should have known..." she hissed, with fury rising like a jet of steam, "That somehow Travis Lazar was involved in this."

* * *

It was most unorthodox for Travis Lazar to have a lunch meeting with Mrs. Evelyn Hathaway, but the producer planned to ooze charm like a perfect gentleman.

They met at an upscale restaurant along Ventura Boulevard where there were white linen tablecloths and the white-gloved servers were so unobtrusive that they were as scarce as truffles. It was a far cry from the venue in which Travis was most accustomed to hold his clandestine liaisons, namely the

Chatsworth Diner, and the caliber of the cuisine was to a mercifully higher standard.

They sat at a round table on a flowery terrace enclosed with glass from the floor to the dome, adorned with a mural of the Amalfi coast and affording a view of the traffic passing on the boulevard.

To maintain propriety, Travis had extended his luncheon invitation not only to the mogul's wife, but also to her personal assistant, who had been a porn star many years before but had made a successful transition to executive aide, or in this case, chaperone. Where she had once been notorious for opening her mouth to swallow immense organs in front of the camera, in her role as an executive, she had achieved much success by learning how to keep her mouth shut.

They all exchanged pleasantries, and Travis steered the subject towards the glamorous world of production into which the director could offer his witty insights and anecdotes most entertaining to the ladies. He offered behind-the-scenes revelations about the celebrated stars and explained how different shots were achieved during the filming. He was unctuously polite, not only to his guests, but also to the waitress, and, with her collusion, he managed to tempt the other diners into a glass of wine. Mrs. Hathaway was so well-persuaded that during the course of the meal, she had two more. They began with bruschetta followed by salads for the ladies and a swordfish with pasta for the producer, and rounded off with slices of cake and gelato. By the time dessert arrived, Travis came to his point, which was just as well because his guests had languished in suspense of his destination all through the appetizer and the entree.

"I don't know if you were aware that Miles Flannigan was a friend of mine," he said out of the blue, and Mrs. Hathaway, three drinks under her belt now, cocked her head, as Travis continued, "I was hoping I could turn to you to mediate with Duncan. I am not at all comfortable taking his award."

"I know that," said his patron, resting her hand on his across the table, "But we need you to do this for us. I am going to confide in you because you have brought us to this lunch, and I wasn't sure what you had in mind, but I had a feeling..."

While the great lady was talking, Travis had the presence of mind to follow the example well-set by her assistant, and kept his mouth shut. She was calling in a marker.

"Duncan is trying to sell the company..." she revealed, not knowing how well-informed and committed Travis himself was to that outcome, "It adds a little sparkle to our portfolio to have a recent Best Picture award. And, between you and me, Travis, I'll tell you what. Yours really was the best picture. I loved it." She gave her assistant a sturdy nudge. "I love all his movies. Even folks who detest him admit that he is a very talented director."

This compliment was the end of the matter, the end of the conversation, and the end of the lunch, in which Travis realized he had painted himself onto the end of a ledge. His purpose was to appeal to Evelyn Hathaway to intervene on his behalf, but her own objectives were exactly the opposite. He had no choice but to comply. She was the hidden driving force behind the green light of *Fireworks*. He could not refuse his ally.

When they left the restaurant, while Travis was still parked in the Mercedes, digesting not only his swordfish, but also how his lunch plan had backfired, he received two telephone calls.

The first came in just as Travis was watching Mrs. Hathaway being chauffeured away in the front passenger seat of the Bentley with her assistant at the wheel.

It was Nicholas. "Did you just have lunch with Evelyn?"

"I did," admitted the producer, recognizing how rapidly the leaks had reached the all-knowing executive. This was obviously the work of the tight-lipped assistant now steering the Bentley.

"Are you out of your mind?" Nicholas demanded.

"I am trying to resolve this Best Picture thing." He did not yet start the car. He felt paralyzed. He had misplayed and he was not sure of his next move. "I wanted to meet in private to try to talk myself out of it, but she came to lunch to talk me into it. I've put myself in a hell of a position."

"You've put me in a position too," said Nicholas, "I am on very thin ice over here. Duncan is on edge. I can't get movies made. Don't do anything to rock the boat now."

The last thing that Travis wanted was to tip his shipmate at the Head of Production overboard into the breakers. He could tell that Nicholas was not pleased, but his second caller was positively enraged.

It was rare for Travis to receive a telephone call from a performer, with the exception of Ginger who clearly had his ear, and it was especially uncommon for him to hear from Tiffany.

"You are the lowest scum excreted from the ass-pit of the universe," she uttered, controlling her emotions. "If I gotta testify, you'll lose a testicle!"

"Hello, Tiffany," said the producer, keeping the high ground, "I am swept up in it the same as you are, and being that we are both witnesses, we should probably not be speaking."

"I have already said everything I have to say," Tiffany said, hanging up.

Not only was Travis not offended by the vicious verbal assault he had endured, but he could not help cracking a smile as he started the ignition.

* * *

On the morning of the trial, Travis began what was becoming an alarmingly frequent routine, getting dressed in his suit, knotting his tie, and making the early morning drive through the rush hour traffic of the valley from his home in the lush suburbs to the government buildings in the center of Van Nuys.

Well-practiced now, he parked in the same underground garage where he had parked for his bout with Howard, and made his way up the same short flight of steps into the sunny plaza. He passed the kiosk selling fruit juices, among the straggle of forlorn souls who had business before the courts. Dark moods hung over them all, including Travis who was heading this time not towards the minor tribunal of small claims court, but into the foreboding criminal division of the federal court building.

The memory of his success against his former production manager was not reassuring, confronted with the daunting criminal process in which he was about to participate. The steely veteran was not concerned about his own appearance in the court. It was a level battlefield. The producer did not feel that the federal prosecutors were a match for the slippery moguls and mobsters he dealt with over the course of his colorful career. He could handle them. Travis was troubled by the toll that the trial placed on Beppo. He could not imagine how the old bear would stand up to the pressure of the proceedings, let alone the confinement of a prison cage, in the worst case, that he was returned to custody. Jailed or innocent, he had paid a price. It all hung heavily on him, and when Travis saw him in the courtroom, in a gray suit with a gray face, the acting President of Majestic Movies seemed weary and beaten.

Beside Beppo, at the defendant's table, was his defense attorney. She had a gentle manner about her, in the way in which she interacted with her client, and the softness of her eyes. She had the tendency to wring her hands, so to combat this habit, a tic of which she was aware, she kept her hands in the pockets of her chartreuse jacket. There was a prosecutor in a tight suit, and he spoke in a nasal voice, pointing his sharp elbows and a sharp pen. His movements seemed staccato, like a cornered lizard or a squirrel. He referred to his notes so much, reading verbatim at times, that it seemed he never looked anyone in the eye – with the sole exception of Beppo the defendant, who wilted under his piercing gaze. There was a jury of his peers, if his peers comprised senior citizens and a diverse ethnic community, who all seemed to have been corralled in the juror's box after losing their way in the building. And, high on his bench, there was a judge, with short white hair parted geometrically on one side, and a short neck, culminating in a double chin and a red face, who wore a black robe looking more like an executioner.

As it turned out, not only had Travis Lazar been watched. He had been scrutinized.

Officer Luis Perez of the Los Angeles Vice Squad had first pointed out Beppo "The Bear" Bari to his fellow task force member, Special Agent Frank Hassenger of the FBI, during the January convention in Las Vegas. Since the aforementioned Bear was not permitted to be involved in any way, shape, or form in the communion of pornography as a condition of his parole, his presence at the convention suggested that he was meeting members of that very industry for that very purpose as opposed to meeting his penal requirements.

Building a case over a period of months, the task force kept their eyes on Beppo, as well as any of his associates. He had been surveilled discreetly – notwithstanding one unfortunate moment at a buffet where the defendant spotted the officer peeking from behind a newspaper. His habits, patterns and behavior had been observed. Long lens cameras had been used. He had been tailed in his car on certain occasions, although that pursuit had been discontinued when all that was uncovered was that the suspect was harboring a secret appetite for donuts. Notes had been taken. Files had been created. Records had been kept. They had secured a court order to eavesdrop on his conversations. A mobile undercover unit had been parked in the vicinity of his office to monitor his appointments. There was not much traffic. Few visitors came and went, so those who did were all the more noteworthy.

A close known associate was identified as Travis Lazarus, also known by the alias, Travis Lazar, a producer of pornographic material. There was no written contract between them to provide any evidence, but it was believed that they were in business together. There appeared sundry exchanges between them, including cash payments, confidential dealings, trafficking in pornographic material domestically and internationally, and other commerce, including the production of pornographic films.

One such cinematic exhibit was called *Hard Time*. The government would seek to show that the defendant had financed the movie, which had been produced by Travis Lazar Productions and distributed by Majestic Movies, of which the defendant was the acting president.

That is to say, his name appeared nowhere on any paperwork, but he appeared to run the company. They believed that the de facto owner of the company, who was also not inscribed on any paperwork, was one Bobby Bellocchio, who was already well into the years of his residence in federal custody. The signatory proprietor was a Mexican national, with the unlikely name of Marco Pollo, supposedly located somewhere in the municipality of Oaxaca, beyond the jurisdiction of the court or the reach of federal agents.

What was relevant to this matter was the extent of the Bear's engagement. The prosecution tried to establish that

Majestic Movies was a functioning business, but that was questionable in the first instance, so hard to authenticate. There were few telephone calls, and those few conversations were kept vague. A search of the premises revealed no appointment books, ledgers of any legibility, or agreements. There were invoices from Majestic Movies which were not matched against any deposits, bills not matched against payments, old calendars, and many scraps of paper with hand-scrawled notes that would only have any meaning to the author.

To the prosecution, this meant a deliberate attempt to obfuscate; to the defense, the shambles of the organization was exculpatory evidence that no efficient enterprise was operating. To this point, if nothing else, the claim of the defense was an absolute fact.

Travis Lazarus told the truth, the whole truth, and nothing but the truth, so help him God, to the best of his recollection. His recollection was not that reliable with respect to a number of the questions which he was asked, his memory being nebulous due to the number of movies which he produced. He could not be expected to remember every last detail that he delegated. This evasiveness made the producer seem shifty. He may have been a gifted director on a movie set, but in a witness box, he provided a weak testimony under direct questioning by the prosecution.

When the defense lawyer turned to the witness, it was stunning to observe how the cool-steeled Travis Lazar melted under cross-examination. The producer collapsed like a flaccid member. Beppo's attorney found many inconsistencies in his statements, and he stammered sweaty responses, which did not seem convincing. He was tense. He contradicted himself. He fidgeted. He looked about nervously. He kept gulping from a glass of tepid water, like a wanderer just emerged from the Mojave.

It may have been the shrewd tactics of the attorney for the defense tripping up the witness. It may have been that the nasal prosecutor had not adequately prepared the witness. It may have been the grim stare of the morose defendant in front of him that intimidated the witness. It may have been the cold glare of the square-jawed Hassenger, and the beady yellow eyes of Sergeant Perez that drilled into the witness. Whatever the reason, Travis was at his worst.

The prosecution did not want to risk any further damage on redirect, so he was excused.

When Tiffany took the stand, it all seemed to go by so quickly that it was a blur and it was over before she knew it.

Was she a professional actress who appeared in sex scenes in pornographic movies?

Hell, yes, she was one of the biggest stars in the industry, but that was not a crime the last time she checked.

Did she star in a movie called *Hard Time?*

Perhaps, was in so many movies she couldn't remember.

Was her memory refreshed by looking at a box cover of the movie?

Agreed that those were her breasts on the cover.

Did she remember seeing the defendant on the set?

Did not.

How could she be absolutely certain?

Was busy blowing a guy and not paying attention to who was watching.

Perhaps, on her lunch break?

Did not eat with the crew and was a vegetarian.

Was the director of the movie Travis Lazar?

It was.

Was she well acquainted with him?

She totally was.

What was her opinion of Travis Lazar?

Creatively or personally.

In each case?

Was a brilliant director.

As to his character?

Was about time she was asked to describe it.

The witness then testified under oath that she would not believe one word out of his lying mouth until hell froze over. The defense lawyer asked which liar was to be believed. All on his own, Travis did not come across as a credible witness, but thanks to Tiffany, his testimony had been tarnished beyond repair. The witness impugning the testimony of another of clearly disreputable character seemed sufficient grounds for the jurors to find reasonable doubt and in favor of the defendant, and Beppo Bari was released.

* * *

Tiffany had finally denounced Travis Lazar, and in a courtroom, and under oath no less. It was proclaimed to the world. It was on the record in the history books. It was hammered into stone. She felt vindicated. She felt liberated. All she needed now was to feel vibrated, which is exactly what she was planning to do as soon as she got home and smoked a bowl.

With the music blaring triumphantly, she roared off in her convertible, keeping just under the speed limit so some stupid ass-wipe policeman lingering in the quarter would not spoil a perfect day. She had the top down, and she was still all dressed up in her professional look, and driving out of the courthouse parking lot, she pretended to herself and the dowdy attendant in the booth that she was an attorney. In her imagination, she was wearing a chartreuse jacket. She took the long way home, because she did not want to taint her mood by driving along

Sunset Boulevard past any offending eyesores. It was all so vulgar to her.

When the esteemed counselor returned to her apartment on the West side, steeling herself for the possibility that Coochie might have soiled on the rug while she had been attending to matters at court, she was delighted to discover that Coochie had been content and continent. The dog was so delighted to see the delighted owner, however, that she began yapping excitedly and consequently lost control of her functions at that precise moment. Tiffany, stoically prepared, quickly got a pad to wipe up the offense, and put Coochie outside on the balcony, and shut the sliding door in case she (the dog) was inspired to any further micturating.

Her bedroom, which was done in white, was clean but not neat because of the clothing, shoes, DVDs, and fan memorabilia scattered around the room, not to mention the bristles of dog hair, and it was beneath her dignity to ever make her own bed. She had a queen size with a white wrought-iron frame and huge pillows, and she threw her court clothes onto the crumpled sheets without hanging anything in the closet because she couldn't get into her sweats quickly enough.

After a quick change, she grabbed her pink Tiffany West-branded personal vibrator and a bag of weed from the drawer on the bedside table, and went to load the glass bong on the coffee table. She kept the TV on mute, so that she could have a quiet moment of meditation before binge-watching reality shows.

She was just settling in on the couch for her afternoon with *moi*, when the telephone rang.

It was Billy.

"First of all, I have your check," he began on a positive note.

"They took their priceless time about it..."

"Now, before you go jangling your spurs, hear me out," the

talent agent advised, "I am calling about work, and you don't have to take your clothes off, or have sex, and it pays good money."

"I'm listening," she said, without giving anything up.

"It's about Vegas. Y'all won the Best Actress last year. For Travis Lazar's picture. That means that this year they want you to be the hostess."

She stretched back on the sofa, with her head against the arm-rest. "I have to be in the spotlight, and on stage for the whole show?"

"Yes. It gets televised too."

Sometimes, the universe could be so cruel, she thought. She had lost her husband, and even though he had his faults, she did not regret marrying him, and there was an emptiness where he used to be, and there was, if she told herself the truth, a black hole where she was once a contract star. So much could be so easily snatched away, and it always seemed to be those things taken for granted. She had borne her share of bad days. She had no choice but to endure. She weathered it out. She had seen so many hopes shattered, like ice-cubes spilling out of a kamikaze, that she hardly dared to hope. But, the wheel turned, and sometimes, in the blink of an eye, the universe evened it out, evened out so much of it, in one day, like today.

* * *

Travis sat at his desk, alone in the production office, rocking back and forth on his leatherette chair. The last russet rays of the autumn sun burned through the blinds, and the office was all in shadows, but the producer had not stood up to turn on the lights. He had been straightening up the paperwork that Howard left behind. He was going to have to find a new production manager for the upcoming winter season. It would have to be somebody who had the confidence of the talent, and who understood production, but he did not have a candidate. He was doing all the office work himself as the year wound down. The white board was wiped clean. Papers were sorted into stacks. Materials were organized. Laid out on the desk in front of him, by way of helping him keep track of what belonged where, there were glossy box covers of his movies. The movies always helped him to keep things in order. They were place-keepers. To Travis, they were a diary of his life.

Sometimes, he had a reoccurring realization while driving home in the small hours after shooting on location. As he drove along the 405 freeway, which flowed so fluidly at that time of night, curving onto the on-ramp from Santa Monica off the 10 east into the valley, and riding above the streets and through the canyons, he passed the landmarks of the city, recalling places in which he once lived or worked or had a meeting. The movies were like that. He remembered every shot, and every angle, and it was a way for him to remember where he was at different moments of his long career. Each movie was like a checkpoint. This movie was when he got married, these movies were when the boys were born, this was Howard's last picture, this was where he first met Beppo.

The story behind the movie was always more interesting than the story on the screen.

He stared at the box covers, in the fading light of the day, and scanned the faces of the performers who had appeared before him. There had been so many – naked, exposed, hungry for stardom – but the director thought that he had been a responsible steward. He did not believe that he had taken advantage of anyone. He had not coerced anyone, to be in it, or to watch it. Careers had bloomed, and bonds had been formed, but all that anyone was ever trying to do was put bread on the table for their loved ones.

The stars stared back at him from the covers, the perfect pout, the shoulders back, the belly in, the arch, the eyes. The frozen images captured the moment. There was Tiffany and Ginger and Traci and Mariana, all different in their moods and their demeanor and their slice of lunacy. They all sparkled with their unique flames. It was a myth that all porn stars were the same; they were all as divergent as any other group of people. It always amazed Travis that individuals had such a range of penchants and fascinations; fantasies were as limitless as human imagination. There was no taste, in appearance or in activity, that was an absolute. In its sweeping range, all manner of human things appealed to all manner of humans. Not all gentlemen preferred blondes. Appetites ran the gamut of opposite choices. Diverse tributaries filled the sea.

He still had work to do and he did not want to tangle with the snarl of traffic, but he was ready to go home. He could finish up quickly. His wife would have dinner waiting. He did not want to miss singing the boys their lullabies before bed.

He was about to get up to turn on the lights when the call came in from Nicholas.

"Congratulations," said the executive.

"Thanks," Travis responded, guessing where this was going but not wanting to anticipate, "What for?"

"Best Picture of the Year. *Fireworks*. You got the nomination."

It was not unexpected, but it meant that the pieces on the board might have shifted. "Does that mean I'm off the hook? Can I say no to taking Miles' hand-me-down award from last year?"

The executive had never known the producer to understand the meaning of the word no, so he responded in no uncertain terms, "I have done everything I can, but Duncan wants to stick it to Selwyn twice as hard, and you're the weapon."

Nicholas paused, but there was more. "Also, in case you don't win for *Fireworks*, he wants something guaranteed."

"Everybody's worried about *Ice Queen*," Travis surmised.

"Blimp was also nominated," Nicholas acknowledged.

Travis knew that he was going to have to do something about that. It was not that he cared about winning any awards for pornography. With the rise in his fortunes, partly as a result of Miles' passing, Blimp was bludgeoning ahead as a heavy competitor, and, being that Travis was in the movie business, his turf was never fully secure. The turf, most in need of tending, was New York Pictures.

"Well, the best of luck to him," the director said, in keeping with his chivalrous reputation.

His influence had extended to other honorees. Mariana and Traci received Best Actress nominations for *Fireworks* and *Cheats*, respectively. Mariana Trench and Sebastian Barge received the nomination for Best Sex Scene, for the blistering rooftop encounter in *Fireworks*. Little did the reviewers realize the amount of sacrifice, persistence, and destruction that was involved in creating the artistic triumph. Ginger Vitus was nominated for best solo performance for her riveting self-pleasuring on top of a roulette table in *High Risqué*. So much time had been taken to film the scene, while they all waited for her co-star to arrive, that it had paid off on the screen. The crew was not neglected. Maria was nominated for Best Make-up for *Fireworks*, mostly as a result of smudging burnt cork on the grimy faces of the firefighters. Jack received a Best Cinematographer nomination for *Fireworks*, an accolade that was well-deserved in Travis' opinion, considering how the nimble cameraman had captured the shot when the fireball did not conform to the rehearsal. In short, there were enough prizes to go around for all, ensuring a lively attendance at the upcoming convention.

* * *

The following week, The Duchess was in production for New York Pictures. She had gone out of turn on the checkerboard while her stable-mate was confronting juristic matters, and, in any event, was without a production manager. Travis could not draw a replacement from her team because, with the exception of Jack and Tommy, whom they shared, all the members of her crew hated him, her production manager most of all.

On location, the set was in a funky dive-bar in North Hollywood, with grotesque mannequins and peacock colors. At night, it was filled with a gothic crowd of local artists, but under the blue skies of the day, it was often rented out as a movie location. The cramped parking lot was first-in, last-out, so when Travis drove up, as a guest long after the call time, the producer had no choice but to block everyone else in, being that he was first-out. He was only planning to stay for a few minutes for an update.

He made his way through the cluttered hallway to where it opened out into the bar. Everything reeked of liquor, as if it had soaked into the walls, an olfactory effect that would fortunately not be communicated on the screen. Jack and Tommy were making the final adjustments to the lights, and, already on-set, Ginger was at one end of the bar, studying her script. She was wearing nothing but heels and a sheer negligee, which was not her costume, but simply worn for the purposes of modesty, since in the scene she would appear fully nude.

As soon as she saw him, she ran up to Travis, with her rolled-up script coiled in her hand, and they hugged in a show-biz way, with Ginger kicking up a heel like a pin-up. They exchanged some small talk in connection with her imminent role as a stripper being just like old times before she got into the business. They each congratulated one another on the nominations, and upon that topic, the star revealed her intentions.

Vegas was coming up, and Ginger wondered if the famous producer would once again be her escort down the red carpet, an invitation which no gentleman could refuse. Then Ginger had to go and douche because it was time for her scene.

Travis could not find The Duchess on her own set. None of the crew had any inkling of where their director had disappeared, and helpfully went off searching in different directions, including a thorough sweep of the craft service area. He went back out to scour the parking lot, relieved that the fumes of liquor had not seeped through the exterior.

He found her on the telephone in her SUV, dressed in black fatigues. She saw him through the window of the driver's side, flung open the car door without getting out, and held up her forefinger to indicate that he should remain silent, which he did, and not to go anywhere, which he did not.

She hung up, and said, "Well!"

"On again?"

"Yes," she beamed, "It was a bluff. Like we thought. They were finding Duncan's breaking point. They always planned to come back and grind again."

"And the poison pill?"

She paused before responding. "Let's just say that a little bird might have tipped them off, and the information might have been helpful in bringing them back to the negotiating table, but it has not been mentioned in the negotiations at this time."

Travis understood what else was not being mentioned. "So, they can discover the loophole after everything is delivered, and when they're supposed to pay the installments, they could void the contract. And Duncan might never see the rest of his money. But Oscar Lowport will still get his commission up-front."

"That's the best part," she laughed, "The argument was that the deal the broker put together fell through, and this was a new deal without him. But they offered him a finder's fee instead."

"So, Oscar got *Lowportimized.*"

"Something like that." She climbed out of the car. "They're going to make the announcements in Vegas. But it's a done deal. Duncan's out of the business. I'll be the new President of AXE."

The production manager, who had also been searching for The Duchess, came out into the parking lot to notify her that they were ready, and she gave a wave to signal that she was on the way. The production manager indicated that he understood and glared at the guest whose Mercedes was blocking the access of every other vehicle.

"I have a request..." Travis advised The Duchess, before she got back to work, and before he removed his vehicle from the privileged first-out pole position, a fitting metaphor for the current dynamic.

"There will be plenty of production." She understood when her fellow producer was pitching. "I am going to need a blockbuster new slate."

"I will try to squeeze you into my schedule," her fellow producer offered graciously, "But that's not what I was going to say."

"Tell me." It was going to be non-negotiable. He was calling in a marker.

"Nicholas stays."

She was not going to argue the point. "I would be a fool to lose him." They threaded their way through the parking lot and

The Duchess had that same strut of confidence again, like she was wearing pearls. "Did you see Ginger?"

* * *

Coming off the 118 freeway, Travis headed south in the Mercedes, as De Soto made a smooth metamorphosis from rural to residential to commercial, on the way into Chatsworth.

He was satisfied that the AXE deal had closed, and deals did not collapse twice. The Duchess would be at the helm in the new year. Immediate problems would disappear, replaced by a prosperous reign in the new Duchy. All he had to do was make sure that she stayed on the throne.

Without Duncan to worry about, the politics were different now. Alliances had shuffled. Nobody expected history to stay in place. It was a time to clear accounts. His conscience would be clean. He could refuse the award, and let Miles rest in peace.

He pulled into the lot at Majestic Movies and could not help glancing at the shady spot where the white surveillance van once lurked. It stood barren, which was scant comfort. The site would be a lingering remembrance. The mint-condition Cadillac was in the parking lot, but there were no other cars. The blinds were up, letting in the sun, and he could see Beppo staring out of the window of his office.

Beppo came around to the front to meet him, because he was the only one in the building. The purple-tipped receptionist had been laid off, and the lone shipper had found another post.

The meeting with Beppo was not as simple as one might think. True, Travis was a hero. Withering under cross-examination, notwithstanding the damning testimonial of Tiffany, the producer had helped to undermine the prosecution's case. Beppo understood that Travis had taken a dive.

But it meant that Travis was holding a marker. Beppo was not going to be pleased that once again he owed Travis a remission. He would not like the loose end of having something on the books. He would be looking to find a way to make a settlement.

"So, we never got to talk," Beppo said, when they sat down in his office, "That thing with Howard." He felt for a cigar in a box buried under some papers on his desk. "How'd that work out?"

"Like you said. Kept my mouth shut."

Beppo rolled the cigar between his palms. "He's a backstabber, and he is a threat because he has nothing to lose."

They both knew enough to be concerned about loose cannons, particularly some underling with a grievance.

"There are a lot of people who depend on me," Travis said, thinking aloud, which played as a non-sequitur in the parlance favored by the Bear.

"You never know if he'll come back some other way," cautioned Beppo, "When you least expect it."

Travis tried to change the subject because he knew where Beppo was angling, but Beppo did not want to talk about the trial, because recent experience taught him that you never knew who was listening, and, in any event, there was not much more left to say. They had known each other for many years, they felt like they had said it all, and everything was on the best of terms.

Beppo lit up the cigar. "Let me do something for you."

Here was the favor.

Travis took a breath. He had to find a way to balance the equilibrium so that Beppo would not feel obligated, or slighted. Sunlight poured into the office. He had never seen it so bright in there before. Everything seemed so clear and airy. The musty smell was gone. He weighed how Howard had turned on him, and the crude way that he had spoken to The Duchess.

"I don't want him hurt, Beppo."

"Nobody's going to hurt him." Beppo rustled some papers on his desk to disrupt any potential microphones. "It'll be my nephews."

"I mean it. That's not a code. He can't be hurt." Travis did not want any misunderstandings on this delicate point, notwithstanding any avuncular connections.

"He won't be hurt. We are just going to talk to him. That's all."

Beppo had a shipment to get out, and since there was nobody else in the building, he was packing it himself, so they walked to the warehouse together. The metal racks were almost bare. Stacks of boxes were piled up, sealed up, ready to be loaded up. There were a few boxes still empty, mouths open, waiting to be filled. The last of the DVDs were on the racks. Some of them were legendary classics that Majestic Movies had released to international notoriety back in the heyday of the studio. It was a wistful moment to recall those former glories at the benchmark of this final consignment. Beppo began sorting them into different boxes. Travis gave him some assistance, helping him choose odd titles from the shelves in different quantities.

They grabbed five pieces in a handful, so they always knew by touch how many they pulled, and they packed them, spines up, fifty to a row, and stacked double in twenty-pound boxes. They dropped a blizzard of Styrofoam onto the top, to protect the goods in transit, and sealed the boxes with packing tape. Beppo scrawled a reference on the top of each anonymous box in a black marker to identify the contents. One by one, they made their way through the inventory until there was nothing left on the skeletal shelves but dust outlines of where the stock used to exist.

"Thanks for all you did," Beppo said, resting his palm on the last box, "But this thing wiped me out. They beat me. I'm throwing in the towel. I'm going to retire in Florida."

This was news, and the producer's first concern was his foreign distribution outlets – a consideration Beppo must have read on his face.

"You'll still keep the international," he assured him, "The Germans are part of the deal."

Travis was relieved to hear that his domain was protected, but surprised to hear that there was even a deal. He had not seen this one coming. But there was no mystery to the identity of the buyer. Travis guessed at once who the new President of Majestic Movies would be.

They heard the grind of the UPS truck pulling up outside the corrugated doors.

Beppo looked around the barren warehouse. "I'm selling everything to Sunbeam."

CHAPTER TEN

WHAT HAPPENS IN VEGAS (PART TWO)

Motti Sunbeam was transfixed by the whirl of the roulette wheel. He watched how the little white ball bounced from slot to slot, selecting its preference. He loved the sound the wheel made clacking around, and the clatter of the stack of chips portioned in front of him as he toyed with them between his fingertips. The rest of his chips were spread across the table on a random assortment of wagers. Some were favorite numbers, which he bet with obsessive regularity, but most were impulsive gambles flung down on the spur of the moment as inspiration struck him. He received impetuous hunches like mystical illuminations. Tiny reflections played on the grooves of the wheel. Lights, numbers, chips were all a blur. He was mesmerized. He could not tear himself away from the table. He won again. He was ahead.

He had a one p.m. appointment, and, anchored to the table, he was already ten minutes late. Luckily, the appointment was to take place at the steakhouse in the lobby across from the casino, so he could be there as quickly as his short legs could carry him. He dared not miss connecting with someone who could solve a major problem, but the betting was irresistible. He decided to let his ventures ride a few more spins. He was in a cheerful mood, and not only because a cocktail waitress in fishnet stockings and a corset had served him a complimentary Bloody Mary at the table.

With grudging acceptance of the constructs of time, Sunbeam swept his chips into his hands, rose from his stool, and engaged in what was for him a rare occurrence, namely walking away with his winnings. He stood in line at the casino cashier – there was only one person ahead of him – which was a new experience for the compulsive gambler. He felt glum at having to leave the roulette game when he was on such a hot streak. When he got to the counter, after a simple transaction, the chips transmogrified into crisp hundred-dollar bills, and he started to feel a lot better. But the proceeds were burning a hole in Sunbeam's pocket, and, like the old saying about fools, the holder and the money would soon be parted.

He sauntered off on his way to the restaurant, from time to time checking that the cash in his jeans was still intact. Like many gamblers, he was a highly superstitious man, so the success at the tables boosted his buoyant mood. Uplifted, he was filled with confidence at the prospects of a successful encounter.

Of course, he was always excited just to be in Las Vegas, with its endless games of chance. He loved the possibility of winning free money, and never considered his losses as mathematical probabilities, but the cost of the opportunity to profit. The thrill of instant gain was so gratifying that it overwhelmed the pain of his inevitable damages. Gambling for Sunbeam was a loss leader. Risk-taking had made him prosperous. That was the way he ran his business, and business was good.

He was consolidating, building, and acquiring. He was investing. He was expanding. He needed more space. He needed workers. He needed shippers, salespeople, drivers, secretaries, receptionists, bookkeepers, collectors, printers, editors, and, most of all, he needed a director.

* * *

The annual adult industry convention in Las Vegas was in full swing on the final day. Crowds had poured into town in anticipation of the awards gala. Hordes crammed the aisles and halls of the hotel where it took place. Starlets, fans, press, managers, producers, and exhibitors all had essential business to conduct before the culminating ceremony in the evening. There was traffic of people in all directions. Some paced through with purpose on the way to an important rendezvous, but most meandered about like stray herds, particularly in clusters where there was no assigned wrangler. At all intersections, further confusion ensued at the great criss-cross of greetings and conversations and the recognizing of long-lost colleagues and former partners. There were many handshakes and even more hugs, and a fair amount of kissing in the air. People bunched around the celebrated performers. The scent of cologne, make-up, and hairspray merged with the honeysuckle infusion of the casino to make the air sweet. Everyone was dressed to make an impression, even those who wore the very least. Nudity was forbidden, but the law was provocatively tested to its limits. Armed sheriffs eyed the proceedings. Fortunately for many, the laws of Nevada which prohibited public undress allowed for twenty-four hours a day of alcohol consumption, although in all fairness, there were just as many who desperately required coffee.

There were meetings, interviews, shoots, parties, and deals. None of this was without conflict. It was always a grueling schedule with the entire industry together under one roof.

They were all bunched in such close contact that there were inevitable squabbles, not to mention outbreaks of flu, hangovers, and various complaints.

Everyone had an agenda.

Myriad strands of intrigue weaved through the political and personal webs, but on the talent grapevine at the convention, the subject which provoked the most chatter was the developing feud between Traci Gold and Mariana Trench. Neither woman was considered the type to get involved in feuds, but circumstances had driven them into opposite corners. Mariana had received two nominations for Best Actress, for her starring roles in the two adversarial Best Picture nominees, *Fireworks* and *Ice Queen*. Competing against herself, she could conceivably split the vote, and consequently, Traci would be the likely beneficiary for her role in *Cheats*.

Hence, the feud.

Factions developed.

Complications arose.

Caught in the middle of the triangle, as geometric and human interaction would have it, was Sebastian Barge, who having recently been spurned by Mariana developed an intimacy with her rival. This catalyst added zest to the quarrel, and much fuel in spreading further gossip. Everyone along the chain claimed some interest or information, or at the very least, a strong opinion.

This grand stir was not even remotely mentioned on the executive grapevine.

The buzz along the executive grapevine during the convention was the headline in all the trade papers: Duncan was out of AXE, and The Duchess was the new President of the major studio.

To show his support for her success, Travis hardly left her side during the convention, and they made sure to parade about, as if they were conjoined, wherever their unity would receive the most prominence. This was primarily in the walkway leading to the exhibitors' hall. The hallway narrowed before the double-doors, compressing the throng of people through security, so it was at this nexus where it was the most crowded, and where they lingered. He was wearing his designer suit and a burgundy tie – last seen on the witness stand – and she wore a cream suit and a string of pearls.

Many came up to offer their compliments to The Duchess while she held court, with Travis standing bodyguard at her shoulder like the crown prince. Stars, agents, crew, news media, and executives from other companies, all sought to ingratiate themselves with the incoming studio boss in a fawning display which Travis – hovering at her ear – found tasteless.

The Duchess took to offering frivolous asides and self-aware commentary in the reflection of her rise to high achievement, basking in her own glow until they were confronted by the President of Paradise Media, Inc, who was the last of the moguls left standing.

"So, you're the big cheese at AXE now?" Selwyn said, with his hands in his pockets and such a smug delivery as if he were holding a secret in each fist.

"Hello, Selwyn," The Duchess said coldly, "Is that how you say congratulations?"

"I'm not on your side." Selwyn dropped his own temperature to a degree as frosty as the Arctic nipples in *Ice Queen*. "This isn't one big happy porn family. I'm looking forward to burying you in the marketplace." He gave a theatrical scoff, and brushed on, before The Duchess was afforded any opportunity to deliver her own chilly rejoinder.

He continued on his way, without looking back, a small, muscular man swept into the currents of the commotion and buffeted along the tide.

Travis witnessed the entire encounter, and discretion being the better part of valor, practiced his ongoing craft in the benefits of taciturnity.

"Well, the first war has started," she said, as if they were confronting Napoleon, "Selwyn wants to move into the number one position. He sees an opening with me in charge."

"We expected this," Travis counseled, "But it's not like him to come out bragging without something up his sleeve."

"How am I going to fight Selwyn right out of the gate?" she asked.

"We watched the end of Duncan," Travis contemplated, "Selwyn will be easier."

* * *

By the time Sunbeam made it to the steakhouse, his lunch companion had moved up the hungry line to the velvet rope at the front. The hostess unbuckled the barrier, just as Sunbeam scampered up to slide into place beside a man with a red beard and a camel beret.

"I with him," he pointed out to the hostess, and to allay any further inquiry, he added, "Alex Zig."

"It's Alec," sniffed the auteur, who did not appreciate the idea of being Sunbeam's place-keeper in the line. "Not *Alex*."

They were shown to a small table on what was referred to as the terrace, which was through French windows and enclosed in a wrought-iron fence with hedgerows, but still technically beneath the soaring ceilings of the casino. From where they sat, Sunbeam had a disquieting view of the roulette tables to which his gaze kept wandering like a lazy eye.

Alec Zig ordered the most expensive steak on the menu, for which Sunbeam, being *the seducer*, was obliged to accept the bill. In the aim of presenting a positive image, the President of

Sunbeam Video took the splurge and ordered the same for himself. Happily, he was able to sustain the expenditure, because he was still possessed of his gambling dividend, the ignited fuse sizzling along toward depletion.

Alec hardly said a word, as they waited for the meal, and when he did it was in his sibilant rasp which the Middle Easterner found hopeless to follow, a difficulty matched by Alec's challenges with his companion's truncated version of English.

"I buy Majestic," Sunbeam said, "I am Majestic now. And Sunbeam Video. I need new movies. Many. You come with me. You make what you want. I give you salary. I put budget."

The steaks arrived just at that moment, on heated plates, with all the trimmings, and the suitor was obliged to wait until the object of his desire had digested these words and a few costly bites before he replied.

"The thing is, Motti," Alec said, between mouthfuls, "I have other choices. With more prestige."

"No choice," Sunbeam said cheerily, "You go in your neighbor house. You come from the jail. You have three months with criminals and mash potatoes." He waved a fork. "Nobody touch you. I give you chance."

Alec stroked his wispy red beard to add a mysterious flair. "I'm telling you I have offers."

"Who? Who offer you? New York? Sylvia she never touch you...."

"Selwyn at Paradise." He dispatched a few more valuable morsels. "He offered me Blimp Pullman's spot."

"Selwyn don't touch you," retorted Sunbeam, but, when Alec just smirked in response, he demanded, "Why you don't go with Selwyn? Why you sit with me?"

"I thought it would be the right thing to tell you to your face," said Alec, although it seemed clear that he was also enticed by the opportunity to consume fine dining at no personal outlay, especially after the aforementioned culinary disappointments during incarceration.

"To my face? To tell me no to my face?" The countenance in question cast over with a dark cloud. The Destroyer was not only insulted, but also on the hook for the pricey meal. He stood up, and grabbed a handful of bills from his pocket, which he scattered onto the white tablecloth. "I pay the lunch."

This gesture of generosity was not considered well-disposed; it meant conclusively that the possibility of any business between them was over forever.

The account was closed.

* * *

Howard had not made it to Vegas for the convention. While all the industry was partying it up in the glamorous suites of the Strip, he sulked in the gloom of his North Hollywood apartment. Bored, he could not resist calling Traci on the convention floor. Given his frame of mind, she was not inclined to talk to him, but Howard prolonged the conversation because he was so lonely and listless. He heard the jingle of slot machines and blasting music in the background, and she had to talk loudly because there was so much noise. She said she was not having a good time. She complained about all the politics among the performers, but he was jealous. He hated that he was not part of the festivities, but he knew that he would not be able to look anyone in the face.

His anger seethed. He kept the core of his emotion contained, like a simmering pot, but he let his mind run wild. He was consumed by wicked fantasies about how he could still turn the tables.

Most of the time, he just hung around in his apartment, surfing through channels on TV, and eating cereal to relieve his boredom. He watched the tick-tock of the lonely tramp on the wall, in the kitchen where Traci had once graced his table. Like the tramp, in his loneliness, he shuffled about from the kitchen to the bedroom to the living-room.

He was not expecting any visitors, so he peered through the peephole when there was a knock at the door as the night was falling. There was a dirty blonde in her twenties on his doorstep. He could not quite place her, but he considered that she might have been someone he had met at Billy's open casting session one Thursday afternoon. She had a waif-like porno look to her, with double-Ds in a sleeveless top and the odd tattoo.

He unlocked the door.

Somehow, as if an evil wizard in a distant tower had cast a horrible spell, the female through the peephole evaporated, and, in her place, two heavy-set toads dressed in sweatsuits, suddenly shouldered their way into his apartment. One of them slammed the door shut, and stood with his back to it, as if to blockade the entrance against any chance of escape of which there was no possibility.

The other one had him by the lapel of his shirt and jerked him around like an inflatable doll.

Howard had never seen either of them before, and because he had no possessions worth the effort of a robbery, was initially convinced that they had the wrong apartment, but then one of his assailants made sure.

"You Howard?" he demanded, giving him a rousing shake, when he did not answer instantaneously, "I said 'You Howard?'"

"Yes," he spluttered.

"What do you think you're up to?" said the man at the door.

"Nothing," he wriggled, "I'm just watching cartoons."

"Don't you ever bother anyone ever again," he said, with a twisted smile.

"I don't even have anyone to bother," Howard said plaintively.

"Keep it that way." The man at his lapels roused him once more and shoved him away so that he landed on the back of the sofa.

And then, they barged out, leaving the door wide open. He shut it with the imagined terror of a second round of invaders, locked it, and dragged the kitchen chair against it as an additional fortification. He was in such a state of shock that he was not sure what had just occurred, but, no matter what, he swore that for the rest of his days he would never bother anyone ever again.

* * *

Howard's presence was strangely missed by his crewmates, Jack and Tommy, who had both been hired as technicians for the live production of the Las Vegas Awards show.

Jack would be operating one of the cameras along the stage. The nimble hand-held skills of the veteran shooter of sex scenes surpassed any broadcast cameraman who was stuck behind the legs of a tripod. Shooting sex was like shooting sports. The cameraman had to have an instinct of where the play was going so that he would never miss the shot. Jack was always on the mark. It was live, there were no second chances.

Tommy's job was working one of the spotlights in the upper rafters. The higher the spotlight, the more plum the post, because the remote placement of the light, along with the responsible electrical operator, allowed for no supervision other than the walkie-talkie, which was, by definition, optional. This consequently made an easy assignment even more appealing, and also a possible prospect for the consumption of an illicit treat to better endure the duration.

At the technical rehearsal, the breaking headline from the executive grapevine had broken a little more on the way to the crew grapevine, where among the garbled news that Jack and Tommy gleaned was that The Duchess had been fired from New York Pictures and AXE had gone out of business.

This muddle caused some consternation.

They felt that the big accounts were drying up, and, without Howard, their crew had fallen apart. An additional factor in the remorse for the absent production manager was that, adding symbolism to their cognitive confusion, they took the wrong door out after the technical rehearsal. They found themselves shut out at the back of the building, in a dimly-lit loading dock with a half-a-dozen ramps. It was at times like these that there should be someone running the production. They had to walk through what was apparently a wind tunnel all the way around to the street, and then to the front of the building to get inside again. They were not pressed for time, as to the call time for the live broadcast, but the biting cold gnawed through them.

They walked briskly to keep warm and to escape the chill as quickly as they could. The cold air being symbolic of where they would be left if they didn't make it back quickly enough to hold onto their employment.

"Okay," said Tommy, out of breath from the pace of the walk, "So last year, I didn't have the money to come to Vegas... my own fault, had a setback, things happen...anyway...this year, I got the job here...spectacular...but now I'm worried that there won't be any work when we get back..."

"No AXE, no New York," Jack summarized, "And all of the other studios have their own crews."

They emerged from the service alleyway and they were

back on the Strip. Lanes of traffic were jammed. Crowds of pedestrians, oblivious to the raw weather, were gathering in anticipation of the event proclaimed on the neon marquee.

"I hate being in this position," Tommy complained, "Back to the wall...what to do?"

With all the flashing signs and distractions, they were momentarily confused about which way to go.

Jack spotted the entrance. "We will have to pin all our hopes on Travis Lazar."

* * *

There was a matter of discussion in Colt's suite, where in eschew of his annual late-night after-party, he was filming a scene for a cheap new line. Since there was going to be sex anyway, there might as well be gain. Some of his fellow performers were open for a little pre-gaming. They were all exhibitionists, so the recording of the action only made it more titillating. Colt had put his own money into the enterprise, rigged a few lights, and was planning to operate the camera himself.

He had rented the same suite, Suite 33013, from the year before, when Tiffany and Mariana had first become acquainted on that fateful January night. For some reason, beyond aesthetics, the furnishing had been redone in a yellow hue. Everything was designed to look very modern, but, notwithstanding the cables, equipment, and Colt's bulky luggage, it was a comfortable room in which to lounge, with a square coffee table and soft upholstery.

Gathered on the oversized sofa were Traci, Sebastian, Summer, and Storm, who were preparing to shoot a foursome by first passing around a bong. Colt, taking his directorial responsibilities seriously, refrained from indulging in the intoxicant until after the completion of the scene. This contradiction in choices motivated Colt's urgency to begin shooting, while at the same time lulling the rest of the company into a more languid pace, thereby increasing his impatience.

Although hair and make-up were ready, the participants were not even undressed yet. Summer was still wearing her glitzy outfit from working the floor of the convention, Traci was in sweats, Sebastian, always dapper, was in a tight button up black shirt and gray slacks, and Storm looked like he had just parked his Harley. Before the scene commenced, as was their right, the four performers discussed their various comfort levels on both physiological and political grounds.

They had very little to enumerate with respect to their limits, because they had all partnered together before, and, in fact, as to limits, they did not really have any. But when it came to the politics, there were always considerations.

Their presence at the intended orgy – if it ever got off the ground – indicated that Summer and Storm had thrown their allegiance to Traci in the feud with Mariana. With such fealty in mind, Summer broached the question of whether she might repeat to the collective ear of the community the appearance of Traci and Sebastian together at the orgy in the concern that the report might reach Mariana.

"You know, it's just a scene," shrugged Traci, her legs crossed in her sweatpants, "It's not like we haven't worked together before. But everyone is making such a big deal about it like we're dating." She took a puff of the bong and sank back into the cushions of the couch. "We're not dating, we're just having sex."

Sebastian nodded, in full agreement, and offered something between a smile and a grunt, and unbuttoned his shirt, taking her remarks to mean that the aforementioned task was imminent.

Summer took it to mean that not only would Traci be content with the airing of the affair, but saw it as her loyal duty to make sure that messages were spread like cheap perfume.

The bong made its way around the group, more than once, and finally, in exasperation, Colt himself succumbed to the enticements of the sweet aroma on the pretext of confiscating the instrument.

"Is that the time?" Summer asked, and began to get naked, "If we are going to make it to the awards on time, we had better start fucking."

* * *

Travis called his wife while he was getting dressed in his tuxedo because he had the usual complications to do with the bow-tie, and he hoped she might offer him some advice on the fastening, or at least, moral support for the struggle. He stared at his own reflection in the windows of the suite with the dotted lights of Las Vegas all around, talked to her and talked to the boys, and then she came back on the line again to say goodnight and to wish him luck for the awards – in addition to the bow-tie. Even though he had only been gone a few days, he hung up reluctantly, not wanting the family to slip away. He wished he was home, singing bedtime lullabies.

Vegas was all business.

Bow-tie vanquished, he got an early start to the evening so that he could mingle with the rest of the industry, while everyone was all dressed up and having such a spirited evening. It was not just fun and games. Deals were always done in these encounters. It was like a tank of sharks, if sharks were swimming around to negotiate.

He was not the only one at work.

Downstairs, The Circle Bar was surrounded easily ten

deep, not counting the cliques that lingered in the vicinity of the bar, all yelling to make themselves heard above the noise of yelling. Every star had an entourage of private security guards, publicists, boyfriends, and sundry hangers-on to form a perimeter that kept the fans at bay. Undeterred, there were fans clustering around performers, and there were performers sidling up to producers, and producers stalking executives.

Among the pack, Travis pounced on Motti Sunbeam.

Sunbeam was dressed in blue jeans and a blue sweater in independent contrast to the prevailing formal attire, eyeing the roulette tables from a vantage point. He had surrendered briefly to the call of the wheel, and returned some of what he had removed, but he had retreated resiliently before he squandered all. He stood back from the bar, with a glass of water and lemon in his hand. He was not a big drinker. The free Bloody Mary he accepted earlier kept him in a mood all through the afternoon.

Travis had vodka, and they clinked their glasses together.

Travis was not going to shoot a movie for him – that bridge had been burned, and the director would be busy enough riding the spanking new gravy train at AXE. He did not need to lower his standards to shoot for Sunbeam again. But, in the first place, the gallant Travis always paid his respects to any brave soul who had ever been daring enough to finance a production, and secondly, they needed to discuss the new ownership of Majestic Movies.

Sunbeam was clear on the point that Travis would still control the international rights to the library, and looked forward to receiving payments, just like his predecessor. This came as much relief to Travis, who five hours earlier, had guaranteed those rights to Klaus from Hamburg Film and Book Company on his annual spending spree. Majestic Movies would receive a piece of the bounty. That business amiably concluded, Sunbeam told Travis all about his acrimonious lunch with Alec Zig, which was most informative, as the producer put the parts together.

As they conversed, Sunbeam allowed the mistake of boasting – with embellishments – about the roulette winnings in his pocket. Travis expressed a polite interest and was making further inquiries, like a predator with a whiff of prey on the wind, when they glanced across the bar at Blimp Pullman. He was in his signature muumuu, exhibiting his unique personality as he ploughed his way through the throng to get a drink, dragging a tow of other thirsty customers behind him.

"Blimpie," Sunbeam said wistfully, "Hot now. Everybody ask for *Ice Queen*. I like to make a deal with him."

Travis gave him a shrewd look, smelling blood. "I can make that happen."

"You swear?" Sunbeam perked up. "You know him?"

Travis gave a white grin. "He owes me a favor."

Sunbeam was of a volatile nature, his emotional range being so swiftly swayed between extremes, that he became as energized as a child promised a treat, bounding up off the barstool. "Make for me introduction."

They both understood the unwritten importance of the request. The introduction was considered to be a guarantee by the intermediary of the good will of the other parties. The introduction would cement the deal.

Travis turned stony. "You owe me one thousand dollars."

"For what I owe you?" Sunbeam responded with a flash of anger, as his emotions oscillated again.

"*High Risqué*. One thousand dollars reward. No questions asked."

Sunbeam smiled meekly. "We find. You no steal. I pay. Make for me introduction."

Travis went around the bar, coming up behind the rotund

director. He called out his name as he approached, and Blimp turned to respond, just as Travis was going around him the other way, so he was obliged to follow a temporary orbit around the girth of the equator before reaching the front, whereupon he was greeted affably by his fellow director.

"I promised you that I would try to find you a home," Travis came to the point, "I think I have something for you."

By way of expressing his gratitude, Blimp said, "You know, I wish people knew how not like an asshole you really are."

Travis accepted these kind sentiments, and warmed up his colleague in anticipation of making the acquaintance of The Destroyer. "He has deep pockets and an insatiable demand for movies. Come and meet him."

Sunbeam was waiting anxiously on the other side of the bar, as Blimp and Travis rolled around, and he beamed and rubbed his hands.

"Blimp Pullman," Travis brought them together, "Motti Sunbeam."

"I very happy to meet you," Sunbeam said, cutting right to the cinematic chase, "I know is finished with Paradise. You come with me. You make what you want. We do a lot. A lot."

"It's good to meet you, Motti. We can do a deal, if Travis says you are okay."

"He's okay, he the best!" Travis offered his whole-hearted endorsement of The Destroyer, appropriating the Middle Easterner's staccato syntax for the sake of clearer comprehension.

Motti Sunbeam's cherubic cheeks flushed with modesty.

They shook hands and the deal was done, although it was standard that they would work out all the details in Los Angeles, more often than not, even after production had already begun.

"I give deposit," Sunbeam offered, showing his good faith by reaching into his pocket and bringing out the wad of bills.

"Give him five thousand," suggested Travis, with which Blimp heartily concurred.

Sunbeam counted out the money, and put it into Blimp's spread hands. He was thrilled that he had found his director, and he did not want his substantial catch to slip away from him.

Then Travis said, with that same intensity, "And one thousand to me."

Having just departed with the bulk of his gains, Sunbeam gave his sheepish smile. "Tomorrow. I give you."

Travis was not going to accept any promises in lieu of cash. "The deal's off."

To Sunbeam's horror, Blimp tried to hand back the cash deposit, a practice that was unheard of within the industry, like a prize fish unhooking itself from the bait and swimming away in the depths of the sea.

"Okay, okay." He smiled pinkly. "I pay."

Blimp reclaimed his deposit, and when Sunbeam counted out another thousand, Travis came in close to collect the money, so that Blimp – whose attention was on tallying his own windfall – could not overhear them in all the racket.

"It's a good deal, Motti," Travis reminded him, as he pocketed his reward, "Remember who helped you."

Motti grinned, which was not a flattering look on him, but he could not hide his satisfaction. "I owe you."

Then, coming in for the kill, Travis tugged on the line, "You're not worried about Selwyn?"

A fresh supply of cheap movies directed by Blimp Pullman for Sunbeam Video was soon to flood the market, which would have the effect of brutally devaluing the contents of Selwyn's vault.

"I am Sunbeam," chuckled The Destroyer, "I go to destroy him."

* * *

Tiffany luxuriated in a long, hot bath in the oversized tub in her hotel suite. The foam from the bath salts lay on the surface of the water like lacy lingerie. She had spent the day in bed, twisted in the clean linen sheets and stuffed pillows. She was trying to relax before the night unfolded. Soft lights reflected in the mirrored walls, which were misty from the steam. There was a basket full of sponges, lotions and soaps, and fluffy white towels rolled into tubes, and the bath water was warm and bubbly. She had made sure to upgrade from the previous year, so as not to be reminded of the catastrophic events, and she wanted a room fitting for her stature as a star. Besides, it was all complimentary, even down to her make-up artist, who knocked on the door while she was still wrapped in a towel.

She was listening for the knock because she had ordered room service, which was also complimentary, but Tiffany knew that they would take their precious time to ride up in an elevator with a tray.

She opened the door for Maria, who wheeled in her kit on rollers, and managed a fold-up make-up chair under her arm. The make-up artist seemed to have it all in hand, having traveled so encumbered all the way from the elevator to the corner suite, so Tiffany did not feel any need to provide any assistance, and besides, she had to make sure that Coochie did not get out into the hallway. There was a basket of fruit and a bottle of wine in the ice bucket on the bar, which came with the suite, and, before setting up, Maria took it upon herself to pour them each a glass.

The living room was spacious, with a big couch and low tables with lamps, statuettes, and lacquer boxes of potpourri. There was a flat screen TV, but Tiffany had not figured out how to use the remote. The floor-to-ceiling windows commanded a view of the lagoon-shaped pool and an artificial volcano emitting gas flares at regular intervals across the street. In the center of the room, where the light was the best, augmented by occasional eruptions, Maria set up her chair, and, alongside, she dragged a high, narrow table that was against the wall, not serving much purpose, to better employ as her workstation, upon which she laid out her cosmetics.

"This is going to be the most humiliating night of my life," Tiffany shuddered, sitting in the make-up chair with her pudendum uncovered. "I don't know why I agreed to it..."

"You're going to be great," Maria offered her support to the star, not really foreseeing any danger that she might cancel her global appearance. "How are you going to be humiliated?"

"You mean besides if Mariana Trench wins Best Actress?" she inquired archly.

This had nothing to do with Traci's dispute. With the incendiary billboard controversy still smoldering, Maria understood how *the* Tiffany might be impacted. "Yes, besides."

"He set me up," she said, through clenched teeth, "And I was too distracted to see it coming."

"Who?" asked the make-up artist, as she adjusted her supplies.

"Travis Lazar." Tiffany froze like a mannequin with a gleam in her eye. "Who else?"

"Now why would Travis set you up?"

"To gloat in his twisted revenge for what I said about him in court," she said, trying to hold her pose, "And also because he's a puckered asshole."

"How is Travis setting you up?" Maria tried to start work on her face.

"Don't you see?" Tiffany was too upset to keep still. "He is going to get the re-awarded prize from last year. The award that went to Miles before the tragedy. And it's been set up so that

I'm going to have be standing right there on the stage while Travis Lazar prances up to receive it. Right in my face." She lifted her wineglass and held it up, without drinking, as if she were offering a toast. "If I don't tear off his nutsack on the spot, then I might as well just leap off the stage myself like it's a skyscraper."

"But, Tiffany, you're wrong about one thing," said the make-up artist, trying to get her subject to settle down so that she could begin her transformation, "Travis is not going to accept that award tonight."

There was a knock at the door, signifying room service. The make-up artist, doing double duty as a butler, went to answer it.

"I'll believe that..." Tiffany said, taking a gulp of wine, as if she were administering herself a dram of hemlock, "...when hell freezes over."

* * *

The award ceremony in the grand ballroom began unconventionally. As the ticket-holders were still settling in, there was an announcement.

This is a special programming announcement concerning what was listed as a special programming note in the program. The special programming note, which was originally listed, has been cancelled.

This announcement caused more confusion than clarity, but, as audience members helped one another decipher the clue, the general conclusion was that the Picture of the Year award for the previous year was not to be re-awarded, as had been advertised, but was to stand in the recorded history of the adult industry, and that Miles Flannigan would retain the previous year's award through everlasting life.

This was greeted without rancor or enthusiasm by the

attendees who were not aware of the machinations of the moguls behind the scenes, and were pleased for the show to go on without the interruptions of special programming notes.

After escorting Ginger – without incident – down the red carpet, through the hall and to Billy's table, Travis paused to shake hands with the talent agent who was once again the only rooster among his virginal hens.

Billy cackled, "You're a genius. Y'all turn down last year's award on principle, so they have no choice but to give it to y'all for this year on the merit. Or they'll look like a bunch of weasels with sour grapes."

Conspicuously absent, there was no grand central table for AXE. Nicholas, alone, represented the mighty studio in the midst of transition, but was seated across the room at the table for the First Amendment Association. Duncan and all his entourage from the former years were gone. A large floral arrangement marked the site, which not only gave the impression of a funeral wreath for the absent fixture, but also obscured the view of the stage for the table to the rear.

Travis took his place at the prime table reserved for New York Pictures. On one side sat The Duchess, who would be presiding over her own table on the next occasion. On the other side of Travis was Sylvia Bern, in from the eastern seaboard for the function.

"With The Duchess taking over AXE..." Sylvia began, leaning in confidentially and speaking out of the side of her mouth, as if she were dangling a cigarette. "And, don't get me wrong, Travis, she deserves it. But it creates a problem for me."

"How can I help?" offered the altruistic producer, who was a few strategic steps ahead, but lagged so as not to appear presumptuous.

"I am going to have an open slot," said the female executive, oblivious to the feasibility that she was performing dialog from one of their pictures, "And I was wondering if you could fill it."

"I already have my own slots with you and I am going to have to fill a big commitment of bookings at AXE," the producer said, but overhanging a little at the end, as if he were thinking aloud. "You're asking me to pick up your entire production line..."

"I tried to catch Blimp on the way in, but Sunbeam already netted him. Well, they are probably a good fit." She tilted in at a more perilous angle. "So, Travis, what do you say?"

"Sylvia," Travis reassured her, "I can never say no to you."

Sylvia leaned back the other way now that they had both got what they wanted. "You're going to be very busy."

Right on cue, a fanfare struck up and the drums rolled, and the lights came up on the stage, and the famous presenter stepped before her audience.

Tiffany was in her element under the spotlight. She hit her marks, spoke in turn, knew her lines, improvised delightful quips, and was effortless in her delivery while having one of the most wonderful nights of her life. She looked glamorous, and gorgeous, all in gold, with her hair down and her boobs out, and every inch a star. The audience was in the palm of her hand.

There was only one stumble, which was anticipated, and could not have been avoided. During the sequence bidding farewell to departed friends, she almost had a breakdown when they came to Miles. On the giant screen, there was that same photo of him sitting at the camera in military khakis like it was a machine-gun. Tiffany went into a tremble. Summer had already rehearsed to take over at that point, and was standing by as an understudy in case of any potential mishaps or absences with respect to the leading lady.

However, Tiffany miraculously recovered her abilities and was able to proceed with the show at the peak of professionalism. Everyone agreed that the diva had never been such a trouper on a movie set, where her demands were legendary.

The show proceeded smoothly. The presenters were captivating. The music was on the mark. The lighting was proficient, with the exception of one lone spotlight which wandered erratically, to the ire of guests seated in the balcony who were blinded for some of the early program.

The first big trophy of the night went to Mariana Trench and Sebastian Barge for Best Sex Scene, which was on top of a burning building in *Fireworks*. The pair came up on stage to receive the award, and they were overwhelmed with such passion at the occasion – less of the accolade and more of their reconciliation – that the audience roared as they coupled together. They actually had to be restrained by Colt, who was the presenter, before they re-enacted the scene for which they were being honored. Mariana and Sebastian walked off the stage arm-in-arm, like a bride and groom, and, in a slight to Traci, and a statement to their fellow performers, it was clear that their union would continue.

The rupture of Traci's relationship with Sebastian was relieved by her award for Best Actress for *Cheats*, with Mariana splitting the vote between her two nominations, as she had feared. As was her annual custom, Traci gave a shout-out to her director, but, in her own snub, did not mention her rival when she accepted the prize. She further stunned the room when she took the opportunity to announce her retirement – not from the industry, which had brought her so much love and happiness – but from performing in front of the camera. She hoped to continue her career working in production or as a brand ambassador or anywhere else in the offices of Chatsworth where she might be absorbed.

Everyone nodded at these vocational prospects, which had been so ably advertised, and Travis wondered if, in Traci, he might have found his new production manager for the slog which lay ahead of the crew in the chock-full winter season.

As Sylvia said, he was going to be busy, but he was never going to be busy enough, because, as was clear to everyone in the room, there was not enough pornography in the world. There were vast oceans. There were many briny rivulets conjoining with the voluminous swells. But the voracity was insatiable. Consumption never ended. That was why they all just kept churning. It was plain human desire.

It was railed against, it was vilified, and it was blamed for the fall of civilization, but it was demanded. The performers were shamed and demeaned by society but they were essential. In an eruption of provocative images, stimuli, temptations and bombardments, the world was in its own merry state of decay. Entertainment was not the cause of anything, it was a mirror. He had not contributed to the coarsening of a culture that was – all by itself – a carnival of vulgarity.

The most fundamental thing in the world was sex. It was the quintessence of life, universal for all species, naked anthropology, basic nature.

"I know that everybody is waiting for the Best Picture award..." Tiffany said, in a strangely somber tone, as if she were about to announce a repeat screening of the roll of the deceased, "But I am going to keep you in suspense a little longer..." She looked into the lens of the television cameras, "This will only take a moment, I know we are being broadcast." She turned back to her live audience again, then thought it better to address the wider network of worldwide viewers directly. "Sometimes, you think you really know someone well. And maybe you think the worst of them. But they can surprise you. It turns out that there can be good in everyone. Once in a gazillion years, maybe hell freezes over." She stopped, tearing up at the profundity of the cosmic moment, and directed her gaze once again at the viewers in the auditorium, who were in silent awe of her extemporaneous revelation. "I'm talking about a producer who is nominated in the next category..." There were some whispers audible in the hushed assembly. "...But as far as I am concerned he should win an award, you know, as a human being. So, on a personal note, I just want to say thank you and good luck to a decent man in an indecent business – Travis Lazar." There was no public reaction, as she had prefaced her commendations by the caveat that they were personal. Having spoken her mind, she gathered her emotions, and went back into her character as a presenter. "To present the award for Best Picture – which gives me a hint as to maybe this is his year – here is the hottest redhead in the house, Ginger Vitus."

The choice of his personal favorite as a surprise presenter was a nice touch, and the insiders understood what it meant. The Duchess prompted Travis to his feet, as cheers began around him, and when Ginger announced his name as the winner, the producer, propelled by the currents of well wishers, was halfway down the aisle.

Spotlights swept the auditorium like rays of the sun.

He crossed to the center of the stage to receive the award, and before he knew it, Ginger had her arms around him in a hug, and one leg wrapped around through a tantalizing slit in her gown. Admirers whistled and applauded. Cameras flashed as Travis embraced her to withdraw his face from publicity.

"Fancy meeting you here!" he declared, in mock surprise.

"You know, people imagine we're having an affair..." she teased, away from the microphone.

The producer laughed, with one arm around the star's waist and the Best Picture award in his other hand. "Imagine if people knew the truth."

AUTHOR BIO

Stuart Canterbury is a veteran producer-director in the adult movie industry, with over 300 major feature films to his credit. With a string of awards and nominations, he has produced and directed titles for studios such as Penthouse, Hustler, Brazzers, Adam & Eve, Arrow, Video Marc Dorcel, and many others. He was inducted into the AVN Hall of Fame for lifetime achievement in video in 2017.

Running Wild Press publishes stories that cross genres with great stories and writing. RIZE publishes great genre stories written by people of color and by authors who identify with other marginalized groups. Our team consists of:

Lisa Diane Kastner, Founder and Executive Editor
Mona Bethke, Acquisitions Editor, RIZE
Benjamin White, Acquisition Editor, Running Wild
Peter A. Wright, Acquisition Editor, Running Wild
Resa Alboher, Editor
Rebecca Dimyan, Editor
Andrew DiPrinzio, Editor
Abigail Efird, Editor
Henry L. Herz, Editor
Laura Huie, Editor
Cecilia Kennedy, Editor
Barbara Lockwood, Editor
Kelly Powers, Reader
Cody Sisco, Editor
Chih Wang, Editor
Pulp Art Studios, Cover Design
Standout Books, Interior Design
Polgarus Studios, Interior Design

Learn more about us and our stories at www.runningwild-press.com

Loved this story and want more? Follow us at www.runningwildpress.com, www.facebook.com/runningwildpress, on Twitter @lisadkastner @RunWildBooks